In the Midst
of Bounty

In the Midst
of Bounty

Kathleen Vellenga

40
PRESS

Design: John Toren

Forty Press, LLC
427 Van Buren Street
Anoka, MN 55303
www.fortypress.com

ISBN 978-1-938473-30-2

To Tom Vellenga, Charlotte Vellenga Landreau and Carolyn Vellenga Berman, my darlings who are living proof of the best of their late father.

Three things are the overthrow and bane of [colonies]: vain expectation of present profit; ambition in their governors and commanders, seeking only to make themselves great; and the carelessness of those that send over supplies of men unto them, not caring how they be qualified.

Good Newes from New England,
Edward Winslow, 1624

1

December 1621
Nemasket Village, Wampanoag Territory

Attitash

It was not the whippoorwill's incessant cry that woke me from my ragged sleep, but its sudden silence. Straining to hear, I did not move. Cold sweat crept down my neck. Even New Life, always active in my womb, lay still and listening.

I hadn't planned to be asleep in my cousin's longhouse. I'd come that afternoon to save her from the approaching battle and spent the day trying to convince her to leave this rebel sachem's nest and return with me to our own village. We would not be here with the rebels if she did not cling to her husband like a sand burr, I'd scolded. His sticky sweet lies spoiled her mind and she believed only Shimmering Fish. Persuading her to leave was like trying to pull a hungry child off its mother's teat. My only hope now was that our friends with firesticks would not come until after we had left with the rising sun.

A branch snapped.

"What was that, Attitash?" Seafoam threw back the furs that covered us. The rustling was too loud for fox or deer.

"Hush!" I said to my cousin and pushed her back down, pulling the furs over our heads to muffle our whispers. "We have to leave before the Strangers try to rescue our Massasowet from your rebels."

"He can't be trusted," Seafoam hissed in a harsh

whisper. "My husband says Massasowet will betray us to those who claim to be friends."

"Stop talking!" I wanted to put my hand over her mouth. Seafoam would not listen to anyone since marrying Shimmering Fish. He stole Seafoam's mind and wisdom along with her heart. And now he and his rebel sachem had taken our leader, Massasowet, prisoner in order to replace him. They were only interested in gaining favor with greedy new Strangers, not living by the treaty of trade and mutual protection we had negotiated with our friends in Plimoth. They would do by force what they could not accomplish through the council of grandmothers' selection. It was for their own small village alone, not that of the Wampanoag nation, that Shimmering Fish and his rebel brothers acted. Even if Seafoam did not believe the truth, she was my cousin and I would try to protect her.

The three fires in the rebels' longhouse were banked. I lifted the fur enough to expose my ear so I could hear.

"Who-whoooo." Was that an owl or my husband's secret call? My husband, Black Whale, had left our winter home at the same time I did, he going by way of Plimoth. He intended to bring my father to help, along with our Strangers. Please let the call be Papa and Black Whale, I prayed.

The entry flap of the longhouse burst open. I could see only dark shapes, but the clanging of the shiny-rock shirts and leggings told me it was Strangers. I was both relieved and scared.

"Massasowet!" a voice called out.

Shouts and cries filled the longhouse. Wind gushed through the open flap and swirled smoke from our fires. New Life now kicked wildly inside me.

"Massasowet, are you here?" the voice demanded in the rock-scraping words of The Strangers. "We know the rebels hold you here."

"He's not in here!" I cried in the Strangers' own words but it came out in our Wampanoag tongue. I could only guess where the rebels had taken him.

A Stranger lifted his firestick, ready to aim its bad-spirit fireball at us. Had my friend Esapett's leader turned on us?

More Strangers came into the longhouse. Seafoam slid down from our sleeping bench pulling me with her. She tried to grab my hand, but someone shoved her and her fingers slipped through mine. Mothers carrying babies pushed children toward the opening at the back. I tried to see through the smoke, but could only make out white faces in dark shapes. A man grabbed my arm. Hot breath burned my cheek. I wrenched my arm away and shoved my hip against him. He smelled of fear. He was bad sickness, matchanni.

"Attitash!" Seafoam called through screaming people. A grandmother pulled me off the bench. I was swept through the flap and outside.

No stars. No moon. Only rain.

The rebel women huddled together. Moving away, I searched for Seafoam in the deep dark. Strangers' firesticks boomed like the sky-fire gods. More shouts, and my belly cramped hard. The firesticks blasted again. A wave of burning flames swept over me. My blood bubbled like seething water as the ground reached up for me.

2

December, 1621
Plimoth, Massachusetts

Elisabeth Tilley Howland

The rain let up gradually as the household awoke. Long after most of us broke our fast, Desire Minter emerged from her curtained bed, her thick dark hair tucked beneath her cap. Her persistent cough allowed her special privileges, like eating someone else's cooking.

"Any sign of our men?" she asked, as Widow Ford served her a bowl of corn mush.

Elder Brewster was standing at the door, looking to the sea through the slow rain. "We hope they return today. Shouldn't take long to drive off a few rebels."

"Can our governor be certain these savages will not turn on us?" asked Widow Ford. "If they do, I would not be the only widow in Plimoth." She flicked her eyes at me.

My hot face surely betrayed my urge to shove her cruel words down her narrow throat. Desire's eyes tightened with anger, assuring me that my own fury was justified. "John Howland will return safely," she said in clipped words and clasped my hand.

I desperately needed to believe Desire. If John caught a rebel's arrow, my beloved husband would die before we consummated our marriage. And should our men not succeed, my own dear husband was not the only one endangered. We all would be back under King James' boot, sent back to live in fear again of being hanged for following God's will.

Elder Brewster turned from the door and took an ember from the fire for his pipe. "Yea, we will succeed. God is surely on our side, Widow. The stakes are not only one husband lost, one widow made." He drew on his pipe and moved back to the door, keeping it open as the rain stopped. "If King Massasowet is not rescued from his betrayers, men of his own people, who hold him captive, our treaty of mutual aid and fur trade would be worthless. The heathens who live beyond the hills west of us, the Narragansetts, would take over the Wampanoag land and attack us."

"I cannot keep all these heathen names straight, 'Wampa—Narra—and Massa,' Widow Ford said quietly so our governor would not hear.

"Everyone has trouble with the names at first, except Master Winslow." I tried to be civil to her. "Their king is called, 'Massa-sew-et.'" I mimicked sewing up a seam and the widow smiled faintly. "His nation is Wampa-noag. Their enemy are Narra-gan-sett. Rhymes with nary-can-get."

"Only the devil can pronounce such words," Widow Ford sniffed. "I won't even try."

The widow and her companions were the first new Christians we'd seen in more than a year. The new arrivals had looked about our little settlement with disdain. Why are the houses so small? When will you build more? There is so little to eat!

So little indeed! We'd had sufficient for ourselves until the ship Fortune arrived full of people and nearly empty of supplies. If I dared speak to their leader, I would have asked: And where are the flour, onions, and nails Governor Bradford wrote and told you to bring?

Weary of her tirades and nearly mad with worry about my husband, I attempted to compose myself and began sorting through the mending. Mother always chastised me when I moped, telling me, "Idle hands are the devil's workshop." Get busy, I told myself. And stop listening to Widow Ford's complaints. At least she had more justification than the other newcomers.

Keeping my tongue was never easy. But I had not yet tried to explain to the widow or any other newcomer, my deep feelings for my friend Attitash. At least I need not worry she would get caught in the rescue. Just before the new settlers landed, Attitash and her family had gone back to their winter home. She would still be at Poanoke until spring and God willing, if He cared how the heathens fared, she would soon be brought to childbed. I wondered what a new Indian babe would look like.

Now, Widow Ford sat on a trunk, holding the babe to her breast.

I kept my head bent so Widow Ford would not see my temper flare. Fear fuels anger. Truth be told, I'd been afraid since our governor sent a party of our men to rescue their leader. I roiled with worry over my John's safety. And I was angry with Widow Ford for not understanding the desperate need to keep the treaty with the Wampanoag. She had arrived at Plimoth Plantation just a month ago and would not understand. Like most newcomers, she was full of opinions about those she still called "savages." The Indians were naught to her but another danger.

When I came on the Mayflower more than a year ago, I too believed that God's blessing was for us, not for heathen like the Wampanoag. After that terrible first winter of death—when God did not spare our sorrow and let half our colony die, including all my family—my faith was shattered. But then God was merciful and led me to a heathen friend. It was Attitash and her "savages" who saved us from starvation and attack.

Earlier that summer Martha Ford left England as Mistress Ford. Before her ship arrived at Plimoth Plantation, she'd become Widow Ford. Her father-less babe was born the day she arrived. I hoped that after living here awhile, she would form a new opinion. Instead, she was afraid and angry.

"You are married, but still live here with the Brewsters," Widow Ford said. "When will ye move into John Howland's bed?"

"My husband must return first." I didn't mention that even if he returned safely, it was months before I would turn fifteen and my John would bed me. I was still a wife in name only—my beloved John and I might have waited until I was sixteen, but when I turned fourteen we'd hastened to make it legal to avoid my becoming an indentured servant.

"I pray your husband and the others return safely, Elisabeth." Widow Ford's mouth puckered and she bit her lip. "I need not remind you that losing a husband is sore troubling. God favored few to live together so long as the Brewsters." She glanced at me. "As you grow up, Elisabeth, you will learn to accept what God ordains." Widow Ford's blue eyes did not hide her thoughts: she knew better. She was in her mid-twenties and already had wrinkles around her eyes.

"I have thought much about death since my mother died. And I don't need you to be my mother, Widow, telling me I should accept what God ordains."

She dropped her eyes from mine, wiping the milk from her babe's mouth.

I continued, "I have learned from my husband and Elder Brewster that no one can discern what God wills. We can only try to understand his will."

She flinched and I felt a small tug of regret that I'd thrown my own husband at one who'd lost hers. That regret evaporated with her next words.

"Elisabeth, I do not comprehend Governor Bradford. Why aid and abet heathens?"

"Why do you think you should comprehend, when you just arrived," I shot back. "We are too few to defend ourselves." I struggled to convey the complicated world we now shared. "You must know, Widow, that we arrived on the Mayflower last year with scant supplies and rampant disease. Half of us succumbed to starvation, cold, and disease the first winter." I did not mention that after I lost my family, my new guardians also died.

The widow sniffed dismissively. Her own loss was fresh and she had no sympathy for me.

"We need these Indians to help defend us from the other heathen nations, as well as from the French. Even if they don't kill us, these enemies would take all the beaver and we could not pay back the debt to our financiers."

She knitted her brows together in silence, her squirming babe tucked under her elbow. "Elisabeth, I do pray thy trust in God is realized and your man come home alive."

"My husband assures me constantly he has been chosen to live." My words did not alter her grim expression. "Did you know John Howland grabbed a halyard as he was washed overboard on the Mayflower?"

"Yea, I did hear he was pulled from drowning in the sea," she answered. "But that does not mean God would not take him later."

"Cease with your predictions!" I said angrily. If only I could stuff her mouth with the babe's clout. "You are withering my soul!" I said, and went to the garden. How could I be civil to her? She wanted me to suffer as much as she had, but I had suffered too much already. God had taken Mother, Father, Uncle Edward, and Aunt Agnes from me.

But God would not take my John away. Not now.

I stood in the little garden. The plants were invisible, asleep under the icy rain. When winter had come and gone, John would finish our house and we would become truly husband and wife. Hopefully, in a year or two, Attitash and I would both be mothers and our children might even play with each other. I shook my head to stop dreams. Her husband and mine were involved in a dangerous rescue. Would Black Whale survive to meet his child? Pray to God mercy be shown even to a nonbeliever.

The wind picked up and blew light rain into my face. I covered myself with my cloak. Hearing the door open, I turned away, thinking it was Martha Ford again, but Mistress Brewster's mild voice called to me, and I turned back.

"Find William Latham," she said. "I don't know where that boy's run off to. I told him we need more water, some for us and some for Priscilla. Since her John Alden's with the rescue party, Priscilla needs help."

There was enough rain caught in the barrel for washing, but drinking water required a trip to the spring.

The mud clung to my shoes, making a squishing noise, but at least the rain stopped. I set out to search for William Latham. The Brewsters treated William kindly and his servitude was relatively easy. But he did take advantage of them sometimes.

Hearing voices near the goat pens, I saw a group of boys tossing stones at the shed. "Make sure none of you hit our nanny goats," I shouted. "And William, come here!"

William recognized my impatience and came through the muck. After giving instructions, I told him to bide a moment, Priscilla might want to join us. She did indeed.

Once we were outside the gate and William set off ahead of us with the yoke buckets, Priscilla and I tried to look up the hill. The path was empty until it disappeared into the trees. I pulled my cloak closer and tried to imagine the long day's march some fifteen miles through a wintry forest path to Nemasket. That was where Hopamoch, Attitash's father, said their King Massasowet was being held. And that was where our men were headed.

"Fill the water pails when we get back, William," I called to him. "Let's just go a little way up the trail until we reach the lookout."

He rolled his eyes, knowing our mistress would not allow this, but William was eager for a view too.

Walking was not easy, what with the mud, rain-slick leaves and wet stones. When we reached the opening in the trees, a fog rising from the sea shrouded everything. Only the bare maples and brown-leaved oaks close to us were visible.

The ping of stones on rock startled me, but it was only William tossing pebbles again. We'd just started back down the trail when we heard voices. Scrambling behind a boulder, we waited with hearts quickened until we realized they were speaking English.

Master Hopkins' two man-servants, Edward Doty and Edward Leister, were coming down the hill. Doty's cock-eye seemed to look at me and the good eye at Priscilla. They wasted no time with greetings, informing us the battle was over. "Though it seems no one has won, since the savages' leader, Massasowet, is still not found."

"Swear to Heaven! Tell us how our husbands fare—and don't deceive us to mollify our fears," Priscilla demanded.

Both servants assured us that the last they'd seen John Alden and John Howland, they were unharmed. I drew a breath of relief, but Edward Doty destroyed my comfort.

"Master Howland is tending the savage wench who got herself shot."

Before I could ask, he continued. "Hopamoch's daughter, the one that's big with child."

"Shot? Killed?" My question came out in a wail.

3

Attitash

"**A**ttitash, can you hear me?"

I knew my husband's voice, but Black Whale's words were lost to me. I understood nothing but that my New Life no longer felt safe inside me. Her silence was not that of a baby waiting to push her way out.

The turmoil of fire and ice assaulting my body burned as the scent of blood flooded my nose and I struggled for breath. "Wolf blood," I whispered.

"There are no wolves, Attitash," Black Whale said, his words forming slowly.

"I smell blood." I struggled to open my eyes. Faint firelight showed my husband's face. I reached for him, but a claw gripped my shoulder. Could New Life feel that?

Black Whale took my hand. "The Strangers spilled your blood." His words were high pitched, too loud to escape.

"Did they spill New Life's blood?"

He gripped my hand harder and put his other hand gently on my belly. His voice went low and quiet. "You only bleed from your shoulder."

"Bad spirits from their firesticks?" I was too weary to listen to the answer. Now I remembered a ripping in my shoulder, hot fire in my body. I found a leather sling pressing moss against my shoulder, dried blood caked on the leather, warm drops oozing down my arm. New Life did not stir, even when sharp claws tore at me again. She might leave my dark nest before she was ready. "Don't come now," I told her. "Stay for two more moons—stay safe inside me."

At last she fluttered, her little body sent waves against my shoulder. I clenched my teeth so I would not sob. The claw shook my body, bouncing New Life hard against my ribs. Sour venison stew pushed up my throat, but I forced it back.

Other eyes watched me from their sleeping-benches. I was back inside the rebels' longhouse in Nemasket. I fought the pain to remember why I had brought New Life here. I saw my cousin and remembered Seafoam's husband was one of the rebels. Through the haze of my trembling mind I recalled Seafoam defending their greedy sachem. The one from Nemasket, this village, who wanted to take our Massasowet's place as Main Sachem for all Wampanoag. My mind crumbled. Why had it ended with my getting wounded instead of our leader being rescued?

A grandmother I didn't know added moss to my wound. I wanted my own mother, my own grandmother back home in Poanoke.

I forced my mind away from listening for New Life's every move, away from my body, away from the wolf claws. A dream enveloped me, sending the pain to a quieter place. It took me from the horror, back home to lie by our Trees-in-Love with Black Whale. We were on furs beneath the tree, listening to the three-note-bird sing. Black Whale stroked my body, reminding me of how he had rescued me when the Narragansett kidnapped me. I laughed, telling him it was not only gratitude that drew me to him. His sparkling eyes and strong arms had attracted me even before that. We looked up at our entwined Trees-in-Love and remembered the completion of his vision quest, when he returned a man. We'd burned for intimacy and joined both sides of our circle with delight.

"I didn't see you get hurt." Black Whale's words brought me back to the pain. "Jon-owland told me the Strangers guarding outside thought you were rebels escaping."

"What we were escaping was Cap-tan's firestick." I managed to say.

He ran his hands helplessly through his topknot. "The women here carried you back inside the longhouse." He paused, folding my hands inside his. "Why did you come here?"

"I came to warn Seafoam." My breath failed me. The pain was a fire that burned up all my words.

He held my hands but would not meet my eye. "I didn't know you were wounded."

"No one could see outside," I said. "We saw nothing but fire."

Black Whale did not speak, but the furrow between his eyes eased.

"Were you with the Strangers when they shot us?" I had to ask.

"Matta, I was with your father looking for Massasowet at other houses in this village."

"Is Papa safe?" Fear stirred my pain.

He finally met my gaze. "Tisquantum told us that the rebels had taken our Massasowet away just before we arrived. To give him to our enemy, the Narragansett." Black Whale's hands gripped mine so tight pain shot up my shoulder. I winced and he let go. "The Narragansett want to kill Massasowet and take over all our people."

"Where is my father?" My mouth said words, but wolf claws gripped my mind.

"Hopamoch went to look for our Massasowet."

My heart squeezed tight, wanting to fly back home to my mother. "I need her. I need my mother." I closed my eyes.

"I will go home, to Poanoke, and bring your mother." He stroked my forehead. "Your cousin Seafoam will stay with you. Sleep now, Dearest."

When I woke again, I saw my cousin's worried face, her

dark eyes spilling tears.

"Oh, Attitash. My heart cries for you." Seafoam's voice broke. "If you had not left your mother's fire and come here to warn me, you would not be wounded."

"I would not be suffering if you had listened to me earlier" I told her. Seafoam had refused to return with me to our home in Poanoke. We were caught in a cold rain that drove us into the longhouse where the rebel women and their warrior husbands stayed. I'd just fallen asleep when the night sounds changed to chaos. Now, the bad spirits pushed through my shoulder into my neck and down to where my New Life languished. "If my father and Black Whale had not rescued us, we would now be Narragansett wives."

"Better wives of a Narragansett than of Strangers," she retorted. "Massasowet would let them take all our young women." Seafoam's words were woven out of lies told by the Nemasket Sachem, Corbitant. "You know how few women your Strangers have. You know how some of their men leer at all of us, including this 'Cap-tan,' the one you say leads the rescue."

There was truth in her argument. Seafoam turned from me. Her shoulders were rigid as she awkwardly stirred the fire. "Who do you think hurt you?" Seafoam kept her voice calm, but it did not hide her fury. "You didn't listen to me when I told you what Sachem Corbitant knows. He says Massasowet believes the Strangers' lies." My cousin sat back, leaving silence between us.

Shivering, despite the warm longhouse, I tried to ease my shoulder by shifting, but pain shot through me.

"Can you not understand, Attitash?" Seafoam drew a deep breath and touched my hand tentatively. "The Strangers wounded you and aimed their firesticks at others. Your pain should convince you that the Strangers will kill our people. Not just the Strangers who live here, but those who came across the Big Salt Water earlier will come back to destroy us."

Could Seafoam be right about Massasowet? The wind tossed cold rain through the smoke holes, but the woven mats of this longhouse were a good tight weave and all three fires glowed. My shivering came from inside my body, where the Strangers' bad spirit lay.

I tried to listen only to New Life. She was silent. "Will the firestick's bad spirits kill my New Life?"

"Drink more tea." Seafoam held the cup to my mouth. "I will take care of you until—"

Cap-tan San-dish opened the flap, followed by Jon-ow-land, holding a firestick! Would Esapett's husband betray us too?

Some of the women cried out. My fear and pain rendered me nearly senseless. But the Strangers' firesticks pointed down and were not lit.

Looking rudely into my eyes, Cap-tan San-dish talked loudly. I understood only "Squanto," their name for Tisquantum. I closed my eyes so they would not reveal my hatred of Tisquantum. There was no way to know if he brought the Strangers here to fire at me. He'd betrayed me before.

Jon owland stood next to Cap-tan, his eyes respectfully lowered. "Attitash, matchanni—bad sickness."

Seafoam released my hand, "Ahhe, Attitash matchanni." Her words were pieces of ice, like the frozen bark that covered our house.

Slowly but very loudly, Cap-tan said, "We take her to Pli-moth. We heal her."

"Matta—No!" I spit the words out.

I looked frantically at Jon-owland. Surely Esapett's husband could protect me. He gave me an encouraging smile, which faded as Cap-tan spoke in his rough words to Seafoam, "Get the wench ready to travel."

When neither of us responded, Jon-owland said slowly, trying to use our words. "We help Attitash, take her to Plimoth."

"Wait!" I croaked. "Black Whale's coming back." I kicked at the hands that reached for me. My legs flopped weakly as Jon-owland picked me up and laid me in a hammock.

"We'll take you to our healer. Elisabeth will be there. We will care for you."

Pain seized my throat, choking me. I tried to tell Jon-owland no Stranger could touch me. Not even Esapett. But my tongue was not connected to my voice. I entered the wolves' world again.

4

Elisabeth

"The savage is not killed—but she's bad sick," Edward Leister told me. Hopkins' servant glanced back up the trail. "Standish and our men are bringing her here. Surgeon Fuller can dig out the musket ball with his sharp knife."

Could Attitash survive Master Fuller's knife?

Priscilla and I demanded Doty and Leister attempt to describe what happened.

"'Twas raining when we arrived in Nemasket long after dark," Edward Doty began. "Captain Standish called out for the heathen king, but no answer came. Standish thought the heathen rebels were holding the king in their commonhouse, so he went in." Doty's good eye skittered to me and then away. "There were a lot of savages hollerin' and they came runnin' out. We'd already primed our muskets and some of us got off a shot."

"But why was anyone shooting?" I demanded.

"Trying to warn 'em—or maybe one of the bloody savages raised a club," Edward Leister chortled as if this were all theatre at a fair. "The wench that conjures up potions for you—was in the group runnin' out. She took a musket ball."

"How badly injured?" I tried not to picture Attitash with a mortal wound.

"Just her shoulder, I think she stopped bleeding." Edward said.

"Ye must know who shot her!" Priscilla spoke to menservants more firmly than I dared.

Doty looked up furtively. "Truth be told, Mistress Alden, no one knows. Captain Standish commanded us not to ask. 'Unavoidable consequence of warfare,' he calls it."

"We've tarried long enough." Doty said. "We must run ahead to warn Master Fuller he's needed as a surgeon."

'Twas no use to persist. These men would not reveal anything. My heart would collapse if Attitash and her unborn did not survive. And what if my John was the one who accidentally shot her? I could not comprehend such a disaster.

Attitash
The wolf claws gripped me everywhere. I could not tell when I was awake and when in dreadful dreams. Even Seafoam's hand on me was a claw as we bumped down the trail. Jon-owland was holding the front rope of my hammock. Seafoam had never been so near Strangers, yet she stayed by my side, giving me sips from her journey-cask of water. Two Nemasket women supported the other end of my hammock and kept up a prayer-song for me and for New Life.

The hammock swung and bumped as we came down the trail from the hills to the frozen fields. New Life usually kicked in protest when jolted, but she stayed quiet.

I raised my head and saw Cap-tan and his warriors clanking ahead of us. Nippa'uus was low in the west, but still shining, making the Big Salt Water dance. If only Black Whale and Mama could catch up with us, but they could not. Black Whale would take a half day to run from Nemasket to our winter home in Poanoke. Then it would take another day to follow us to the Strangers' village.

Elisabeth
Preparations for Attitash were seething like the hot water in the large pot outside Mistress Brewster's house.

I helped Desire lay out clean cloths by the curtained bed. We did not know if Attitash needed a musket ball removed first or if she was already brought to childbed. If she was in travail, Mistress would help her. We had no midwife, but Mistress had delivered at least five babes of her own and sat at all the childbeds.

The sun was setting over the western hills and to the east the sea sloshed in darkness when at last we heard a shot fired to tell us our men approached. I was tending the fire under the water pot and looked up to see our soldiers and some Wampanoag coming down the hill to the open fields. I couldn't tell if the Indians were singing or wailing in despair. The fire needed my tending and I could not go closer. I tried to search for my John in the fading light. At last, the party came through the gate and I could see him carrying the front end of a hammock. As they neared the house, the bundle in the middle jerked and Attitash groaned. My John raised his moss-green eyes to me, dark with despair. Two Indian women lifted Attitash out.

"She's soaked in blood!" Mistress Brewster exclaimed. "My Lord, save her!"

Attitash
It was growing dark when I woke from dreaming that a wolf stood on my stomach. New Life was still quiet, but my belly and back were squeezing together so hard the pain pushed away any awareness of my shoulder. Warm liquid ran down my legs. Someone lifted me out and laid me down. Mis-tess cried out. The men backed away.

"Attitash." Esapett took my hand. She squeezed hard as I groaned. I did not want to push New Life out, but my body would not obey. The Nemasket grandmother tending me was between my knees. Mis-tess told Esapett not to look.

My push ended, but I heard no cry. New Life had left me.

The fire in my shoulder seared hotter than ever when I tried to hold out my hands. The Nemasket grandmother moaned as she wiped New Life.

"Put her here." I patted my good side and the grandmother laid my too-early-baby in the crook of my arm. I wanted to follow her to the Spirit World.

Elisabeth
Mistress told me not to look, but I could not turn my eyes from Attitash. Her babe was not blue, it was gray like the sea when it rains. My friend lay very still, her babe cradled in her right arm. Her babe would never see light, never see the sky.

I would not have been present if Mistress had known Attitash would be delivered, because women were not allowed at childbed until they'd given birth themselves. When the still-born babe was born to Mistress Allerton on the Mayflower, I'd not seen it. But after its mother died, I'd caught a glimpse of the blue babe before it and Mistress Allerton were shrouded together and dropped into the sea.

Attitash looked so small lying on the bed, though she was much taller than I. They had stripped the furs from Attitash when they laid her down. Her soft hide dress, rusty red with blood, was pushed above her belly. I pulled the soiled dress down to cover the dark mass of bloody hair covering her secrets. Attitash opened her large dark eyes and gave me a look that stopped my heartbeat. Her long black hair, usually contained in a knot, now snaked out in tangles. I wanted to run my fingers through it and stroke her face. If we'd been alone, I would have.

The Indian women sang to Attitash. Mistress Brewster laid out cloths to catch the blood. My mouth was so dry I could not have spoken even if I'd had a coherent thought. The realization that Attitash might follow her babe chilled my whole body. I moved away from the blood-soaked bedding, then came back to her side to see if she still breathed.

Attitash

"Esapett?" I whispered, as she put her hand on my cheek. Her eyes still looked like quiet water, even when filled with tears. I remembered how they looked when she saved my little brother from drowning. But no one could save my daughter, my New Life.

She made a rocking baby motion and then laid a hand under my tiny child. "May I?"

I nodded. Esapett held New Life in her arms a long moment and then lifted her up for me to see. Her face was so small, no lashes feathered her closed eyes. She had a scant mat of hair. Her tiny fingers splayed out and her skin was gray.

"My nitka—mother—must come help me," I said.

"She will come." Esapett touched New Life's still face and put the little body back beside me. "When your nitka comes, she will help bury your babe."

We could not bury New Life here, not in Patuxet as we used to call this village. Would Esapett care when she discovered Jon-owland made me come to this terrible place? Her husband brought me here like I was a deer he'd caught.

Elisabeth

Attitash's tiny stillborn felt like a baby rabbit. The old Wampanoag woman took the body and Attitash turned away. She did not look up when my John brought our surgeon. More interested in healing than proving his own importance, Master Fuller consulted with Mistress Brewster on whether to remove the musket ball so soon after

Attitash's travail. They did not consult with Attitash, but the old Indian woman talked to her in a low voice, touching the place the musket ball had entered and placing her hand on Attitash's slightly raised belly, massaging it gently. We could not understand the words, but her gestures told us Attitash needed sleep.

Mistress sent Master Fuller away until morning. The young Indian women went to camp at Hopamoch's homesite, a quick walk down the hill and along the shore from our settlement. We cleaned up Brewsters' bed with new cornstalks and fresh linen so it no longer smelled of blood and put bedding on the floor for Attitash and the old woman. I don't know what was in the brew the old woman made, but Attitash did sleep.

The rest of us found sleep troublesome. The tiny house was crowded. I slept with little Humility and Desire, whose coughing woke me in the middle of a dream. I could hear Attitash moaning softly in her sleep and wondered if her dreams were of her lost babe or following the child to the grave. She would blame my people. How could I stay friends with Attitash? How could I live with my husband if he had fired at my friend? How could I myself carry a child and give birth without a husband? There were no answers. I finally drifted back into confusing dreams.

Attitash was still breathing, praise God, when I rose in the cold dark. Surgeon Fuller and Squanto were careful not to awaken her. By that time, Mistress and I had more hot water and clean cloths prepared. Attitash's eyes opened slowly when Squanto spoke to her. She did not welcome him.

We lifted her onto the table, padded with fresh reeds and worn linen. When Surgeon Fuller approached with his knives, Attitash shrieked and tried to twist away. Our surgeon commanded us to hold her down. I took one arm, Mistress the other. Attitash kicked. The Indian woman grabbed her feet. We used all our strength to hold her still as our surgeon tried to wedge a polished stick into her mouth. When she bit him, he shouted, "Do you want this musket ball to poison you? It will if I can't take it out!"

Squanto leaned over Attitash, talking rapidly. Her eyes rolled back in her head. Master Fuller began removing the poultice that covered her shoulder. Chanting loudly, the old Indian woman took the poultice. Attitash's young friend burst through the door, other Indian women behind her. The door stood open, cold wind blowing in.

Squanto spoke to them harshly. They closed the door and gathered around us, wailing. Their strong odor of unknown herbs and strange smoke made me gag. They stood on the benches and Master Brewster's chair. They crowded in front of the hearth, cutting off the heat from the three fires. In the best of times, six people made the room crowded. Now there were at least ten.

"Give us room!" Our surgeon motioned broadly with his knife. Two of the women shrank back, the others pressed forward, bumping up against me.

Squanto spoke again to the women, but they did not leave. Attitash's eyes opened, darting back and forth like an animal caught in a trap. I wanted to pick her up and fly with her like a bird, take her back to her mother.

The surgeon cut swiftly into her shoulder. She arched her back and screamed. Her pain throbbed into my own body. I felt her heart hammering away at the pain, trying to destroy it. Instead of pushing down on her arm, I stroked it, following her blood down through her strong forearm muscles to her hand. My unspoken words wrapped around her pain. Attitash, stay alive! You must live! Her fingers dug into my arm, carving red streaks. I could not contain my tears.

Attitash

The wolf claws were as bad as when New Life left me. The Stranger's healer was trying to cut out my heart. Even Esapett held me down. I vowed never to look into her eyes-like-quiet-water again. Only Mama and Black Whale could save me now.

Esapett let go of my arm and gently patted. I felt her meaning without needing to hear words. Live—live—live. The pain eased and so did my anger. I opened my eyes and saw hers filled with tears. Exhaustion pulled my eyes shut again. It filled me like heavy water dragging me into a deep hole.

The Stranger-who-pretended-to-heal was talking. A voice that sounded like Black Whale's was telling me to open my eyes. I kept them shut.

"Attitash!"

I opened my eyes and saw my husband's, bright with tears. "Take me home, Black Whale," I whispered. "I want my mother."

Tisquantum, standing by the Stranger-who-pretended-to-heal, spoke to Black Whale, just loud enough for me to hear. "The Cloth-Man knows how to destroy their fires-tick's Bad-Spirits," Tisquantum said. "This healer says the Bad Spirits were in your wife's shoulder, not in her woman-place. It did not cause the unborn to come too early."

Black Whale did not answer. He knew the Strangers killed New Life. He nudged Tisquantum away and massaged my feet. He looked over his shoulder at the crowded room. "Your mother has come."

I heard her voice. Esapett moved back and Mama held my head, moving her strong fingers across my forehead.

"I lost my New Life."

Mama leaned over me until her cheek touched mine. "I wanted to be with you." She stroked my hair gently.

"You're here now." I breathed in my mother's scent

with several slow breaths. It was like smelling sweet grass. "Where is Papa?"

"At home. Your father found our Massasowet. They got away from the Narragansett." My mother moved her hands gently to my belly. "I have lost more than one New Life before it saw light. It hurts our hearts."

I nodded, remembering her baby who died when I was young.

"Rest and heal," she said, shushing me when I tried to talk. "You are strong. You will have another."

"But it would not be New Life. I won't stop loving her!"

"You will love them all."

"Look at what the Cloth-man's healer took out of your daughter," Tisquantum's voice disturbed the soothing feeling Mama brought. He pointed to something the Stranger-who-pretended-to-heal was holding. "It's the hard stone they put in their firesticks, like a poisoned arrow to send the Bad Spirits into their prey."

"And why was Attitash their prey?" Mama asked Tisquantum.

"My New Life was their prey," I said. But Mama was right, I was their prey too. The Strangers could kill me. If I followed New Life, Black Whale would lose both of us.

Elisabeth

Was Attitash giving up? Her mother spoke to her with urgency. Squanto showed them the musket ball—disgusting, bloody thing. My gorge rose in my throat. Attitash turned away, but her mother only winced. Turning away from Squanto, her mother asked if she could see the stillborn babe. I went with her just outside the door where the box containing the sad bundle had been placed.

I tasted tears when Attitash's mother unwrapped the remains. The Indian women had wrapped it in a soft leather cloth, but its tiny face was uncovered. Black Whale came out and touched the smooth cheek. Then Attitash's mother carried the box back to Attitash.

"Praise God we were able to bring your daughter here and remove all trace of the unfortunate incident." Elder Brewster said to Attitash's mother when we returned to the house. "Unfortunate incident," was not what Elder Brewster called it when our own women lost babies.

Squanto said something in Wampanoag—his version of, "unfortunate incident," I assumed. Attitash's mother bit her lower lip so hard it turned almost white, but did not look at Squanto or Elder Brewster.

"We will take Attitash home, to her mother's fire," Black Whale told Master Brewster.

"Yea, that's where you belong, at Hopamoch's homesite." Master Brewster nodded with relief. Widow Ford was not the only one who thought it dangerous to harbor an injured heathen.

Attitash's mother bundled her in furs and Black Whale helped carry her in the hammock to their home. I followed until they started down the path to Hopamoch's homesite. My husband was building new houses, but I'd hoped he'd show up to bid farewell. As I turned to go home, I met Widow Ford and her children.

"Is it safe to come back?" She looked at the procession, pulling her young Martha close and hugging her babe. "Will Master Brewster cleanse his house with prayer before we enter?"

"Yea, prayers will be said," I answered somewhat evasively. I'd given the widow several pieces of my mind already, and I realized that if Mother were alive, she'd be as fearful as Martha Ford. "The Lord looks upon us with favor, and these heathens are on the Lord's side," I told her, liking that I sounded wiser than the widow. "The corn

He bent his head to my ear, "Would ye like to see thy letter from home?"

"For me?" I'd waited all these months for letters to come back from my brothers. When the ship, Fortune, arrived, the packet of letters had gone to our governor to be sorted. With the tumult of the rescue battle and horrific consequences, I'd forgotten. "Where is it?"

"I have it in my desk. If ye've had enough of this cold night air we can fetch it."

Governor's house was filled with men smoking and talking, John got the letter and we settled on the bench by the fireplace. The thin paper rattled in my hands, but I could still make out the words, *"To our beloved little sister, Elisabeth."* All ability to contain my emotions fled. I collapsed in John's arms, oblivious to the sudden silence in the house. John patted my shoulder, and then asked quietly, "Shall I read it out to thee?"

"If ye please." I wiped my eyes on my apron and took a deep breath. "After ye've read it, I will read it again myself."

We received thy letter and were sunk in Grief and Despair. Only our loving God can Understand why He would take our Father, Mother, Uncle Edward, and Aunt Agnes. We are grateful our Heavenly Father spared thee and Aunt's little niece, Humility. Word has been sent to the widow Cooper that her Daughter is with thee and thy guardians. Thy sister Rose sends her Love and wishes ye to know that Every day she joins in Prayer for thee. Rose, like the rest of us who remained in England facing King James's threat of hanging, prays constantly for our parents and all the others who met God through pestilence in His Promised land instead of at the hand of our treacherous monarch."

A sob slipped from me and John asked, "What is thy sister Rose like?"

"Rose and I told each other secrets every night in bed."

I remembered the distant sound of sheep bleating softly and the wind carrying the smell of new-mown hay. "That is, we did until Rose got married when I was eleven. Our bed was taken by Rose and her husband and I was alone on a cot by Mother and Father's. She has children now, but will never see ours—if God grants them to us." I nestled against John's shoulder. "Read more."

There are many Fears in our hearts for thee, alone without Family. Our prayers beseech God to find thee a Master capable of Molding thee when ye are indentured. Submit freely to thy Mistress and Master when they must Chastise thee. We pray that Satan's snare Releases thy left hand. As Jesus sat at the Right Hand of God, ye must always use thy Right.

My left hand tingled, remembering the rod's futile pain. That pain had been but a sliver compared to the burden of the Cur's violation of my body on the sea voyage to this New Land. I thanked God my family knew nothing of this and thanked Him again for using Attitash to heal me.

John continued to read for a moment, then stopped. He took my left hand in his and kissed it. "Both thy hands do the Lord's work, Love."

I thanked him for his soothing words, then asked him to finish the letter. My brother surely had more admonitions.

Dear sister, we Pray that ye be kept Safe from the savages, who set the Evil One's snare for him. We hear Loathsome tales of Satan's heathen people, far more Dangerous than the Lions and other fearsome Beasts. Never wander from thy Christian guardians' keeping.

We await Better News with the next return voyage. Give our Thanks to the man who reads this out for thee and ask him to once again write to your loving Brothers and Sisters.

"They will not be so indifferent to 'the man who reads,' when they discover ye now carry my name!" John gave my cheek a possessive peck and continued, *We were Pleased to see ye had learned to make your own sign. It is very Elegant.*

"What would thy brother think if he knew ye used thy left hand?"

I grimaced. "Robert would be on the next boat—or he'd abandon me."

"Would he not want to save thee from the accusations that could have thee hanged?"

I shook my head. "That I can't say, but I do know that ye saved me." I kissed him quickly and he returned to the letter.

Sister Rose has made a charcoal rubbing of the Betony flower for thee. In God's name and in His keeping, Brother Robert Tilley

John handed me the slip of paper with the rubbing. Rose had delicately brought out the whorls of the flower and I could picture the red-purple color. A faint remnant of the astringent scent clung to the paper. If only Rose could have preserved the stalk, a concoction from the juice could cure breath ailments and soothe childbirth pains.

I began composing a return letter in my head, but most everything that came to mind would be too thorny, my marriage-in-name-only to a man twice my age, conspiring with Attitash to convince Squanto to teach the English proper planting, or her heathen ceremony which purged me of the curse. And nothing of Massasowet's rescue and Attitash's wounding. That I could not even discuss with John! Truth be told, my family's life in England was a world to which I no longer belonged. My family would not recognize me, but once they accepted that I was a married woman, they would surely approve of my John.

He took my hand as he walked me home. He gave me one last kiss and a reminder that in a few months we would live as man and wife.

As soon as I sat down, little Humility climbed on my lap and asked me to sing the "Foggie" song. I'd not sung to her since she was sent to stay with Winslows during

Attitash's trauma. It brought joy to the Brewster household to have Humility back singing songs, and giving us kisses. Three-year-old Martha Ford, just a bit older than Humility, happily joined in, "Froggie went a courtin' and he did ride." By the time we finished all the verses, Humility was nearly asleep. I removed her dingy white dress and helped little Martha out of hers, then put both girls in Desire's bed. Widow Ford got out our bedding and laid it on the floor, then put her babe down and lay next to him. As I pulled up our covers, I prayed our psalm, *"Shout to Jehovah all the earth. Serve ye Jehovah with gladness. Before Him come with singing mirth. Know that Jehovah He God is."* I would come before Him singing mirth, if God put his merciful hands on Attitash.

5

ANOTHER WEEK PASSED before I dared go to Attitash. A cold wind brought snow and kept other women inside where they could not see me when I went to fetch water from the spring. It was mid-afternoon and the men were at work building houses. When I came to the spring, I scooped up my own cupful. It was ice-cold, bubbling up through snow. Leaving the yoke and water buckets, I took the path to the shore instead of through the woods. Anyone seeing me would assume I was collecting sand to scrub the pots.

The snow stopped and blue sky appeared between fat clouds. They danced, reflected in the waves below like heavy old women slow-stepping to the music. Pulling my cloak tight, I ducked my head out of the wind until I came to the A-shaped rocks that formed a barrier between Plimoth and Hopamoch's homesite. When I checked back to make sure no one observed me, I glimpsed a flutter of dark cloth beside a large boulder. As I watched, a face peeped above the rock and I recognized Remember Allerton. She ducked down again, but I ran back and pulled her up to face me. Her freckles stood out like cinnamon on her stark white face.

"Please, Mistress Elisabeth! Don't tell Father."

"What would I tell him?" Isaac Allerton had done me so much harm with his attempts to make me his indentured servant, even using this daughter to spread rumors that I was in Satan's snare, it was not likely I'd give him any information. "Why are ye here, child?"

"You are going to the heathen hut."

It was not a question. Remember Allerton and her little sister followed me there some months back. 'Twas their revelation of my secret cleansing ceremony that ignited vicious gossip.

"Why should I tell ye where I'm going? Thy father will bring forth new accusations."

"Nay, nay!" Her nose was dripping—from the cold or swallowed tears—and she wiped it on her cloak. "Please, let me go with you. I saw how quickly your Humility's burn healed, whereas my sister's burn left scars. I want the heathen's salve. Promise I won't tell." Tears pooled in her eyes.

"Her name is Attitash." I turned to the A-shaped rock. No salve could help her sister now. Remember would tell Widow Fuller where I was going regardless. Mayhap if I let her follow me, she'd have to keep the secret or risk inclusion in any rumors.

After we climbed through, the rocks slippery from snow, I did not stop until I came to the little round hut. Pausing at the entry flap, I called "Halooo."

"Esapett" came back a faint voice.

I told Remember to wait outside and I went in. The fire crackled in the center and most of the smoke floated up through the hole in the roof. Attitash was lying on one of the fur-covered benches that circled the little hut. The knot between her eyes was gone, but she looked very weary. The hut was surprisingly warm, free of the wind that found its way between the chinked clapboards of our houses. Attitash's friend adjusted some furs and motioned for me to sit down. I hesitated, wondering if Remember had already fled back home to tell on me. I turned back to the entry flap and found Remember still there, her face scrunched up against the cold wind and her cloak pulled tight. Waving my hands from Remember to Attitash, I attempted to ask if the girl was allowed inside.

Attitash

The memory of the deafening sound and foul smoke of the Strangers' weapons came back as soon as Esapett entered our moon lodge. She brought the sour Strangers' smell and looked out of place. Seafoam told her to sit, but she just stood there, snow melting all over our dry furs. Esapett looked back to the entry flap, then motioned to the spotted-faced girl and back to us, stumbling with our words.

Without waiting for Seafoam to understand, she brought in Spotted-Face. I gulped and forced myself to sit up. Why would Esapett bring that grimy runt in? The girl kept her head down, her shoulders stiff.

I closed my eyes so Esapett could not see the pain behind them. With my eyes shut, I might hide the image of her husband and all the other Strangers shooting their firesticks. I'd pushed away that memory during the sadness when the blood washed away my New Life before she could breathe. Now it was back.

Touching my arm gently, Esapett asked about my wound. Her voice was so familiar, so worried that I opened my eyes and tapped my shoulder to show it no longer throbbed. I flinched when Esapett lifted the poultice on my shoulder. She looked closely and smiled with relief.

Seafoam peeked at our guests warily as she gave a wooden cup of brew to Esapett, who shared a few sips with Spotted Face. I told Esapett how to say Seafoam's name in her own words and she made waves with her hands like the Big Salt Water dancing. Seafoam's smile flickered before she ducked her head. Esapett then put her hand lightly on my flat belly and touched her own heart. Neither of us had to say anything. We knew a poultice would not stop this pain.

Mama brought me the green cloth blanket Esapett had given me before I lost my New Life. Holding it out to

Esapett, I said, "Catabatash, Esapett. T'anku. New Life."
I swallowed down the lump of sorrow. "New Life is not."
I put it in her hands. "For Esapett's baby."

Esapett tried to give it back, "Matta—no. Keep for babe."

I had no more words she would understand, so I simply closed my eyes and prayed for both of us. I prayed we would both bring babies safely to the light.

Elisabeth
How could I tell Attitash to have faith that God, whom she called Kiehtan, would give her another babe? She refused to hear what little I knew how to say. Aunt Agnes' shawl smelled of the pungent smoke Attitash's mother used when she healed me of Satan's curse. Perhaps Attitash had been given a similar ceremony to erase her pain and she no longer wanted the reminder of her loss. Though it no longer smelled like Aunt Agnes, I could wrap it around Humility to remind her of her auntie-mother. I tucked the shawl under my cloak.

"Don't forget to ask for salve," Remember whispered.

Who knew what Remember would do with it, she had done nothing to prove she could be trusted. 'Twas fortunate she spoke no Wampanoag.

"This girl would like some of the ointment you use for burns," I told Attitash in English, rubbing my fingers. Attitash's widened eyes showed she understood. "Nun'squa matta netop." I said. Remember Allerton did not understand I'd said, "The young girl is not a friend," but Attitash did.

She spread her hands dismissively. "Ahhe, Esapett." Picking up a small jar, Attitash showed us that it was empty.

"Maybe she'll have some later, next time someone gets burned we'll ask," I told Remember. "Anyway, your

Mary's hand already has a scar. You must use the ointment when the burn is fresh."

"Catabatash," I thanked Attitash and nodded farewell to Seafoam, taking Remember's hand to lead her from the hut. Remember bobbed her head as she prattled, "Much obliged, Goodwife Awededash," and I hastily pulled her away.

Remember was full of questions. Why did I give away my late aunt's shawl? Why did Attitash's babe die? Why was their hut warmer than our houses? Before I could answer, I saw two Indians coming down the intersecting path from the hill. Each carried his bow over his shoulder with a small quiver of arrows. I recognized the first as Toka, a Wampanoag who spoke some English. Another Indian followed with a bundle. His face paint did not look like any of the Wampanoag. Something I could not identify made my skin crawl.

Remember yelped and tried to squeeze behind me on the path. Toka stopped short and turned to the man behind him. "Run back to the hut," I hissed. As we neared the longhouse, Black Whale came out and I pointed to the heathens.

He called out, "Toka-mahamon." When his kinsman responded, Black Whale motioned for us to hurry. We picked up our skirts and skittered down the path to Attitash's home, disheveled and out of breath.

Attitash

Esapett's voice brought me upright on the moon-lodge sleeping bench. Mama had gone back to our wetu and Seafoam was guarding the entry.

"Toka-mahamon came with a Narragansett," Black Whale reported through the flap. "I've brought Esapett and Spotted Face."

Seafoam opened the flap to our moon lodge for Esapett

and the girl to come in, and then closed it again. "Black Whale is showing Toka and the Narragansett to the Strangers' village," Seafoam told me.

Esapett and Spotted Face huddled by the fire, Esapett trying to reassure Spotted Face, her own face stark white. I was not exactly feeling calm myself, with a Narragansett's appearance in our place.

My friend and the girl were still trembling when we heard Black Whale return and call out, "Toka-mahamon says the Narragansett brings a message from his Sachem—Canonicus—to Sachem Bad-ford."

That reassured me somewhat. Unlike the betrayer, Tisquantum, we could trust Toka-mahamon and he knew many Strangers' words.

"I will lead Esapett and the girl back home before anyone misses them." Black Whale called.

He needed to take Esapett home, but that left Seafoam and me alone in the hut with a Narragansett close by. If only I could leave the moon lodge, where Black Whale was not allowed. I needed to be with him, feel his arms around me.

Seafoam opened the flap so Esapett and the girl could get out, then closed it just enough to talk to Black Whale. "Where should we hide?"

"No need. You'll be safe here," he assured my cousin. "He's come to see the Strangers, not us. Take care of Attitash." I heard their footsteps sloshing in the snow, then only the sound of wind in the trees.

What if our enemy arrived at Esapett's village with arrows flying only to be met with firesticks? I felt the searing pain of the Bad Spirit ball in my body again.

Elisabeth
Black Whale walked quickly and we stayed well behind him. Remember was not the only one who felt strange

walking with a heathen. I held Remember with one hand and lifted my skirts with the other. My heart was running away with my breath but I could not stop to rest. When we reached the spring to collect our buckets and fill them, Black Whale turned back.

6

Most of our people were gathered near the Common-house. Governor Bradford and Edward Winslow were with the Narragansett and Toka. I saw my John. He flicked a glance of relief my way, then turned back to the Indian. Widow Ford motioned to Remember to join her and they stood at the back of the crowd. I was able to slip back to Brewsters' house so I could stow Aunt Agnes' shawl before anyone asked why. I had no easy answers for why Attitash gave it back to me. Desire was tending Humility, so full of speculation over the Indians she did not notice the shawl.

"There's a Narragansett here—with a message from their king," I hastily told her, then went back to witness the confrontation.

I edged through the crowd to my husband and slipped my hand into his. He held it fast, keeping his eyes on the scene.

Master Allerton pushed in next to John, his eyes narrowed to slits. "Ask thy wife if she's seen my daughter."

John did not respond, knowing full well I'd heard.

"She's over there with Widow Ford," I told Isaac Allerton. "She and I went with to fetch water." Master Allerton stomped over to where they stood. He took his daughter's hand roughly and departed, ignoring the drama in front of us.

"What's happening?" I asked John. "I can't see over all these people."

"The Narragansett is giving something to Governor

Bradford." John grabbed me by the waist and lifted me up so I could see. Governor Bradford and Master Winslow faced us. Their faces were white with control, eyes focused on the Indian, their mouths a tight line—a model for all Christian men. Captain Miles Standish was incapable of such demeanor. He bounced up and down, face flushed and eyes darting. The Narragansett's face was fierce. It amazed me that he dared come into our stronghold. He held out a bulging object.

John set me down again and continued to narrate. "Governor's taking a quiver full of arrows from the Narragansett."

"What does it look like?"

"'Tis not leather—looks like snakeskin," John whispered.

"What vile purpose would a snakeskin quiver serve?"

He gave no answer as our governor consulted with Master Winslow and Stephen Hopkins. Captain Standish had hold of the Narragansett. "He is taking him to Hopkins' house."

Our governor turned to all of us, announcing in a loud voice, "This messenger is from Canonicus, king of the Narragansetts. Our friend, Toka-mahamon, tells me the snakeskin filled with arrows means Canonicus threatens us with war. If we do not submit, he would war against the Wampanoag as well." Murmurs from the crowd caused our governor to pause. "Hear ye now! I have sent for Squanto, he being our trusted translator. Until he arrives, this messenger shall be kept under armed guard." Governor Bradford paused and looked into the eyes of all the men of our settlement. "If the understanding of this message is confirmed to be war, do ye all agree with me that our answer will be to defend ourselves, as well as Massasowet and his people?"

"Yea! We will fight!" The great shout went up from the

men assembled. My John's voice rose with the others. The newer men joined lustily.

BEFORE DAWN, Governor Bradford went to meet with Squanto. By the time I'd prepared the morning porridge, our governor came back with news that Squanto confirmed Toka-mahamon's translation.

"I must answer this threat with a clear indication that our arms are superior and we will respond to arrows with guns," the Governor announced.

"Then you should replace the arrows in the quiver with gun powder," John suggested.

Captain Standish pounded the table with glee, spilling the cup of ale I'd just poured for him. "The savage king should know what that means without a translator."

A small smile relaxed our governor's mouth. "Good thinking, John. There should be enough in our bandoliers without retrieving more from the magazine."

I was not privy to the sight of the enemy's messenger accepting the snakeskin quiver filled with gun powder but he was sent home promptly and our men gathered in the Commonhouse.

When John and Governor returned, it was to announce the plan. He and Captain Standish agreed there would be daily drills to prepare against an attack. My John and the other men were divided into four companies.

I hated the sharp reports of muskets. It brought back the horror of Attitash's wounding. Despite every attempt to suppress the vision, I still imagined my own husband aiming his musket at my friend, an image that filled me with nauseating chills. The image would disappear when John was with me, but returned when he was out shooting muskets.

The second part of the plan our governor announced was that we would no longer live in an unprotected settlement. Plimoth would be impaled—surrounded by tall, sharpened logs.

As the wall was built, my view of the sky and the forest became framed by uneven stitching. I expressed my mixed feelings to Desire. We had walked to the new gate at one corner, which marked where we took the path to the shore. From our position near the fence, we could not see the shore or the water. Even the wheeling seagulls would disappear from view.

"Someone will always have to let me in or out, like I was a child kept in a garden," I told her.

She did not answer for a moment. I thought perhaps she did not hear me with her heavy woolen cloak hood pulled close. Finally, Desire turned to me. "On the other hand, no one can come in without being seen." She raised her hood back so she got a clear view of the hills. "Do ye really think we women can gad about like the birds and rabbits?" Desire laughed wryly. "Have ye not heard that these heathen kidnap people—young women being part of their game?" When I did not respond, she continued. "I heard Elder Brewster and Mistress speaking of it. Worrying about their daughters, if they come on the next ship."

"Well, they needn't worry now," I answered. I did understand the need to protect us all, but it chafed my spirit and I wondered if it would do any more to protect us than our current practice of keeping lookout guards.

Attitash
Papa showed us the foolish wall the Strangers built. "They know that any Narragansett could send a flaming arrow over the wall and set afire the dried grass roofs of their houses." To prevent that, my father told us, Sachem Badford would have men guarding the wall. "They will call an alarm if any Narragansett is sighted. The guards carry big

firesticks. Each of these has more black-sand fire powder than that quiver-full they sent back to Canonicus."

Mama paused in her work drying the squash slices over a fire. "The Strangers could start a fire themselves, shooting at the Narragansett." We'd already seen fires started by sparks from their chimneys. Some they were able to put out, but one of their houses had burned down before they finished building it. "This is a dangerous place. I think Attitash should go to Poanoke as soon as she's strong enough."

There had been much talk around our fire about where I should live during my healing. The journey back to Grandmother's fire in Poanoke might be dangerous, but to remain near the Strangers was even worse. Even if they kept their firesticks to themselves, they might be a draw to Sachem Canonicus and all the Narragansett.

It was finally settled that Black Whale could protect me and Seafoam, and that our small party with two women would not be seen as dangerous to any Narragansett spies.

Seafoam and I were eager to leave, but Black Whale was worried about my endurance. I had been doing light work without any pain for a month, but still did not carry heavy packs. He was worried that if we had to flee Narragansett, I could not run.

"Are you sure you're ready?" Black Whale stroked my cheek. He meant his touch to be tender, but I longed for the time when he could touch me everywhere. Tenderness that lacks desire feels more like pity.

"Husband, I am ready to travel and I am certain I will also be ready to ask for all your passion before the river-ice-gone moon comes."

"I will wait until you invite me, but then be ready for a strong man to melt you." Black Whale cupped my head gently and for the first time in many moons warmth gathered in my empty womb.

7

Elisabeth

God allowed a late winter storm to interfere with our plans to have a home ready by early March. John expected to use all the short hours of winter daylight to work. He'd adjusted his plans when Captain Standish demanded the men spend time every day exercising their arms. John reminded me that the marching and shooting were necessary to prepare for a Narragansett attack. Then the late February storm shut down the arms exercises, building the house and even any opportunity to see each other.

All of us were trapped in our crowded little houses, John in Bradford's and I in Brewster's. The wind whirled the snow so thick we could see nothing outside. Everyone indoors was underfoot. The Brewster boys vented their restlessness with quarreling, usually with each other and at times with the younger children. Elder Brewster, usually so calm, gave his sons the rod more than once, to little avail.

Desire and I made an effort to keep Humility and little Martha occupied. After singing "Froggie Went a Courting" ten times, I was ready to break into "Greensleeves," even though it comes from the foul King. And "Peas Porridge Hot" became tiresome even to little ones. Humility's big brown eyes grew even larger while listening one more time to the story of baby Moses being rescued from the bulrushes. When she was a little older she might recognize a parallel to her own life. But a three-year-old only knows the wonder of finding a baby. She peeked at Widow Ford's three-month old babe.

"Did you find him in a basket?"

Widow Ford managed a bleak smile. The babe had been fussy all day, the house too noisy to allow a child to sleep very long. "If I could count on someone to find the babe, I'd put him in a basket right now."

Her daughter started to protest and the widow shook her finger in little Martha's face. "And ye will be in there with him if ye don't stop sniveling."

Humility and the babe's big sister grew very possessive, each standing by infant John, putting a finger out for him to grasp and waving away the lazy flies that woke from their winter slumber when the fire warmed the house.

I awoke the next morning to the quiet sound of melting snow dripping from the roof onto the wet ground.

The Brewster boys were glad to be the first out, scooping the heavy slush from the door. John was at our door in his tall leather boots, grabbed me right in front of everyone and gave me a sweet kiss.

"Don't think ye get to bundle now, John," Mistress laughed. "Too much work to do."

The snow melted within a day. Their arms exercises resumed, bringing back the boom of their muskets. Of course the servant boy, William Latham, took great delight in any arms drills. On his way to fetch more powder or musket balls, he'd interrupt my chores, wanting me to applaud his imitation of "our men, returning Narragansett fire."

"Cap'n tells our men that we must fire at them before their flaming arrows land on our houses Mistress," William told me, his young face filled with pride that he could use his second-hand knowledge to inform me.

"And how will a musket put out flames?" I demanded.

The pales surrounding our village could not stop these, and the boy knew it. I thought of our own home that was rising under John's hand, my heart fluttered imagining it filled with our rude furnishings. Would I have to worry each night that our thatched roof might catch fire?

"Cap'n thinks of everything, Mistress." William said.

I did not give Captain Standish much credit for thinking. My face must have revealed my doubt. William drew himself up as though he were already a man.

"By your leave, Mistress, there is indeed a plan. Just ask Master Howland." He then turned and ran on.

That thought was kept at the back of my mind when I found John working on the roofless frame that was our home.

"I could stop worrying about the Narragansett," I told John, "if I knew there was a plan to keep our houses from being set afire."

He continued studying the pile of newly sawn clapboards and did not answer. Were all wives left ignorant?

"Should I ask Master Brewster about a plan?"

John finally looked at me and grinned. "'Tis a clever plan, and ye shall know it. A company has been formed to respond if the enemy fires."

"What would a small company do?"

"While others put out the fire, our small company will take up our arms to prevent treachery," John explained.

"So the company would be on guard to shoot any enemy storming the pales?"

"We would indeed. Ye listen well, Wife."

"Ye explain well, Husband." I waited for more details, but he was studying the clapboards again. "Ye are part of this company then, John? Who commands it?"

John's smile revealed his pride. "I will."

"Well deserved. Ye have proven ye can fight," I saluted his small pride. Truth be told, however, both his reputation and his new responsibility troubled my heart.

When I arrived back at the Brewsters, Desire and Widow Ford were in the garden washing up. I took advantage of a rare moment alone with Mistress. "John is honored to be responsible for his group of guards," I told Mistress Brewster as we plaited our hair for bed. "But there is something about his soldiering that troubles me." I described my disturbing image when the muskets sounded. "John may carry the knowledge that his musket ball wounded Attitash."

Mistress Brewster raised her hands in prayer, and I thought she was ignoring my words to carry on with her bedtime supplications. She said nothing, then lowered her hands and took mine in hers. "It's time the two of you bundle again."

I removed my hands from hers. We'd be in our marriage bed soon. Why would she suggest lying in bed with a board between us and the whole household listening to us now? "What do you have in mind, Mistress?"

"Thy friend has healed, she'll have another babe." Mistress continued. "And whatever it is that John Howland did or did not do, he may have sought forgiveness from God."

"And so?" A pulse of regret for not trusting John beat in my throat.

"Ye must speak with him." Mistress' quiet voice sunk to a low whisper. "With our village fenced and guards watching anyone beyond the pales, there's no opportunity to seek privacy. The curtains 'round the bed might allow intimate conversation."

Intimate conversation while bundling could go all wrong, however. What if John refused to answer my questions? We'd be trapped in bed with each other—already married and no longer wanting each other. John and I could surely find a more private place for intimate conversation than in a curtained bed surrounded by the household. I knew Mistress enjoyed a bit of juicy gossip. When we'd bundled the first time, she may have discovered through the curtains that John touched my breasts and reached below my navel.

Regardless of Mistress's motive, John and I would find a way to have the conversation.

I caught John alone again next day, working on our house, and told him Mistress offered us another bundling.

His response was quick. "Why now? In a week or two I'll have ye in a proper marriage bed." He looked into my eyes. "Dear heart, I don't think I could resist thy charms, even in a bed surrounded by the entire listening household. Ye deserve better for thy first time as my true wife."

Despite the warmth spreading over my body, I continued. "She knows we need to talk."

John waited a beat, examining his hands. "Have ye more to tell me?"

"Nay! Have ye more to tell me?" The warmth turned to cold fury. "I've already told thee my secrets—the abuse I'd suffered on the Mayflower and how I was cleansed by the heathens. Is there nothing polluting thine own heart? God save us, John, Attitash carries a wound and lost a child!"

Before John could answer, Captain Standish shouted from the lane by our house. "Howland, we are assembling to exercise our arms."

John turned and I was left with a hollow feeling, wondering if God wanted my life to be like Desire's—without a man and glad of it.

John kept his eyes cast down during supper and scarce spoke to Governor Bradford or Master Eaton while they smoked their pipes. When I'd finished cleaning up, John rose from his chair. Without a word, he touched my hand and pointed to the door. I hurried into my cloak and followed him out. The night air chilled my face and I pulled my cloak tight. John went into the little garden and turned to me. The sliver of new moon hung over the palings to the west, just above the hills. I could barely make out his face.

"We may be going into battle again." John's voice had an edge, betraying his effort to keep it calm. "Do ye understand what that means?"

My back became a straight beam. "Why must ye ask that? Do ye think I am still the young girl I was before we left England?"

He shifted his feet. "Nay, I do not. I ask because, thank God, ye've not yet been caught in a battle." John took me by the shoulders and I could see the intensity of his eyes in the faint starlight. "I'd never been in a battle before we came here. So, listen. In battle we do not know what will happen. We prepare for the worst. We are defending ourselves, our people." John leaned toward me. "I am defending thee."

I nodded, every part of my body straining to understand.

"Standish told us to stand guard when he went into the rebel Indian's house. We all thought Massasowet was held captive there. He told us to shoot if Massasowet's enemies ran out." John paused and took a deep breath. "We lit our muskets. When we heard people running we shot." John's hands gripped my shoulders so hard I felt their heat through my cloak. "That is God's truth." He released me and looked up at the sky crowded with stars. "It was raining. Dark. We could see nothing. Who knew there would be friends not enemies? Who knew it would be women— thy friend among them!—running out?" He pressed his hands against his temples. "My musket worked, everyone's worked. Only God knows who hit her."

John pulled me to him. "Never—never in my worst night-terrors—did I dream any of us would shoot a friend." He hugged me for a long moment and I sank into his despair. "Never did I imagine a woman great with child would run out of that house." A shudder took his breath. "Never Attitash."

I could no longer ask a question for which there was no answer. John had been honest with me. The memory of that night and its terrible consequences would live on. I lifted my face to his. "Your suffering is my suffering, John."

8

After John Finished the clapboard framing, I helped spread the daub for our walls. Spreading wet mud on the walls didn't work as it had back in England, we'd learned. Plimoth mud had no heft and the walls fell down on the first house they'd built. John said there was no sediment in the soil here. By trial-and-error we'd learned to mix straw for sufficient binding.

Once the walls were dry, and the roof thatched, John built a cupboard. Mistress and Desire helped me place my mother's housekeeping bits: two towels, two trenchers, spoons and beakers, one kettle and two pots. Humility put things away, then took them out again, continuing until Desire slapped her hands lightly and played pat-a-cake to distract her. With a braided reed basket near the hearth to hold wood and another hung high on a peg to keep the food away from vermin, all looked tidy. Mistress and Desire dissuaded Humility from emptying the kindling basket and took her with them.

I was scraping salt from the cone when John came at noon to survey the result. He frowned, then paced off the tiny house. "Our bed will be up against the table, can ye abide such crowded space?" He sat down on the chair which Master Carver had left him and pulled me to his lap.

"It will do." I brushed salt from my hands into the bowl. "I know ye can make the table and bed fit the space."

John nuzzled my neck. "As soon as the bed's ready, I'll have thee in it. Can we move in day after tomorrow, the Sabbath? I can make the bed and table in one day."

I blushed. "No need to hurry." My courses had just come that morn. By Thursday I should be ready.

I recalled one of Mistress Bradford's recent lectures. "Ye'll know that John's got thee with child when thy courses stop," she had said. "Let's hope ye don't feel pleasure 'til ye bleed two months in a row." I waited for her to explain. I'd heard idle talk about women with only two children, like Goodwife Billington, who could not get with child because her husband did not pleasure her. He was such a brute it was a wonder they had any children. "Ye must understand," she continued, "the gossips will claim he'd bedded thee too fast if ye come up carrying after just a month. A young maid needs a patient mate."

I stood, realizing John's lap was not exactly a safe place to be sitting this time of the month.

That night I was awake far into the night—imagining what might transpire when at last my husband took me for his own. A rustling from Brewsters' bed, followed by faint moans intruded on my dreams. I was not surprised someone as old as the Brewsters still wanted delight in their bed. These rustlings had become familiar when I lived with Master and Mistress Carver. Once John and I had bundled, I had more idea of what was causing the nighttime noises. But now, instead of covering my head with the blanket, I paid attention. It did rather surprise me that it seemed to take so long. Was Master Brewster strong enough? I pulled the pillow over my head. I wanted only to picture my husband, not my master.

THANKS-GIVING SERVICES WERE HELD before sundown each Thursday. I spent the day getting ready so we could return from services to our home. The new tick was stuffed with straw and all was in place before supper. I reached into the stores and brought out a small beaker Constance Hopkins had filled for me from her father's bottle, saying her mother recommended it for virgins. I had only tasted the strong drink once since the night Constance brought some top-deck during our voyage across the ocean. I poured out the little beaker into the slop bucket. I wanted no reminder of that night.

When Humility saw me moving my trunk, she wanted to bring her little poppet and come with me. Desire gently took the poppet and placed the rag doll on her own bed. "Poppet wants ye to sleep here with me, Humility."

After supper, we walked separately, as we always did to services, the women in front and the men carrying arms behind us. I sat across the aisle from John. Everyone was looking at us. Even Elder Brewster looked my way, then John's, as he gave thanks for "All those who have survived to come before Thee today as man and wife."

The sun was still lighting the timbered hills to the west when we finally entered our house and shut the door. I helped John unlace the points on his breeks. He took them off and shook the dirt onto the hearth. His long shirt covered his knees and he brushed it off as well.

As he pulled the curtain over the window, Capt. Standish's loud voice called to me, asking if I needed any of his weapons to defend myself. Then another voice, which seemed to be Constance Hopkins' brother, Giles, "Do you want a boy to practice on first, Elisabeth?"

"I'll practice on thy head!" John yelled back. It seemed we were surrounded by at least ten men guffawing and making lewd jokes. John just grinned and banged his beaker of ale on the table, telling me in a loud voice that we needed some bread and cheese, "to last until the vermin flee the night."

I giggled and thought, "Three blind mice..." but did not give voice to the song.

John took his flint and struck a flame to light a candle

as it finally quieted outside. I stood with my back to him so he could work on my laces. The fresh rushes on the floor tickled my bare feet. When my stays were free, I turned around. "It's still light outside," I whispered.

"Yea, just a bit." He pulled me onto his lap and settled me. "We have a minute to read the Bible."

It was not what I had in mind, but I leaned into his shoulder to listen.

"Time for Solomon." John turned the pages and showed it to me.

I traced the words and read, *"My beloved is mine and I am his."*

John blew out the candle. We found the bed in the dark. My shift had already slipped off my shoulders and I involuntarily arched my back to boldly present my tingling breasts. My husband took his time exploring. John's touch was enhanced with his spoken endearments. Even in the dark I blushed to hear the eagerness in his voice. I responded with loving words to each of his, but was too shy to let my hands respond to his touch, except to grip his shoulders. My only thought was to belong to each other at last. Truth be told, there was no thought, only feelings. When he entered me, I tried to keep perfectly still to stop the pain. That was impossible, but the pain diminished with the flood of warmth as he shuddered and sank into my arms.

When we could both draw breath, he raised himself on an elbow and traced my mouth. "I hope I did not harm thee, Dearest Love."

"Is making me thy true wife harm?" I leaned into his chest, listening to his heart. The slight ache between my legs was nothing compared to the lovely warmth filling my body and soul.

"I take thee, Elisabeth, to be my wedded wife. To love and to cherish."

"I take thee, John, to be my wedded husband. To love and to cherish...'til death do us part...as long as we both shall live."

John kissed me slowly. "And we shall live as husband and wife for fifty years."

I laughed. "I will be an honored grandmother instead of a too-young bride!"

He put his arms around me and I sank immediately in sleep. It was still dark when I awoke. I could not tell how long before sunrise. John was breathing deeply beside me. It was so strange and so wonderful to have him there. My secret place was only a little sore, nothing compared to the great swell of realization that I was a true wife—that I was a woman! Snuggling close to my husband, I slept again until he woke me with a kiss.

John went out in the pre-dawn light to relieve himself. I checked the bedding. The smear of dried blood from losing my maidenhead would have to be washed. I pulled the covers over and set about building up the fire and making breakfast. John's smile was tinged with concern when he came back in. Once I'd assured him I not only felt fine, I felt womanly, he laughed and kissed me thoroughly.

"Next time ye will find what a true wife can enjoy," he promised before he left for the fields. After I cleaned up from breakfast, I began work on the stain. Glad for the sunny day, I pulled all the bedding and rubbed soap on the spot, then set it to soak in cold water. It was a small stain, but it reminded me of the efforts it had taken Mistress Brewster and me to wash out Attitash's blood after her great loss. Could I suffer such a loss? It did not require a musket ball for a babe, or a woman, to die in childbed. Maybe I was too young to deliver safely. The lingering warmth in my body chilled. Surely I had not felt the delight a wife must feel for her husband's seed to take hold. Gratitude, amazement, love, but not the kind of delight

Priscilla described as "wanting more and more."

Priscilla herself found me rinsing the soaked sheet with hot water and laughed. She stroked the small bulge in her belly, telling me that young women do better in child-bed than old ones. My worries faded and were gone with John's sweet kisses when the sunset brought us back to bed again. He was right, I did enjoy his entry this time, but I made certain that I contained myself and did not cry out for more.

9

January, 1622
Attitash

We began our journey early in the morning. Black Whale kept his spear ready, on the alert for Narragansett. The dogs, Mowi and Suki, pulled a travois and Seafoam carried a pack. Toward evening the path up the hill grew steep and Black Whale carried me. Leaning into his shoulder, I whispered, "I will carry my own weight soon." He huffed, a reply that seemed to both gasp for air and expel my concerns.

It was almost dark when we reached a level place. Black Whale cut pine boughs and Seafoam piled them thickly for our sleep. I felt as if I were watching Seafoam and Black Whale prepare to lie down together while I floated in the dark sky. I slept between them, waking often to the strange sensation of my cousin on one side and my husband on the other. We trusted the dogs to alert us if Narragansett approached, but I listened for footsteps anyway. When I did drift back to sleep, the dream came again that disturbed my sleep since I lost New Life. A little snow fell during the night, not enough to get under our furs.

We munched journey cake as we started out next morning. Sleep crept back to me and I stumbled. Black Whale carried me more than I walked. When we finally arrived home, I was so exhausted I could barely return my sister White Flower's embrace. I hardly even listened to Grandmother's news about the snakeskin quiver. No one in our village knew where it was, only that Canonicus had banished it from his sight.

Seafoam touched my face in farewell before she went to her mother's fire, hoping her husband would return to her. I wondered if Shimmering Fish was indeed loyal to our Massasowet now.

After sleeping for a day and a night, I felt well enough to eat and talk with my Otter Clan family. My shoulder no longer demanded my constant attention, only when I forgot and moved my arm quickly.

Aunt Blue Sky's little daughter toddled about the neesh'wetu until Uncle Seekonk picked Ice Feathers up and bounced her. It was good to see Black Whale's clan uncle as father to his own child.

When Uncle Seekonk and Black Whale went to set traps, I told Grandmother the dream that tore sleep from me so often since my loss. "I was a grandmother like you."

She smiled, "Ahhe, and you will have children soon. And they will have children."

My eyes closed to see my dream. "My grandchildren were grown too," I told her. "I was very old. But I could still see. Bad spirits controlled everything."

Grandmother murmured softly. I could not hear what she said.

"I saw such horrible things, but the dream began with pleasure," I continued. "I saw our children—ahhe, we had healthy, beautiful children. Esapett also had many, healthy, beautiful children. My children carried firesticks. As they walked, more and more Strangers walked with us. The path they walked widened and then lost its soft surface of leaves and earth. It became hard, with many little rocks that hurt our feet. The forest filled with Strangers' dwellings. The Big Salt Water was filled with the Strangers' Big Wind Canoes. All of them had our trees holding up their white cloths."

Grandmother put her arm around me. "Who knows what the Bad Spirits will bring, or whether we can keep them out of our bodies. You needed to leave Patuxet, Attitash. The bad spirits still live there. Was that the end of the dream?"

"Yes," I lied. The rest of the dream could not be told. Even awake it stiffened my body. Unbearable noise. Thick, black smoke. Blood running into the Big Salt Water.

She poured me some of the healing tea.

"Where are Black Whale and Uncle?" I asked Grandmother.

"They have not returned from the trap line."

I became aware of the howling wind and snow coming down our smoke-hole. It had been so warm when Black Whale left that the remaining snow was disappearing. A storm during the ice-melting-moon was dangerous, bringing heavy, wet snow that could pull a strong man beneath it and keep him there.

"Black Whale and Seekonk know how to survive. They'll take shelter in a hollow log or build one from branches, as Black Whale did during his vision quest."

"What if the Narragansett find them?" I asked.

"If the snow holds our men hostage, so does it also hold our enemy," she said, and stroked my forehead. "Now sleep some more."

My dog, Suki, was snuggled up against me and I tried to use her comfort to bring back sleep, but it would not come. Singing prayers softly, not wanting to wake my family, I'd passed into dreams. A dog whining was part of my dream, but when Suki nudged me with her wet nose, I realized the whine was coming from outside. Suki's whines changed to yips, but she did not move. Pulling my fur tight about me, I called into the night.

A faint voice answered. Suki started toward the sound, looking back to make certain I was coming. Quickly wrapping my feet, I stumbled behind the dog through the wet snow. Twenty or so paces away, Black Whale was crouched, so covered with snow he looked more like a tree stump than a man. I squatted in front of him and he fumbled to uncover the furs over his face.

I pressed my cheek against his icy one. He trembled so violently that words were impossible.

Finally, he whispered, "Get help. Uncle Seekonk twisted his ankle. He's many paces behind me. I tried to carry him."

Suki howled and Black Whale's dog, Mowi, joined in. Aunt Blue Sky opened the door flap and I called to her.

Black Whale stood up and leaning against me walked to the neesh'wetu. While Grandmother and I tended Black Whale, Aunt Blue Sky ran to Massasowet's home and soon four men were following the tracks in the snow. Once Black Whale had changed to dry moccasins packed with fresh moss and had a quick gulp of broth, he insisted on following them.

It seemed like another full night before the first rays of Nippa'uus revealed the men bringing Seekonk, his arms around their shoulders. Grandmother massaged his feet with tepid water and then Aunt Blue Sky pasted her husband's ankle with a woundwort concoction and bound it.

Grandmother firmly reminded Uncle and Black Whale to watch the sky spirit's signs. Then they were allowed to sleep.

I curled up next to my husband, pictures behind my eyes of Black Whale struggling home after his clan uncle was injured, remembering that he'd learned on his vision quest to look ahead ten paces and keep a tree in sight, trying to see too far ahead would only get one lost. Now, I gratefully listened to my husband breathe the deep breaths of the weary. My womb ached for his seed. I knew that within a few circles of Nippa'uus, the river ice would melt,

Uncle's feet would heal and my husband would be my strong lover again.

A FEW NIGHTS LATER, I brought a small pot of the new syrup with me as Black Whale and I walked to our Trees-in-Love. We had mourned our first new-life, now it was time for a sister or brother. The two trees wound even tighter about each other than last year when we'd joined beneath them. Dipping a finger in the warm syrup, I gave it to Black Whale. When he'd licked my finger clean, he passed his sweetened tongue over my wrist, then up my arm. I took off my fur and laid it over the damp grass.

Once settled on the furs, I dipped into the syrup again and frosted my nipples. As Black Whale tasted them, I traced his straight nose and the small dent above his mouth. My woman-place was slippery, ready to receive his seed. With a small moan, he proved he was ready to give.

Elisabeth

John was too eager. He could not hide his anticipation as he loaded powder into his bandoliers. My husband had made me his true wife only a fortnight ago, but now he apparently felt no regret at leaving me to run off with Captain Standish.

"Do ye expect a fight with the Massachuseuks?" I held my breath for the answer.

"We don't expect a fight with anyone," John said. "But we must be prepared."

Rather than argue, I put my hand on his and looked into his eyes. "Ye are filled with excitement. Just to go on a trading mission?"

He flushed. "Ye know me too well. Yea, there has been some dissention on whether to go at all. Hopamoch claims the Narragansett are allied with the Massachuseuks. But we have no food and the Massachuseuks sent word they will trade us beaver and also more corn to feed all these new people." He looked up as my sigh escaped. "Dear Heart, don't worry! I'll return in a few days and ye can welcome me back to our bed as warmly as ye've done each night!" John put down the bandoliers and took me in his arms. "Who would have thought such a young maid could be so passionate?"

Now, I turned rosy. Maybe my new husband needed to rest. Most nights, I'd eagerly accepted every gentle kiss John bestowed on my tender places. He brought me to new delight and soon I'd found ways of my own to bring pleasure to his wondrously strong body. My earlier fears diminished.

"Remember me each night." He kissed me again.

"I will," I assured him, then whispered to myself, "But I will be alone." Alone and empty.

"And know I shall make up for every night lost." John picked up his musket and went to the door, pausing to let me through.

My earlier fears came creeping back and settled in my throat. After joining with him completely, I would now be hollow without him. I swallowed hard. He must not see my girlish lack of courage. We walked silently to the shore. Amidst the bustle of loading the shallop, I did not have an opportunity to speak again. As he climbed into the long-boat, I called out one last, 'fare thee well.'

10

April, 1622

Attitash

I went outside our neesh'wetu to tend the supper fire when Black Whale and Uncle Seekonk came running home, their faces agleam with sweat.

"Do you know where Shimmering Fish is?" Black Whale called before he reached me.

"Not here," I said.

"Is he with Seafoam?" Uncle Seekonk was puffing.

"The last time I talked to her, they were together," I said. "Why do you ask for him?"

My husband and his clan uncle exchanged glances as Aunt Blue Sky came from the neesh'wetu with her baby in the cradleboard. Uncle Seekonk went to nuzzle his daughter, then kissed his wife's cheek. Black Whale put down his bow and arrow and finally came to my side.

"We don't want to frighten anyone." He glanced at Aunt Blue Sky and her daughter."

"Frighten us about what?" I repeated. "I'll worry less if I know what's happening."

"We saw Tisquantum and Shimmering Fish. They were speaking very quietly together and when they saw us on the path, they ran in opposite directions. Tisquantum went towards Patuxet and Shimmering Fish toward the Big Salt Water."

"What is so frightening about that?"

Black Whale scooped up some stew from the bubbling pot with the wooden ladle, letting it cool before he ate.

"Probably nothing. We just always worry about Tisquantum." He put the ladle back, then pulled me close. "Don't worry. Stay safe. Uncle Seekonk will talk to Massasowet and he'll go to the Grandmothers' council. If we can't find Shimmering Fish by next circle of Nippa'uus, I may have to go to Patuxet and see if he is there."

Elisabeth

Priscilla and I took little slips of chive, rue, and parsley. Even the sharp smell of chive was soothing. We used left-about boards to build up beds for the seedlings. "I'll be big with child before we harvest," Priscilla laughed. "Won't want to be kneeling on the ground."

I hoped that speaking of her new condition didn't tempt the bad faeries. The old wives at home said such faeries could snatch the life from a babe before it even moved in the womb.

We were carrying water from the catch-basin to the new plants when William Latham came running.

"There's a savage with blood on his face come to the wall! Governor's sounding the alarm."

Before we could ask William any questions, the boom of our cannon broke the soft spring air. Men from the fields scurried in the gates.

"God in heaven! What is happening?" Mistress Brewster pulled us back into her house. Martha Ford's babe was screaming and her little girl clung to her skirts. Elder Brewster came in, his face gray.

"The Indian made signs to warn us. He waved a yellow feather—their king's symbol—and Winslow says he claims Massasowet is betraying our compact and is now marching to attack us." Elder Brewster sat down heavily and took a long breath. "The Indian insisted we shoot our cannon as an alarm so that Standish and the men in the shallop will come back to defend us. The shallop was still within earshot and is coming to shore."

"Are ye certain that's what the Indian meant?" Mistress Brewster asked.

Her husband shrugged. "One can never be certain."

"Where's the heathen?" Martha Ford demanded.

"He's secured with chains in the commonhouse, until we find out if the messenger is telling the truth." Master Brewster answered.

The back of my neck broke out in sweat. Would Massasowet's soldiers fire upon our men in the shallop? Massasowet was trusted by all the people I trusted. Only Isaac Allerton spoke up against him.

Priscilla's mouth was blue and she seemed unable to speak. I took her hand, needing reassurance myself, but concerned for her condition. Mistress dosed Priscilla with a strong tea. Her color was returning when a cry came that the shallop was near.

Amid a hullabaloo of shouts and attempts at explanations, I struggled to see my beloved among the group coming through the gate. John found me quickly, hugging me so hard his muscles pushed against my ribs. We all stood outside the commonhouse, trying to listen while Hopamoch and Edward Winslow talked with the bloody-faced Indian man, then consulted with our Governor.

Attitash's mother arrived from their homesite and stood near me. Her younger daughter stood next to her, the little brother on the girl's hip. Attitash's mother touched my arm and indicated the messenger in chains. The man's head was bent. When he looked up, I nearly cried out. A gruesome face indeed.

Attitash's mother leaned to my ear. "Seafoam's man."

"Husband?"

"Ahhe." She said the affirmative as if it were a foul word. I had not even known Seafoam had a husband. I realized that since Attitash was living in King

Massasowet's village, her cousin Seafoam would be there too. This husband must have come from there. Was Attitash safe? Was King Massasowet protecting her or endangering her?

Hopamoch seemed to be making a great effort to control his rage and speak our language. "Massasowet friend. More friend than Tisquantum—Squanto." He continued, switching to Wampanoag as Master Winslow translated. "Hopamoch says this Indian, Shimmering Fish, who claims he is a friend, is Squanto's family. Squanto disappeared as soon as the shallop landed. Hopamoch says Squanto is the betrayer, not King Massasowet."

I clenched John's hand, digging my nails into his palm so my fear and anger would not be revealed. Seafoam's husband was a betrayer of King Massasowet, our compact, and our peace.

"Squanto speaks more English than Hopamoch does," John whispered. "If he works against Massasowet, our negotiations with other Indians are doomed and our compact useless."

"We are in danger—and so is Attitash!"

John tightened his arm around me. *Calm down, stand tall*, I told myself.

Governor Bradford's face knitted into a pattern of frowns as he pondered Hopamoch's words. Hopamoch now bent to the prisoner's face and wiped the blood with dried plants he took from his string belt. With the blood cleaned off, Hopamoch traced the long, narrow cut on the prisoner's face. Master Winslow leaned in close to observe, listening to Hopamoch's tense words.

"Hopamoch says no enemy caused this wound. It is straight, such as could only be made carefully," Master Winslow announced. "This was an intentional cut, such as he might have made himself or for purposes of deceit."

"Pshaw! Lies!" Isaac Allerton said, then continued in

private converse with Governor Bradford, who grimaced as if the words were putrid meat.

I wondered if Allerton's false face was obvious to Governor Bradford. Our governor had held firm against Isaac Allerton's plans to make me his indentured servant. Bradford knew that Allerton had harried me mercilessly with accusations of witchcraft. But Governor Bradford and Mistress Brewster both seemed to assume Isaac Allerton would easily be redeemed. Our governor had agreed when Mistress Brewster proclaimed, "All Isaac needs is a good woman to replace his dead wife."

Deputy Governor Allerton was now murmuring with his little band of allies in one corner, ignoring our governor's request for civil discussion. He certainly was not respectful of Governor Bradford, but I could not assume this meant Isaac Allerton was practicing deceit with Squanto and this rebel.

Master Allerton did not look directly at Seafoam's husband. Perhaps he did not want to reveal a connection with the rebel.

Governor Bradford spoke loudly to Allerton. "Isaac, how do you propose we verify the truth? Who can prove that what Hopamoch says is the falsehood you believe it to be, or whether this bloody man practices deceit?"

Isaac Allerton stroked his beard, sneering at Hopamoch. "This is a falsehood! Hopamoch knows nothing of what Massasowet is doing. He only hopes to remain in your good graces."

Governor Bradford rubbed his forehead, then turned to Hopamoch, "I have a plan, Hopamoch." He pointed to Attitash's mother. "You must send your wife to observe your king's actions. She will then return to us and report if she finds that King Massasowet is preparing to attack us."

Hopamoch spoke to his wife, then replied, "My woman, White Cloud, go to Massasowet."

I glanced at Attitash's mother. Her face was firm, her eyes flicked at me in friendship, then lowered respectfully. Even though she had healed me, I'd not known her name was White Cloud.

Hopamoch spoke to our governor. "Is dangerous. Squanto try to stop my wife—and his warriors could harm her—but she braver than this man." Hopamoch dismissed Shimmering Fish with a flick of his hand and continued. "White Cloud go see Massasowet. She find truth. Keep aquene—peace."

How would White Cloud learn the truth? I could not even picture a village filled with huts like Hopamoch's, much less imagine how a woman could approach her king to discover his loyalty.

"Hopamoch's wife risks traveling through the enemy's path," our governor said to us all, then turned to Master Allerton. "Isaac, do you agree White Cloud can discover the truth?"

Before Deputy Governor Allerton could answer, we heard a rustle from the back of the crowd and turned to see a tall young Indian coming through the gate. I did not know if Isaac Allerton or William Bradford recognized Attitash's husband, but Hopamoch and White Cloud both hid their surprise and looked down. Black Whale ignored our leaders and went straight to the bloodied man in chains. He knelt down to speak to Seafoam's husband with a voice so low I could not tell if his words were friendly or hostile.

Master Allerton waved his arms as if we'd missed Black Whale's entrance and shouted, "Send this man with her. He will see the truth and the woman will not be able to lie about it." I felt the slight shake of a suppressed chuckle from John and dug my elbow in his rib.

Governor Bradford nodded and spoke with a loud voice to all. "This savage's story must not destroy our compact of mutual aid with King Massasowet. Hopamoch's wife will go, at peril to herself and discover the truth about her king's actions." Our governor turned again to Isaac Allerton and I detected a hint of sarcasm in his voice. "And this young man will accompany her, as you suggested, Deputy." A muscle in Governor Bradford's cheek twitched, and I knew he did indeed recognize Black Whale. I glanced at White Cloud. Her face was impassive. She trusted her daughter's husband.

A few murmurs arose from John Billington and others in Allerton's corner. "We can't trust any of the savages," and "They all lie."

A grim-faced Allerton shushed them and thanked Governor Bradford for heeding his advice. Black Whale turned from the bloody prisoner to confer with Hopamoch. They spoke quietly, gesturing broadly to White Cloud, then to the hills that stood between us and the trail to Massasowet's village.

It seemed that the terrible threats from Squanto and his followers might be diffused without bloodshed, but I did not like the snarl of satisfaction that settled on Deputy Governor Allerton's face. Was this all a plot to discredit Hopamoch or to harm Attitash's husband and mother?

I sent White Cloud and her children a gesture of farewell, discreet enough to be observed but not understood by the gossips.

It was good to go home. We held each other for a long time, ate a bit of supper and went to bed before the sun was quite set. John was asleep immediately. I snuggled into his arms, breathing in his scent and feeling the beat of his heart in the soft spot under his neck. Would our little home survive? I sank into sleep but a dream came to me of my husband being tossed out of the shallop into the sea. I woke enough to realize John was out of bed. He returned and asked if I wanted water, but I could not wake up enough to answer, still feeling as though he needed to be saved from the watery depths.

"Thanks be to Jehovah ye are safe." He took a long breath and gently stroked my face. "Ye can't imagine the terror I felt in the shallop when we heard the alarm. I feared I'd never hold thee again."

It did my heart good to know John could fear for me. I raised up on one elbow and looked into his warm green eyes. "But I *can* imagine. That's how I felt when the shallop left with ye waving farewell and my not knowing if ye'd be coming home alive or dead."

John's eyes lit with surprise. "How could ye doubt my survival? Ye know God saved me from the depths of the sea for a purpose, not to let me succumb to some skirmish with Indians or the waves of Cape Cod!"

"So I'm the only one whom God might not save?" I tried to keep my voice light, but wondered if John thought he was the only one deserving God's mercy.

My husband traced my mouth with a gentle finger. "Ye do tell me the truth, always. Only God knows when either of us will be saved and when He will bring us home." He kissed me slowly and I savored his marvelous taste of salty water, ale, and new chives.

"Husbands don't seem to worry as much as we wives do, or mayhap they hide it well." I kissed him back then settled again against his shoulder. "Do ye think Hopamoch worries about his wife?"

"It surprised me," John answered. "Sending his wife off on what must be a dangerous journey with so much distrust swirling amongst their people. Thank Providence that Allerton's ignorance allowed Black Whale to accompany her."

"White Cloud is very strong. Did you notice her calm demeanor today while talking to Governor Bradford?" I remembered her muscled hands when White Cloud held me during my healing. She had washed away the stain of the Cur's hands on me.

John quieted as though he were going back to sleep, I snuggled against him. I could not return to sleep until I got something off my mind.

Speaking as much to myself as to him, I said softly, "Squanto is not the only force of evil threatening us."

John mumbled a sleepy assent and we lay spooned. I was almost back to sleep myself when he whispered, "Ye need not be doing everything thyself, Elisabeth."

"Yea," I assured him. "I won't meddle into what others can settle." But I knew that John and our other men would not stop Squanto and Isaac Allerton. They were both snakes coiled to strike. Squanto was filled with envy of Massasowet just as Allerton craved William Bradford's position. I could do little myself without Attitash. But together we might find a way to undermine both Squanto's and Isaac Allerton's deception.

11

Attitash

White Flower arrived, breathing hard, her hair streaked wet from running. "Where is Black Whale? Is everyone all right? Why are you here alone?" I demanded. My sister sat down without a word, gulping water, which increased my apprehension. Did she bring bad news? Good news?

"Your husband and Mama are coming with little brother. I ran when I could see our village." White Flower gulped more water and I waited. "Does Seafoam know where Shimmering Fish went?"

Her question increased my unease. "She said he went with Tisquantum," I told her. "Why?"

"Mama has to prove to the Strangers that Shimmering Fish lied about Our Massasowet betraying the Strangers."

I heard her words, but their meaning was impossible to believe. Surely our friends among the Strangers would not believe our Massasowet was betraying them. White Flower pointed up the trail. Black Whale waved to me, but there was no joy in his bearing. Our mother was behind him, carrying Little Fish.

After taking water herself, Mama described Tisquantum's latest attempt to wrest power. Tisquantum was using Shimmering Fish against our beloved Massasowet.

"Go find Seafoam, I want her to come with us to give my husband's report," Mama told White Flower. "She may finally get rid of that shallow Fish husband who speaks against our Massasowet."

"Tell me, White Cloud, do all the strangers believe this story?" Grandmother asked. "Do any believe Hopamoch?"

"Sachem Bad-ford and Win-sow trust my husband—Jon-owland and Esapett do too," Mama answered.

"Then why, Daughter, must you play this game of having to prove Massasowet is loyal to the Strangers?" Grandmother asked.

"Some in Sachem Bad-ford's council trust Tisquantum." Mama handed our little brother to me.

I buried my nose in the familiar smell of Little Fish's hair, then said, "Does Allerton—the father of the spotted-face girl—believe Tisquantum?"

Mama kept her voice even. "Why do you think of this Allerton?"

"He has the same cunning look on his face that I see on Tisquantum's. And his daughter hints that Esapett is prey to evil spirits." I knew Remember Allerton repeated her father's words.

"I've seen that look. It's his terrible need to take away Sachem Bad-ford's power." Mama smacked her hands together hard, as if Allerton and Tisquantum could both feel the blow.

Grandmother gathered the elder women in their council to hear Mama, and decided to bring this trouble to our Massasowet and the Pniese council.

"WELCOME TO our fire," Massasowet said to my grandmother. "And welcome back, White Cloud. How is your husband? And our friends Sachem Bad-ford and Win-sow?"

Black Whale waited near the open entrance flap where he could listen. Massasowet's wives brought cool drinks. Mama accepted the hospitality of the wives. "Hopamoch is well. He finds all is agreeable with our friends."

Massasowet nodded quickly to Seafoam and me. "I see your daughter has recovered." Though his face was quiet,

I saw from the firm line of his mouth that Massasowet knew we had not come just to exchange pleasantries.

Mama looked intently at Toka-mahamon, alerting Massasowet's trusted translator to retell the story to the Strangers in their own tongue. Toka-mahamon would not attempt to be both Wampanoag and a Stranger, as Tisquantum did. "I have a question from my husband," Mama said, returning her gaze to Massasowet. He nodded and she continued. "Tisquantum was with my husband and Capan San-dish when they set out to trade with the Massachuseuk, but Tisquantum disappeared when their wind-canoe returned. Has he come here, Massasowet?"

Our Massasowet frowned. "I have not seen him, and don't want to." He lit his pipe. "Tisquantum is untrustworthy. He threatens me *and* our treaty friends."

Toka-mahamon nodded in agreement. I saw Seafoam square her shoulders on hearing, but she would not look at me.

"Then I must tell you disturbing news, Massasowet." Mama politely kept her eyes down, but her voice was strong. "Shimmering Fish came to Sachem Bad-ford with a bloodied face."

Seafoam choked off a cry. I could see the pulse beat in her throat and felt her tremble when I put my arm around her.

"I have told the Grandmothers' Council what he said," Mama continued. "He claims your warriors bloodied his face to prevent his warning the Cloth-men of your treachery. He admits that Tisquantum gave him this 'duty,'" Mama's voice showed her disdain for Tisquantum's lies. "He claims you are allied with the Narragansett to attack Sachem Bad-ford and his people."

Our Massasowet yanked his pipe from his mouth and tossed its smoldering tobacco toward the fire. Mama continued as his second wife rushed to tamp down stray embers. "Shimmering Fish told the Cloth-men to light their loudest firestick, so San-dish and his warriors in their small wind canoe would come back to defend against your attack."

Our Massasowet jumped up. "My attack? That empty-hearted husk!"

Seafoam shrank back, holding onto my arm. Massasowet smacked his hands against his broad chest, shouting, "These lies are from Tisquantum. Does the Grandmothers' Council want his head? If so, I will inform Sachem Bad-ford he must deliver it to me."

I thought for a moment that Massasowet might immediately send his warriors to kill Tisquantum. It would give me great relief to see Tisquantum's head on a pole. Seafoam's fingers dug into my arm. "Shimmering Fish should not have trusted Tisquantum," she whispered to me. "Tisquantum used my husband. Massasowet would never break the treaty! It keeps the Narragansett and the Strangers from seizing power over us."

Mama was aware of Seafoam's distress but left it to me to contain her anguish. Massasowet's first wife brought him a jar of mint tea. He closed his eyes as he drank and slowly his seething anger abated. I looked to where Black Whale stood at the door, observing the proceedings through the open flap. His eyes caught mine and gave me patience to wait for Our Massasowet. Finally, our sachem opened his eyes and spoke. "This was Tisquantum's ruse to prevent the Cloth-men from negotiating with the Massachuseuk." he said.

"What did your husband do, White Cloud?" Toka-ma-hamon asked.

"My husband protested, of course, that Shimmering Fish was the mouth for Tisquantum's lie," Mama replied.

"Did the Cloth-men believe this foul Fish or did they believe Hopamoch?" Massasowet asked.

"Massasowet, my husband assured Bad-ford that you had not taken action. I think Bad-ford believes Hopamoch, but another man from his council, Allerton, did not. To prove to Allerton, Bad-ford wanted me to hear this from your own mouth. Seafoam will return with me to be a witness that you knew nothing of this betrayal until I told you." Mama glanced at Seafoam, who nodded her agreement, though beads of sweat trickled down her brow to her cheeks.

Our Massasowet looked to Grandmother, who had been listening silently. "Does our grandmothers' council agree this betrayer must be punished?" When Grandmother nodded, he continued. "What words should White Cloud carry to Sachem Bad-ford?"

Grandmother took the pipe from Mama. "Listen carefully." She drew herself up, taking a long draw on the pipe, then laid it by the fire. "We are most offended by the betrayer Tisquantum. White Cloud must carry a message to Sachem Bad-ford. We must think carefully how to approach these weak-kneed men who doubt our trust."

I clenched my fists, seeing Remember Allerton's father's shifting face. It would feel good to knee him where he was weakest.

"What we want to tell him is that he makes our skin jump with outrage when he believes such lies." Grandmother's voice rose, "But we are forced to cover our real words with syrup and deliver a calm message so they do not attack us. Do you know what these men would understand?"

Our Massasowet took the pipe, drew deeply and blew out slowly, "White Cloud should tell Sachem Bad-ford that we thank him for his willingness to think good thoughts of us despite Tisquantum's lies. White Cloud must assure him we will continue to follow our treaty of mutual aid."

"Ahhe," Grandmother agreed. This was no time to

remind my elders that I carried a terrible loss from the Strangers' last attempt to give us 'mutual aid,' I thought. I laid my hands over my belly where my New Life rested, as Grandmother continued. "We will give warning if we discover any further danger to the Cloth-men—as they will warn us should they discover any rebellions against our people."

Massasowet handed the pipe back to Grandmother and said to Mama. "Our grandmothers are wise. White Cloud, tell Cloth-men we will keep our treaty. And we expect them to remember what they promised us."

Grandmother grimaced derisively. "They can't remember anything, but maybe their little pictures will remind them."

I whispered the treaty's words again to myself. Tisquantum had broken the trust and now Esapett's people must help mine. Black Whale held the flap open as we left Massasowet's home.

"You heard what must be said to the Cloth-man's sachem, Black Whale," Grandmother told him. "Now I must take Attitash to our moon lodge and discover if she and her New Life can journey with White Cloud to Patuxet."

I WAITED while she lit a braid of sweet grass and the sage leaves. Their fragrance filled the moon lodge as the smoke drifted up the hole. Grandmother settled beside me on the bench, then placed her hands on me.

"Tonight the fat moon comes again, the third since your life-flow has stopped," she said.

"Ahhe," I nodded, putting my hands over Grandmother's. I closed my eyes and shut out the sounds of fire crackling and wind blowing. Breathing as slowly as Grandmother was, I let my ears listen into my body. For some time, the only sound I heard was my own heartbeat. Then I felt a much smaller beat. It was like the tiny drops from a spring, bubbling one at a time onto the moss. The heartbeat I felt was calm and strong, like the strength of a butterfly's soft wings against a stiff breeze.

"The New Life is ready for a journey," Grandmother said. Her hands turned up and held mine. "You will protect this life safely when you return to your mother's fire."

BLACK WHALE AND I would accompany Mama back and carry the words with us. My new-life was secure in my womb and my heart was ready to return to my mother's fire at our homesite near the Strangers. We would tell Esapett and Jon-owland in the words we both knew.

12

Elisabeth

I shook corn from the bottom of our dwindling sack. "There is little enough corn in our storehouse to replenish this. What will we eat?"

"I'm going to the pond to shoot some birds so we'll eat tonight. And we'll have more corn when Standish can finally take an expedition to the Massachuseuk." John grabbed his fowling piece. With the ducks and geese returned from the south, I welcomed the sound of the men's fowling pieces, lighter than the muskets. The geese and ducks they shot filled our empty bellies.

"But if White Cloud can't convince our governor that Tisquantum lies about King Massasowet, we not only can't go to the Massachuseuk, we can't get food from the Wampanoag, and we can't—" I clenched my teeth at the thought of no trip, and thus no more corn. We could not survive alone in this wilderness.

John drew the bar back and opened the door to the soft April sunshine, then pulled me to him, both of us breathing the fresh green of spring. "Trust in God, Dearest. Pray at all times. God did not send us to this Promised land to starve."

I did not want to question my husband, but it did seem to me God was putting a lot of responsibility on the Indians to feed us. "When will ye go again?"

"Standish is ready to leave as soon as Hopamoch's wife returns and she refutes the false allegation." John kissed my cheek and released me. "But I'm telling Standish I want to stay here. Let the men without wives go running about."

It would have been easy to keep him at my side, but we would not get food if this mission was not successful. "Captain Standish picked ye to go because ye are good with the shallop sails, ye are a good shot, and ye are learning well from Winslow how to negotiate." I recalled John's eagerness to go just a day ago. "Susanna Winslow does not need her husband to stay home. Just because I'm young, that doesn't mean I need my husband to protect me," I argued. "I want ye to be the man I fell in love with, who's a leader among men, not a man tied to his wife's apron strings."

John's silence told me he would not contradict my opinion. He put a finger under my chin and lifted it to look into my eyes. "Ye are a brave woman, but I would not have thee waiting here trembling with terror."

My laugh reassured him more than my words. "Have I ever trembled in terror?"

"Nay, never." John pulled on his jerkin. "I'll be back soon, and then when ye've collected enough mussels I'll stop at Bradford's. I want to know what he and Isaac Allerton were arguing about when we came home."

Constance Hopkins, Priscilla Alden and I brought our baskets to the shore, with Constance's brother Giles standing guard. As we returned with yet another supper of clams more suited for feeding hogs, we met my John carrying a freshly shot duck. I took it to Governor Bradford's house that I might prepare pottage for all the menfolk of his household.

Governor Bradford was alone and before John could ask a question, our governor took his pipe from his mouth and told John to close the door and sit. "Isaac Allerton never ceases to make trouble."

Was Allerton once again accusing me of witchcraft? I

did not dare ask, but John's swift glance in my direction showed me that the same fear we'd lived through a year ago had caught him again.

"What does your deputy governor want now? "John asked Governor Bradford.

"According to Isaac Allerton, the messenger insists Hopamoch is party to the rebellion against us. Allerton demands we free the imprisoned messenger and put the chains on Hopamoch instead,"

"Surely you don't believe this?"

"Believe this sniveling messenger over our friend Hopamoch? Nay, I do not." Governor Bradford puffed for a moment on his pipe. The only sound in the little house was my scraping mussels from their shells.

"Hopamoch's wife should be back here by the morrow," John said. "Then we will learn the truth."

John's conversation with Governor Bradford cast a web of questions cluttering my mind. What was Allerton up to now? As I took the knife and hot water out in the garden to prepare the duck, John caught up with me.

"Did you have any trouble bagging this duck?" I asked, to divert my mind from a conversation I perhaps should not have been privy to. John picked up the shimmering green head, the body hung limp. He smoothed the feathers, drops of pond water flicking off. "Glad Rogue was with me to retrieve—the water was deep."

Taking the knife, John slit the bird and pulled out the entrails. After sorting out the heart, gizzard and liver, he dumped the entrails in a bucket and whistled over Peter Browne's dog, Rogue, to eat them. "Ye heard what Governor said about Allerton."

"Yea. But I don't know what it means." Taking the gutted body, I felt deep under the breast feathers and began plucking out the soft eider down.

John retrieved the bucket which Rogue had emptied of entrails, her reward for retrieving. "Good bitch," he ruffled her head as Rogue wandered off in search of more supper. "It means Deputy Governor Allerton thinks the good meat all belongs to him and we get the guts," John said, wiping his hands on his breeches.

Knowing John was not speaking of fowl, I continued to pull feathers. When I'd filled my sack, John took the duck and pulled its dark body out from the plucked outer layer.

"Of course, I mean all the bounty of this land—beaver, trees, corn, and the Indian's wampum shells." He finished skinning and gave me the naked duck. "That should do for a good soup tonight."

I took the bird and began cutting it in pieces. "I still don't understand what Isaac Allerton has to do with taking away worldly goods. Even if he got more from Tisquantum and his rebels, how could one man be able to keep more than the rest of us?"

John went to the rain barrel and ladled water to rinse his hands. "Isaac Allerton is our treasurer, ye know." As John ran his hands through his hair, the chill wind blew it about. "The bloody man keeps our books."

Master Allerton and Governor Bradford did pour over ledgers, but I had paid no attention. So much went on in Plimoth that I was just beginning to understand. I wondered if Susanna Winslow and Mistress Brewster knew any of this. Placing the duck meat in the bowl, I set it down, then held my hands out for John to rinse. "How does Allerton keeping books make him want to turn us against Hopamoch?"

"Allerton may be holding back some of the Wampanoag trade for himself. He must think Hopamoch hinders this. If Hopamoch and others loyal to Massasowet lose our protection, Allerton could align with Tisquantum's rebels and control their trade."

Wiping my hands on my apron, I mulled over this puzzling accusation. "Doesn't it all go to England?"

"Yea. To pay back the rich men in England who provide the supplies we need." John waved his arm at our little settlement. "The ships, crew, the voyages, tools, salt, everything to build this village."

I nodded, adding under my breath, "But the Indians give us food."

"So, we must pay the investors back. That should be easy enough," John continued. "We sent hundreds of pelts and other goods back with all the ships. Yet they write us letters that they did not receive sufficient goods." He looked at the bowl. "Is that enough meat for a good pottage?"

"Yea, and I should get to it." I hefted the bowl, then continued my questions. "How could Allerton get what the rich English are due?"

"William Bradford told a few of us—Winslow and me among others—that he has reason to believe that Allerton's got someone in England pulling out a share for him and leaving us short in paying the debt." The fair spring day seemed to get duller, as if the sea fog had moved up and wrapped itself around the sun. "Why doesn't Governor Bradford stop him?"

"Isaac Allerton was elected to be deputy governor, and no governor could turn him out without sufficient proof for a trial." John looked out to sea, watching the ebb tide crawl slowly out to sea.

"What will happen to us if these rich gentry don't get the bounty?"

Turning back to gaze at the sun, gleaming on the western horizon above the palings that held Plimoth Plantation, John said quietly. "Ye can't even think that, it won't happen."

"Don't coddle me," I protested. "I'm thy wife, not a child."

That made him look at me. "So ye are. And ye know more than most wives here." He went to the door to make certain it was closed and none could hear him. "I'll only tell thee if ye understand it will not happen." Drawing a deep breath, John leaned close to me and spoke so softly I could still hear the surf crashing. "If we could not pay our debt, the investors would stop sending all supplies. They would tell the king to relinquish our right to live here." I looked at our humble homes, now the only ones I knew. The sea surged in the distance, a sound I woke up to and went to sleep with every day. The sea birds called above me, flying up and back to the rocky beach. "Where would we go?"

"Stop. Ye must not consider this." As though shielding me against a gale, John put his hands firmly on my back and pulled me close. "We would be back under the king's rule."

"Ye mean King George or King Massasowet?"

John grimaced. He did not comprehend that I was serious. When I understood more of our new world, I would ask him how King George got this land from King Massasowet.

May, 1622
Attitash
Our homesite was barely visible under the trees when we stopped to look down the last hill. Beyond our neesh'wetu, the tall peaks of the Strangers' houses rose above the poles surrounding their village. And beyond that was the sea, lapping against the rocks of the shore. Beside our trail a little stream wound its way down to be swallowed by the Big Salt Water.

Grandmother's words tumbled in my mind: "I never dreamed my daughter and my granddaughters would be living with the Strangers." Before we left her, she'd embraced each of us fiercely, hugging me so tightly my breath struggled in my chest. Releasing us and kissing Little Fish, she put a gentle hand on Black Whale's shoulder. "Do what you can to protect them. But do not believe that any of our men can stop what the Strangers would do."

"Sachem Bad-ford is our friend," Mama said. "Do not fear for us."

"Ahhe, he is our friend, Daughter." Grandmother replied softly. The fire rose in her eyes, but we did not hear it in her voice. "He may be a sachem, but he is just one Stranger, and your other friends are few also. Our people are but the stones beneath the waterfall. So many Strangers are coming, like a spring river that grows faster and greater with every rain. They pour over us and will eventually break us."

13

Elisabeth

Our corn sprouted and hoeing released the pungent smell of earth. Worms burrowed away from my hoe, and I began to sing, *Sommer is a cumin' in, loudly sing cuckoo.* Priscilla sang back, *Groweth seed and bloweth mead and springeth life anew.*

Priscilla, Constance, Mary and I worked hard, as did most who'd come on the Mayflower. But too many of the new people did little work or found some excuse to neglect the planting. Saying she was too busy with her babes, Widow Ford at least had more excuse than many of those who'd come on the Fortune. And, being the only woman without a man, several men were willing to help her. However, many of the new men seemed to think God would provide manna, or any kind of bread, without a lick of work on their part. The same men were dismissive of the need for our treaty with the Wampanoag. Heedless of the tension over Shimmering Fish's allegations, they followed Billington's rude behavior and spat upon the chained 'messenger.' When Shimmering Fish, protested, no one replied.

Knowing we must wait for Attitash's mother to return from King Massasowet with her witness I kept my own counsel and so did my husband.

My friends and I kept working the soil, still singing softly under our breath until a shout came from Wrastling and Love Brewster. The boys had left their work to chase each other up the trail and their call alerted us to the line of Indians coming down the hill.

Hopamoch ran up the path to meet his family. Black Whale and Toka-mahamon—the translator I called "Toka"—were in the front and the women behind. Governor Bradford left his digging to greet them. My John was with him as well as Master Winslow. At first I didn't see Attitash but when she appeared around the bend just behind her mother, I felt a warm rush in my throat. She looked healthy and happy—much more like she'd been before the terror and loss of early winter.

We kept our distance, letting the leaders greet each other, but our smiles reached across the crowd. Once everyone was settled just outside the commonhouse, Toka stood by Attitash's parents, White Cloud and Hopamoch. It was then I noticed Attitash's cousin, Seafoam. She looked most distressed and I wondered if she intended to defend her husband or to side with King Massasowet. Shimmering Fish was still inside the commonhouse, though his raucous voice could be heard shouting. Seafoam's eyes filled with tears, but she did not speak.

Toka did not have the quickness and ease in translating that Squanto did, but White Cloud waited patiently for him to find the words. She nodded in agreement as he spoke in English, telling Governor that Massasowet was very angry to learn of Squanto's accusations. When Toka paused, White Cloud spoke fervently to him. The only word I understood was a passionate, "aquene, aquene," or peace.

Toka emphasized King Massasowet was in no way preparing for an attack, desiring only to keep the compact. Repeating the words from our compact, he described mutual aid if either of us were attacked. Would anyone wonder whether this referred to attacks by French and other Indian nations instead of his own rebels?

Attitash took Seafoam's hand, as Toka said, "Wife of Shimmering Fish be loyal to Massasowet. She say Squanto trick her man." Seafoam said something in their language so low that White Cloud repeated it to the translator.

"Seafoam say Massasowet show pure heart." Toka slapped his hand against his own heart. "Both women say much aquene at king's house. No war."

John stayed close to our governor, but he glanced at me with a quick smile, which assured me that Governor Bradford had enough testimony to resist Master Allerton's interests.

There was a small conference the rest of us were not privy to, and then our governor spoke. "We believe King Massasowet is loyal. We are assured our compact is being followed and we assure him we also follow it as loving friends. As to Squanto," Bradford looked about as if he knew the translator was lurking within earshot, "we will admonish him for believing the worst of his king. If Squanto asks our forgiveness and promises to bestow his trust upon his king, our friend, he may return."

John hastened to my side as our governor finished. "We leave soon for the Massachuseuk. Come help pack." His brief words were softened with an arm about my waist.

I hurried to keep pace with my husband. "John, how could Governor accept that conniving turn-coat, Squanto?"

"Expediency."

"Use words I understand!' I was already out of sorts from his imminent departure and in no mood to guess what he meant. Opening the door to our little home, John began loading his bandoliers with powder. "It means he must do it in order to make the compact work." He opened the crock looking for food. "Have ye any biscuits?"

"Little enough, but I'll pack what I have." I tossed the hard biscuits into his pack. Surely my John did not think of me as an ignorant young servant-maid. But I still had questions which I needed answered if I were to understand why a snake must be permitted to lurk in our midst. "Why can't Toka translate?"

"Because he's King Massasowet's."

"Yea, and isn't King Massasowet our friend? Winslow knows as much of their language as Toka knows English. Can't they converse well enough?"

John paused, his eyes on his pack, obviously anxious to leave, not to linger teaching me. "Yea, King Massasowet's our friend. But a friend for purposes of survival. As more and more of our people come over, Massasowet might not feel as friendly. So we need Squanto to tell our own side of the story." John gathered me in his arms, his bandoliers clanking against me. "We shall have plenty of time to talk when I return. And we'll have sufficient corn with us that we can speak without hunger pangs interrupting." He kissed me rather too quickly. "Remember me in thy prayers," and then patted my bottom possessively. "And remember me in thy bed." There was no need this time for me to add that I would be alone and afraid. I would sleep at the Brewsters and it was obvious that everyone in Plimoth would be fearful.

Attitash

Shimmering Fish had already been released when we gathered on the shore, and was back at our homesite trying to persuade Seafoam he was truly done with the rebellion when we gathered on the shore. We were watching the Strangers depart again to the Massachuseuk, when Tisquantum appeared. Papa waited impatiently for Sachem Bad-ford to put Tisquantum in the chains, but instead the snake's pleas for forgiveness were listened to and he was allowed to remain in Pli-mot. It was many moons since my family had restrained Tisquantum and warned him that we knew he had betrayed me and White Flower by delivering us to Narragansett warriors. Our rescue from the Narragansett by Black Whale and Uncle Seekonk spared us and gave Tisquantum leave to claim he was innocent. Now he was flaunting our warnings. At least Sachem Bad-ford did not allow Tisquantum to go with them on their wind-canoe. But that left him with us. Tisquantum was talking with the spotted-faced girl and her father when the rest of us waved farewell to Papa. Black Whale had assured Papa he would watch for any conniving, but simply talking was nothing—even when it was talking to a Stranger we did not trust. I waited until the wind-canoe was out of sight and Esapett had dried her eyes before I approached her.

"Jon-owland will come back to you safely," I told her in my language with motions that made it clear.

"Yea—ahhe," she said with a reassuring smile. "Netop—friend." Esapett did not take my hand in front of so many of her people, but the tingle in mine told me she wanted to. I saw the spotted-face girl looking at us. She had grown close to Esapett's height since I'd seen her before we left for our winter home. I smiled at her and she gave me a quick smile back, then glanced at her father, worried that he might notice our exchange. Esapett and I walked back toward the poles surrounding Pli-mot, but did not go in. She pointed to the field and motioned chopping. Only one circle of the seasons ago Esapett and I had persuaded Tisquantum to teach her people how to plant the weachimin kernels. We walked together to where Mama and White Flower had planted. Our weachimin had burst tiny two-leaved plants from mother earth. We both breathed in the smell of New Life in the ground. I took Esapett's hand and put it on my belly.

"Attitash! Bessyu," Esapett gave me a quick hug, then stepped back, looking about to see if we were observed.

I knew she did bless me. She was glad for me.

Elisabeth

Understanding that Attitash was blessed to be with child again, I felt both grateful and worried. As I joined my friends in our field to continue hoeing, I wondered if Attitash could birth this child safely. Perhaps her body had been permanently injured by the musket ball. I said a prayer quietly, knowing I would continue to do so until she held a live babe in her arms. And what of my own future? I was relieved when my courses arrived promptly. At the same time, I wondered when I too would be blessed with a life to carry.

"The Lord won't get thee with child 'til He knows ye are ready to be a mother," Mistress Brewster assured me. Seeing me stiffen my shoulders, she'd laughed. "Oh ye could manage a babe, but ye need more meat on your bones. Pray God keeps thee free of a wee burden until we have sufficient food for ye to be eating for two." Indeed, we all gave Martha Ford any extra tidbits so she would not lose her milk—and thus her babe. The child was very frail and his mother was nothing but bones and breast. Peregrine White was now over two years old and thriving, but other babes born since we left England, like Oceanus Hopkins, had died.

"Elisabeth! Why do ye stand there looking at the sky? Expecting thy husband back already?" Constance Hopkins laughed, but her words set me to work again.

The atmosphere at home did little to distract me from the oppressive dread that my husband would not return safely. Squanto sauntered about Plimoth Plantation as if he'd never caused a minute of trouble. Governor Bradford ignored him, but Master Allerton was often seen conversing with Squanto. Black Whale came by with food—some fish from his weir, a brace of rabbits, a couple of geese. After he handed them over to Mistress Brewster to distribute as needed, Black Whale lingered, talking briefly with Squanto. Only their tight faces and straight shoulders demonstrated the chill in their conversations.

I saw Attitash briefly when we both worked our fields. Seafoam was helping her the day after our men left but was not to be seen after that. Shimmering Fish had also vanished, so I assumed they'd gone off together. Attitash and her sister were planting their beans in hills around their new corn. We planted our seeds as the Lord directed us in the Bible—each to its own field—never mixed. God would surely provide a good crop, if only we had planted more seeds.

A WEEK LATER, in the cool of the morning, our servant boy, William Latham, called out and pointed to white sails. It seemed the sun would set before the shallop finally came to shore.

Finally, I breathed in my John's deep scent, so familiar to me I no longer identified its particulars. Laughing with relief, we walked up the hill from the shore. Sprinkles of rain got bigger and we ran, holding hands and laughing. When we neared the gate, Captain Standish waited for us, carrying his musket and a sack. When we reached the common-house, he eyed us. We were bedraggled with rain, but scarcely concealing our glow.

"Rough winds do shake the darling buds of May," Captain quoted with a grin. "Do you know Shakespeare's sonnet?"

John nodded. I was shocked to hear the name of the blasphemous writer who consorted with Satan in theaters.

"You should have Howland recite it to you, Mistress Elisabeth. Stephan Hopkins and I keep a copy of the sonnets. Take it any time you want it for your reading lesson." Picking up his burdens, he left, calling out greetings to all.

"Do ye really know the sonnet?" I asked John, as we followed in Captain's shadow.

"Yea, while standing guard with Hopkins, we recite poems to pass the time. This is a favorite."

"But 'twas written by that foul Shakespeare!"

"'Tis just like any country song—only prettier than most."

Mayhap all our country songs were first sung by sinners like Shakespeare. It did indeed fall prettily on my ear and made me eager to get back home together. John's pace was so quick I had to trot. When William Latham caught up with us, John sent him off. "Don't need thee at home, William." William made a face and John laughed. "And don't come back 'til supper, just before the sun sets. I've a great need to recover."

As soon as John hung up his bandoliers it was obvious his recovery would take place in bed. He barred the door, then pulled me tight against him, kissing me urgently. When we both paused for breath, he pulled off his boots. I kicked off my shoes and we landed together in bed. John fumbled with his laces with one hand, his other one attending to me until I pushed him away and helped him shed his breeches. 'Twas sweet indeed to join quickly, knowing we would be back together in the dark.

Only the sounds of life outside our home finally brought us to rest. John pulled his breeches back on and turned his back so I could help lace up his points, talking to me over his shoulder while I worked.

"Let me tell thee a bit now and sometime we'll read the whole sonnet in Standish's book.

Shall I compare thee to a summer's day?
Thou art more lovely and more temperate,
Rough winds do shake the darling buds of May
And summer's lease hath all too short a date."

"When I read the sonnet with ye, the meaning will come clear," I said. To think, I'd been given the rod for trying to read the Bible little more than a year ago. Now I would read a sonnet.

His lacing finished, John turned around and stopped my hands so I could not tuck my breasts back into the stays. "Ye are so beautiful." His voice was thick with emotion. "We've not made love in the daylight 'til now."

"And if William returns soon—or anyone else comes by—we'll regret doing so this time." I reluctantly moved his hands away and completed my dressing.

14

Attitash

"I have evidence I must show you, Hopamoch," Tisquantum said loudly. "This will prove what I keep telling you about the harm the deceitful Strangers plan against our people." Black Whale started to go with them, but Papa motioned to him to stay with us. I thought it dangerous for Papa to go with Tisquantum, worrying that there might be more betrayers ready to ambush him. Mama assured me that my father could take care of himself. They went up to the Strangers' big house and disappeared inside.

Papa came home alone later, his face too quiet. We all gathered in our wetu and Papa lit the pipe, took a draw and passed it around. When Mama, Black Whale and I had taken our puffs, Papa took another draw himself.

"Tisquantum tells me that the Strangers have their worst evil spirits, the ones they call 'plague,' hidden in their big house."

We greeted his news with snorts of disbelief and comments about the newest lie being told. "Of course, that was my response." Papa shrugged his shoulders. "But he wanted me to see where they hide these evil spirits. I asked him how he knew and he said one of the Strangers told him. And this man told him that their Sachem, Bad-ford, can take the plague-spirits out whenever he wants to and make us all sicken and die."

"Does Tisquantum actually believe Bad-ford would do this, Husband?" Mama asked.

"Tisquantum says that's what the Strangers did to our

people when this place was our Patuxet. After all our people were killed, or kidnapped and carried away on big wind
canoes, like they did with Tisquantum, they buried the
rest of their evil plague-spirits here."

We'd heard this many times. Uncle Seekonk had lived
here and lost his first wife and children here. He was spared
only because he was on a long hunting trip. Even knowing
all this, however, I did not trust Tisquantum to tell the
truth. "Did you see this place, Papa?" I asked.

"I did," he said.

We all waited while Papa took another long draw on
the pipe. Mama's mouth was firm, but her tightened eyes
showed her worry. Black Whale was clenching his fists
together.

"It was where they store all the fire balls for their shooting sticks. He showed me where the earth floor has been
dug up and covered over again to hide the spirits." Papa
spoke slowly, as if each words did not want to leave his
mouth.

"How do you know it was spirits buried there? Did he
show you?" White Flower asked.

"Of course he wouldn't, little daughter. That would
send the evil out into our world. And we couldn't see
them anyway." Papa was gentle with White Flower, but
she blushed to still be called "little" for asking a foolish
question.

"Did Tisquantum say who told him this?" Mama asked.

When Papa shook his head, Black Whale spoke up.
"While you were gone, Hopamoch, Tisquantum talked
with the man Sachem Bad-ford calls, 'De-puty Ah-leton'.
I heard this Ah-leton say that Sachem Bad-ford would not
send out these plague-spirits, but that the Strangers' god
would." The sparkle in Black Whale's eyes had changed
from their usual warm glow to fierce fire.

We were all quiet for a while. Finally, Mama sat up

straight. "Maybe he does not trust this Al-ton. He is father to the spotted face girl?" she asked me. I nodded. "You must ask Sachem Bad-ford about this, Hopamoch."

Papa squeezed his eyes shut. I thought he must be picturing Sachem Bad-ford's response to such a question. "How will I know if Bad-ford tells the truth?"

"How will you know anything if you don't ask?" Mama reached over and put her arm on Papa's shoulder. "You know how to read his face. And we have more reason to trust Sachem Bad-ford than we do Tisquantum."

"I don't trust either one of them." Papa took her hand from his shoulder and pressed it to his lips. "But you're right. All I can do is ask."

"Take Black Whale with you to speak with Bad-ford." Mama said. "He can learn more about these Strangers and you will have another witness." She turned to me. "You go behind them, Attitash. You can witness what is there, but stay back in case Tisquantum is telling the truth and Strangers' evil is buried there."

I followed my father and husband to Sachem Bad-ford's house. Papa called out and Esapett opened the door, a large black pot in her hands. She invited us to sit on the bench outside the sachem's door. A few minutes later, Sachem Bad-ford came out. After conversing with Papa a moment, Bad-ford waved his arms about, his voice growing louder with each word. I understood enough from his motions to know he demanded a chance to prove Tisquantum wrong. Esapett watched through a crack in the door and when the men left for their storehouse, she came out. We exchanged a discreet touch of our fingers and I bid her a quick good-bye and followed the men. When I looked back, Esapett was catching up with me.

When we reached the storehouse, I waited near the door so I could leave quickly if there was danger. I tried to motion that Esapett should stay with me, but she continued to follow the men. Bad-ford led Papa and Black Whale past huge firesticks and a small stack of fire-balls like the one that killed New Life. My arms and legs were trembling with that memory as I tried to keep my breathing soft. Sachem Bad-ford stopped at some mounds of earth and brushed the dirt off the top of one, revealing a big round pot.

"Stop. Don't release the plague-spirits!" Papa said in Wampanoag, forgetting his English.

Esapett approached the men, setting her little pot on top of the big one.

Elisabeth
"What are ye doing here, Elisabeth?" our governor demanded.

"Just came to see if we have enough corn to refill my pot, Sir." I used my sweetest voice, hoping my esteemed leader would not catch the concern which led me to boldly follow him. Hopamoch and Black Whale obviously were very distraught over accusations from Squanto and I did not want to be waiting and wondering.

"The corn's not in this barrel. Don't you know it's over there?" He pointed to the row of barrels which I knew full well contained our remaining store of corn.

"But I thought those barrels were almost empty, and I thought mayhap Hopamoch or his son-in-law brought more." While I chattered, I scraped more dirt off the barrel in question.

Hopamoch looked more distressed than Governor Bradford, whose face only revealed impatience. I glanced to where Attitash hid and saw her waving her hands at me to remove myself from the barrel's vicinity. Whatever it was Hopamoch was looking for, it appeared to be a danger to me as well as to him. "Do you need this one for something else, Sir?" I asked, brushing all the dirt from my skirts. "Why is this all covered in dirt?"

"Mistress Howland, please remove thyself from this place," Governor Bradford's effort to be polite while admonishing me to get out almost made me smile. Whatever was he hiding? I nodded politely and went to the corn barrels, keeping an eye on the men as I dislodged the corn barrel top and scooped out a pot-full of corn from the dwindling supply.

Attitash

Sachem Bad-ford was digging up the dirt from the bad spirit pot and I backed up even more. He took a tool and used it to open up the top. I caught the scent of the acrid black sand they use for their fire-sticks and began a soft chant to keep the bad spirits from my New Life.

"This is hidden here in case the Narragansett or French attack," Sachem Bad-ford explained, lifting out a handful of the black sand. "We have no plague in our barrels."

Esapett watched from her position on the other side of the room. She had a look of protection in her eyes that I knew meant she might be carrying New Life. Was she trying to protect herself or me and mine? I called her to me and she came, bringing her pot of weachimin.

"Come." I told her, taking her hand and walking with her to the door. When we got there, I put my hand on her belly, then on mine. She seemed to understand what I meant and we both went to our own homes. This was a time when our need to take care of New Life meant the men had to take care of their own squabbles.

Elisabeth

I hurried home after Attitash made clear it could be dangerous for both of us. I did not understand, but there was so much I could not understand that I no longer wasted effort.

Governor Bradford arrived by the time I'd fixed the corn porridge. As I was setting the trenchers on the table, he called my John from the garden where he was splitting wood.

"Sit down, Howland and hear this tale."

I stood still, wondering if Bradford would tell my John how I meddled.

"I had to open our buried ammunition powder to persuade Hopamoch and the young Indian that we were not storing a plague in there," Governor said.

Storing a plague? Was that what Attitash was trying to protect me from? Could Attitash, her father and her husband believe Squanto's wild tale? At least there was not a word about my presence in the storehouse.

"Plague in a barrel?" young William Latham piped up as if he too believed it.

All the men laughed, including my husband. "I had not thought Hopamoch so full of superstition he'd believe this," John said.

"Yea, all the savages are so full of magic tales, they can't understand what's real and what's imaginary." Governor Bradford wiped the remains of his supper from his mustache. "But I was able to prove Squanto wrong and put Hopamoch's fear to rest."

"Did you find Squanto and demand an account for this?" John asked.

"Yea, when we came out of the commonhouse he showed up, claiming another one of us told him this. And that God controlled the plague in the barrels and could send them forth to destroy our enemies without our leaving the plantation." Governor Bradford shifted his shoulders, loosening his muscles. "Whoever told him that told him a half-truth. Only God knows where the plague resides."

My hands banged the pots onto their hooks as the men

went out to smoke their pipes and gossip. None of our men understood the danger of Squanto's deceit—this story of the plague was but another ruse to undermine our mutual aid treaty. Who had told Squanto this lie? Was Squanto inventing another tale or had Allerton started this? I needed to talk with Attitash, if we could again find privacy and understand each other's words.

"Why would Squanto want Hopamoch to not trust us?" William Latham asked when he brought the water for me to clean up.

John had come back in for an ember to relight his pipe, but ignored William's question. I ignored John and pondered an answer. It was more than I could manage with my temper seething. "Bring me more sticks for this fire, William. And figure out with thy little mind what Squanto gains."

"Is this what Captain Standish means when he tells Governor to defend ourselves against the savage, we must attack them?" William asked, not granting me the favor of showing any humiliation.

I gave him a quick push out the door, admonishing him to hurry with the sticks.

John blew out smoke and grinned at me. "Now ye are a teacher too, Wife."

I gave him a look that would have wilted fresh mint. "Why must ye laugh at Hopamoch's fear? This could have led to big trouble."

John's grin did not fade. "Could have but did not." He kissed my cheek as if that would cool my fire. "Don't let thy feathers get ruffled. We face too many obstacles to worry over the ones quickly solved. Ye must admit that whoever thought this story up can conjure a good tale."

"So, ye don't think it was Squanto?"

"I don't know. Squanto would also believe the tale if a Christian man told him."

"Like Allerton? Or Billington? Or—" My list was too long and John's laughter caught me up this time. I let him put his arm around me.

"Too many scoundrels in our midst, Love." He squeezed my waist. "And I was not joking about thy teaching William. A good teacher makes the student search for an answer before granting one. I'll give him some hints later."

"Speaking of thy teaching, it's a good thing Desire gave me more reading lessons while ye were gone, since ye've never time thyself." I shot back. "But she didn't know what 'expectedent' means either."

John chuckled. "Did ye ask Master Brewster?" He waited a beat but I remained silent. "It's expediency—expedient."

I muttered the word to myself so I'd remember it properly.

"I'm not making fun of thee. No maid, nor any mistress for that matter, needs to know words like expediency."

I leaned away from his embrace. "But if I don't learn such words, I won't understand thy answers to my questions."

"Good point, well done!" He nuzzled my ear. "Truth be told, I didn't know what it meant when Governor Carver told me to write it in a message."

"So, how did ye learn it? Did ye ask him?"

"Nay. If ye remember our dear departed Governor Carver, he moved too fast to wait for questions. I listened and learned. When he and Winslow had discussions, I figured out it meant 'worth doing for practical reasons, or suited to one's end'." John sat down on the bench again. "Such as, it suits me to help ye finish up cleaning up so we can go to our own house. Do ye need anything else?"

"Two more hands would help." We never did uncurl until the early spring light woke us again.

15

Elisabeth

"Come quickly, Master!" William came in the door with the buckets full. "King Massasowet's brother has come and he's shouting at Governor Bradford!"

We could hear the commotion as soon as we left the house. It brought most of our village outside. Hopamoch, Toka, and King Massasowet's brother, who'd been part of our treaty negotiations, were gesturing and shouting at Governor Bradford as he stood in his door. John went immediately across the lane to our governor's side. William joined the Brewster boys crowding close enough to hear. I held back as Priscilla and others joined me by our house. King Massasowet's brother held up a knife and brandished it about as though he were about to slaughter a cow—or perhaps a man. The knife must have come from earlier traders as it was glinting steel.

"Our Massasowet want Tisquantum's head," Toka proclaimed. "He sent own knife for Sachem Bad-ford to cut off head. We carry it back."

A vile taste filled my mouth. 'Would they really cut off Squanto's head?" I asked Mistress Brewster. Certainly I'd heard of this punishment and I knew the London Bridge was lined with the heads of our King's enemies. John had told me that the heads stuck on poles along London Bridge had their eyes pecked out by birds. I could have done without that gory detail, but I'd not thought about who did the chopping!

Mistress had her eyes closed and hands lifted—obviously

seeking God's will and not listening to mine. I focused instead on my husband. I could just see his noble profile as he leaned into the conversation between Governor Bradford and Master Winslow. His clenched jaw told me he was worried. Isaac Allerton pushed his way over to our governor and began gesturing violently at Hopamoch and King Massasowet's brother.

William Latham pushed through the crowd to me. He was almost as tall as I and his voice reached my ear easily. "Governor and Master Winslow worry about how to trade for more corn without Squanto," he reported. "Master John says Hopamoch and Toka talk for us, but Master Allerton says only Squanto can speak our words changed into the Massachuseuk."

William hushed as Governor Bradford turned back to Massasowet's brother. "I am sorry, Quadequina, but I cannot do what your brother, the king, asks." He waited for Toka to translate. As soon as he did, the brother let out a foul sound and slashed the air again with his knife. Toka and Massasowet's brother turned on their heels and left before Governor could explain further. Hopamoch glared at all of us as if he were setting a hex on us, then followed his leader's men.

"Where is Squanto?" I asked William. He shrugged.

Without King Massasowet our treaty was only a piece of paper. I looked about our little village—the small homes surrounded by the pales and only a few cannon to defend us. It felt as though our shelter was transformed into useless sticks, exposing us to the storm of winter.

John and I walked home silently, his arm around my shoulder until we entered our own home. Waiting until the door was closed, I asked, "Why does King Massasowet demand Bradford behead Squanto? Isn't hanging him enough?"

John sat down heavily in his chair, grabbed the ale

bucket and poured himself a beaker. "I suppose it's the same reason kings and queens back home chop off their enemies' heads. Without the head on the body for three days, the soul won't go to heaven or hell—dead forever."

"Do the Indians have a heaven?"

Taking a long drink, John paused to wipe his mouth "Ye always ask questions I don't have answers for. But when we took the things from the Indian grave, Hopkins told us they put food in their graves for the dead to take on their journey to their spirit world. That must be their version of heaven."

"So Squanto would be dead forever," I said, "without a head he couldn't eat or travel."

"Evidently." John passed the beaker to me and I took a drink. "King Massasowet probably also wants the head as evidence that Squanto is dead."

"Does anyone know where Squanto is?"

"He must be hiding—no one knows where." John glanced out our little window.

"It seems it would be expedient for Squanto to die," I said.

John gave me a smile acknowledging my understanding of the word.

"So what do we do now?" I asked him.

"Something has to change," John responded, "but I can't change our governor's mind and I don't think anyone can change Massasowet's mind."

I didn't know what could change, but I knew who could help.

Attitash

I saw Esapett come out to her field. When she signaled to meet her in the trees by the river, I went quickly. It did not take words to know she too was troubled that our leaders were arguing. We took hands and for a long moment enjoyed the moment of finally being together again. "Sachem Bad-ford is netop—friend of Tisquantum?" I asked.

"Nay! Matta! Not Squanto's netop. But Bradford needs him." She gestured to their field where the weach-imin plants had sprouted and some of the new people were trying to get rid of the weeds. "We need Squanto talk Massachuseuk, get more food." Esapett used many of her own words and I was not sure what she said, but knew they had trouble feeding all the new people.

"Must kill Tisquantum." I ran my finger over my throat and bobbled my head.

Esapett put her hands over her own throat protectively. "Bradford say NO."

"Someone must kill." I said again.

Elisabeth

"I've never killed a man," John said. He sat with his hands clenched, his eyes fixed on them. "At least not that I know of." He glanced at me and his shoulders shifted as if adjusting a burden. "In battle, one might not know if it was his own gun or someone else's that killed or wounded another." He paused and I remembered Attitash's bloody wound, but said nothing. 'Twas true she'd not been killed, but it seemed that wounding someone in battle was worthy of note.

"That first encounter, when ye were still living on the Mayflower and the Indians attacked us, we heard a heathen yell but didn't find a body. Maybe someone was killed. Maybe I did it."

It was the first time he'd mentioned that encounter. We had just arrived in the new world then. My parents and all the Mayflower passengers were still alive. That was not quite two years ago, but seemed like someone else's life.

I took his hands in mine. "Ye make a brave soldier,

Jack. But I didn't say ye should be the one to do the killing. I just said it would bring our leaders together again if Squanto died."

John's face softened when I used his childhood, "Jack," but he quickly reverted to his serious demeanor. "Must ye take on solving every problem, Elisabeth? Haven't ye learned how much trouble this causes?"

My own face got warm. "Can I not even ask thee if a solution can be found?" I turned to dish up the last piece of cornbread for him. At least I was allowed to do that.

"I must think on this," John said, giving me the crumb of considering my idea. "However he dies, neither Bradford nor Massasowet must know who did it. Only a secret killing would keep our governor and their king from quarreling over whether he deserved beheading. So, it must seem a natural death—no cutting off heads. Squanto should go to hell and that's his due." John finished off his cornbread. "We won't act yet. The feud can simmer between our leaders for now. Squanto must be alive until we are successful in trading for more corn." He stood, brushing the crumbs from his beard. "Keep thy thoughts to thyself and we'll talk when it's time." He gave me a quick kiss, then a long look. "Can I trust thee not to seek aid from thy friend?"

"I'll wait, since ye think best."

Attitash
Papa listened to my idea of arranging a secret end to Tisquantum's life. "Matta, daughter." he said gently. "We'll let their sachem Bad-ford try to survive without any help from our Massasowet and no help from me. Then maybe your friends could convince Bad-ford to kill Tisquantum."

Listening to my father, I realized that the men on both sides—Bad-ford's and Massasowet's—had drawn a line that neither would cross. Esapett and I were both helpless. The Strangers were leaving soon with Tisquantum to seek more weachimin from other nations. We had to have a plan to get rid of him by the time they returned.

"WHO IS THE best healer? I asked my mother. "The grandmother who knows plants with both good and bad spirits?"

"A medicine that could become a life-taker if given too much?" Mama could always see my thoughts and was one ahead of me. Mama's brow knit as she considered. "Nashaquitsa." She saw my blank look. "She is an Eagle Clan grandmother, my brother Red Hawk's wife's mother—Seafoam's grandmother. She's at Nauset and you can walk that in one day easily."

"But Seafoam can't find out about this!" I wished I could trust my cousin, but she was still caught in her husband's net.

"We can trust Grandmother Nashaquitsa." The raucous noise of crows descending on our garden interrupted Mama. She called to Little Fish to stop playing with his little stones and clap his wood at the crows. With a heavy sigh, Mama returned to our discussion. "Believe me, Grandmother Nashaquita prays every day for an end to Tisquantum's snake-bite rule over Seafoam."

"When can we go?" I asked, eager to take action.

"Our crops are all thriving, go today and you'll be back when Tisquantum and the Strangers return from the Massachuseuk. The snake is hiding now, but he'll go trading with the Strangers tomorrow."

16

Elisabeth

I was preparing noon repast when Governor Bradford brought Squanto in. Masters Winslow and Allerton came too and sat at table with our governor while Squanto stood. It took some effort to keep my eyes on my work, but I directed my dark glances, intended for the betrayer, at the mussels in my hands instead.

Squanto was all false exclamations of surprise and denial—comical in their mangled structure had they not revealed the level of his deceit. "Nay, Gov'ner. Quadequina talk lies—talk evil. My king, Massasowet, love me and is love you. His brother, Quadequina, not talk what King feel."

This was accompanied by much bowing and scraping, as if our governor would be appeased by the appeals to the vanity which King James and his court demand. Nevertheless, these empty promises were enough for Isaac Allerton to persuade Governor Bradford and Edward Winslow that Squanto was ready to do their bidding. He would go with them to the Massachuseuk.

A flurry of preparations for the expedition cluttered the next two days. I'd not paid attention to how the trading was accomplished before. Now John explained the complicated process. Early on, as with all the trading ships before we settled, we had traded some tools and utensils for corn. After our treaty of mutual aid, our governor used Squanto to help negotiate with the Indians living north of us. There the beaver were thick and their pelts in great demand back in home in England.

"We need something beyond our scarce tools to buy pelts," John told me. "Our financiers in England demand beaver pelts, worth even more than the tall pine logs used to make ships."

"What will ye use?"

"Wampum, the purple and white shells," he answered.

I knew the beautiful shells, Attitash wore them, as all her people did. "They give them jewelry?"

"Nay, the shells are exchanged like coins." John told me those shells were not to be found on northern shores. The Wampanoag gathered the shells, polished them and prepared them for trade. In exchange for providing Massasowet and all Attitash's people with protection from other Indians, we used their wampum to buy beaver pelts. I realized our treaty of mutual aid was not only defense, but a way to pay off the English financiers.

The night before they would leave, John and I went to the shore to watch the sunset. The high tide was receding and John took a stick to the wet sand and drew. "Do ye know this?"

I clapped my hands. "It's my mark—the one ye made me last year."

His eyes lit up. "And used on the letters I wrote for thee. But how did ye remember?"

"I practice every time I come here and the sand is right, unless someone is near who might misconstrue what I'm about."

"Were ye using thy left hand? Who's seen this?" John's voice was casual, but he had reason to fear my attempts could be portrayed as witchcraft.

"I tried using my right, but it was impossible. I only did it when I was sure no one saw me but Priscilla...and Attitash."

"Why Attitash?" He kept his voice low.

"Why not? She would never falsely accuse me."

"God's truth, we have more to fear from some of our own than from the heathen." He nodded in approval as I copied with large lines his rendition of my mark, an E with designs and curlicues. "We have a bit more light and little time, Love. I'll get out ink and paper at home so ye can practice."

I had yet to try ink and a quill. My fingers stiffened at the prospect. As we walked up the hill to where our village was hidden behind the palings, we crossed the path coming from Hopamoch's homesite. "I've not seen Attitash," I commented. "Mayhap she's come down ill."

"Her father mentioned that Attitash and her husband left to visit relatives."

Relatives! Her cousin Seafoam? Was this part of Attitash's plot to kill Squanto? Such thoughts tumbled from my mind when John brought out his little desk. He put the inkpot in its hole and got out a piece of paper with a bit of writing at the top, which he'd obviously discarded. He trimmed a goose quill, then dipped it into the ink, held the quill over the pot until the big drip fell off, then made my mark on the paper. He held it out for me to try.

My first attempt resulted in a dark blob of ink on the paper. John said nothing, which I appreciated. I dipped the quill again and waited over the ink pot until a blob fell, then made my E. It looked rather like John's with only a couple of ink blots marring it. When I tried to add the curlicue's my E was nearly obscured. I put the quill down and shook out my fingers.

"I can't," I said, discouraged. His laugh did not amuse me.

"We all did that. Keep trying, fill up the whole page. I have to sharpen my knives." His knife made a soft zzz-ing sound against the wet-stone that made my fingers and shoulders relaxed. It seemed a waste of precious ink, but I kept making my mark until the paper was half filled.

"Should I try it with my right hand?"

"Nay, wait until 'tis easy with thy left." John looked up from his sharpening to inspect my work. "Well done. Now write *expedient.*"

We both laughed. I would never even try "Elisabeth," much less some word I could scarcely say.

John sanded my paper to dry the ink, shook the sand off, and then gave it to me. "Put that in thy trunk." He wiped his knives dry and wrapped them in their carrying leather, then began removing his boots and untying his garters. "'Tis good ye can make thy mark now. Should ye be widowed, God forbid, ye'll need it."

My hands, warm from my efforts, chilled. Of course, there was always the danger I'd be widowed, but we never spoke of this. Perhaps John feared, as I did, that Squanto would bring betrayal and death upon their heads while in the Massachuseuk territory. I tried to keep my voice as matter-of-fact as his.

"But ye always remind me God saved thee from the ocean depths for a reason," I teased. "Has His mercy towards thee diminished?"

"Nay, God is still with me." He ceased undressing and pulled me against him. "I will return from this trip. We all will." He kissed me thoroughly, then held my face in his hands. "God is with us, but I must show Him I don't take His mercy for granted. To be prepared is to show The Divine that I'm ready for whatever He delivers."

How easily my husband could allay my fears! I gave him a quick kiss back. "So as long as ye've prepared me to make my mark, God will not make use of it for my legal rights as a widow?"

"Not for fifty years," he laughed. "Thy quick mind is only one reason I love thee." He turned his back so I could unlace the points holding his breeches up. "But if ye can prepare me to bed thee, I'll be required to do so." He turned and slid his hands down my back 'til he cupped my bottom. His voice was husky with desire as he declared he was indeed well prepared.

It was not until I woke in the dark of mid-night that my fears resurfaced. John's arms were wrapped around me, his breath and limbs heavy in sleep. Sliding away, I sat up and went to catch the sea breeze by cracking the door. What if I had to sleep alone again? What if I were indeed with child and would be like Widow Ford—raising a new babe alone. Pushing my damp curls away, I crawled back next to John. His presence soothed my fears, but he was leaving in the morning on the boat, with Squanto. I recalled how fervently Attitash declared, 'must kill him.'

Attitash

"Attitash, don't ask this!" Seafoam kept her eyes on the low fire in her Eagle Clan's moon lodge. "Shimmering Fish is just gaining the Strangers' Sachem's trust. He'll be blamed for the death of their translator."

Her grandmother blew on the sweet grass and fanned the smoke. "Attitash is only asking for all our people, Granddaughter." She put a gentle hand on Seafoam's arm. "Go back to your husband if you cannot forget him. Leave the moon lodge now, so the spirits can speak to me. I invited you hoping you would understand what is needed, but you do not."

Seafoam's mouth turned down, making her pretty face hard. My hand reached out to her, but Grandmother Nashaquitsa's eyes told me to let her go.

Aunt First Star, watched her daughter out the door, then turned to Nashaquitsa. "You say you can find a Stranger who will put big doses in strong drink and give it to Tisquantum?"

"Yes," I said.

Aunt First Star held out a leather bag. "We collected

the roots last season of falling-leaves. Attitash, give this
to your mother. She must crush these and take five big
hands-full, seethe in a small pot of water, then give it to
the one who will dose Tisquantum's drink. They may have
to mix it in several drinks to give him."

The grandmother closed her eyes and breathed slowly.
"The snake's heart will beat so fast it will crack in two."

17

Elisabeth

When a week passed with no word from our men I could not help but worry. Desire had come to stay with me and I did not want to seem childish to her, but finally mentioned my fears about John's safety. Each night I took out the small scrap of paper he'd handed to me the morning he left. It was just a line, but reading his firm script with the gentle words, "Love me always as I do love thee," eased my aching loneliness. I'd not mentioned to John my pile of clean clouts sitting in my trunk unused for seven weeks now.

"What worries thee, Elisabeth? Thy husband is famously blessed by God to live a long life." Desire could usually shake me from the doldrums by teasing me about John Howland's rescue from the sea, but I did not laugh easily now. She persisted, "Could ye pray for a storm that spares thy husband and drowns that worm, Squanto?"

I almost smiled at that. "Truth be told, I worry that I'll be a widow with a fatherless child." I patted my still-flat belly. Desire caught the reference. Her hands flew to cup my face and she kissed my cheeks.

"God's truth? Already with child?" Her agitation threw Desire into a fit of coughing so I was spared responding.

"Will ye tell thy husband when he returns? And he *will* return." Desire picked up the Bible and opened it. "Now, let's concentrate on thy reading. Whatever ye do with thy big surprise, it will be a nice small one when ye can read this passage to him." She opened it to Solomon's song, still her favorite to practice on. We'd read it so many times I could say it from memory, but I picked up the Bible to read, *"Behold, thou art fair, my love; behold thou art fair; thou hast doves' eyes within thy locks."*

"Pardon, Mistress." William Latham entered without knocking, startling me. "One of the heathens brought fish."

Black Whale stood in the lane, several nice fish on a string. As I took them, he said quietly, "Attitash has more for you." Black Whale pointed to the sea. "Go now." He said something else in his language, but I knew where to find her.

Attitash was on her side of the rock barrier. I'd not seen her for a few months and was glad to see a bump beneath her poncho that meant she carried a growing child.

With no more return than a glimmer of a smile, Attitash handed me a clay jug wrapped in deerskin. She pulled off the leather wrapped around the mouth and an astringent odor wafted out. The jug appeared to be some kind of remedy. "This cohosh kill Tis-Squantum."

"Kill?" I glanced about the shore to make sure no one heard us.

She mimicked drinking then choking. "Bad gods in cohosh."

"Poison?"

"Ahhe. Kill Tis-Squantum. No blood. Sachem Badford be happy."

My hands shook. I put the jug down carefully. "I can't kill anyone!"

"You do not kill. Cohosh poison kills." She gripped my wrists so fiercely my hands clenched into fists. "If Tis-Squantum lives, our people do not keep each other safe." She patted her belly. "No one lives."

My breath was caught in my chest. I gulped for air. "Who would do it?"

"Your men have strong drink."

"Yea, Master Hopkins does."

"Hop-kins give Massasowet strong drink." It was an oft-told story. When our people toasted the treaty with Stephen Hopkins' aqua-vit, Massasowet reportedly had broken out in a sweat.

Attitash used a mixture of her words and English to explain her plan. I then repeated it back as best I could.

"Squanto likes strong drink," I said. "I must tell Hopkins put big cohosh in Squanto's drink."

She held out her hands wide, which I understood meant a lot of cohosh. "Put *all* cohosh in drink, then Squanto will die."

No blood spilled. I would do anything to save our people and Attitash's plan was a clever one. Hopkins hated Squanto. Like Captain Standish who hired him, Stephen Hopkins belonged to the King's church. He believed that a priest could save him from going to hell for poisoning Squanto. He would be willing to deliver the poison drink and Squanto would take it laced into aqua-vit. This clever plan would only work, however, if I could figure out how to approach Master Hopkins privately. And if I had the will to carry out the plan. Those of us Hopkins called, "Puritans," understood that God decided before we were born if we were saved or damned. If this was murder, and it felt like murder, then I was breaking God's commandment. But if it was God's will that Squanto be poisoned, I was part of the Lord's plan to save all our people. But how was I to know what God wanted? Goosebumps rose on the back of my neck despite the weather. When I returned home, I would pray to discern God's will.

The wrapped jug fit into the bucket I'd brought for collecting mussels to distract others from my visit across the rock barrier. Attitash dumped sand in the bottom to steady the jug and we piled mussels in to cover.

As I rose to go, Attitash said. "Tell only Hop-kins."
Then she smiled, "If some ask what this is, say small cohosh is good for women with no moon blood." She put
her thumb and forefinger together. "Small cohosh good
woman medicine." Attitash swept her hand just below
where her growing babe pushed out her belly.

To show I understood, I tried to repeat her instructions
in Wampanoag, which probably came out, 'Squanto likes
Hopkins. Hopkins likes Bradford and likes us. Much cohosh
for Squanto. Little for us women if we don't bleed.' I could
not understand the women part: for young maids who had
no courses, for women with child, or for old women who
no longer were fruitful? Attitash took my hand and leaned
her cheek into mine. I understood when she said, 'Netop,'
her word for friend. But the rest of her words must have
been the Wampanoag version of, 'Go with God.' But was I
going with her idolatrous deity or with God?

It was a warm afternoon and no one was about as I
came through the gate, nodding at the guard. Captain
Standish had left Stephen Hopkins at home to guard while
our men were on their trading trip. Catching him while
my husband away would be most helpful. My breath came
quickly as I glanced around for Isaac Allerton, Goodwife
Billington, or others who had accused me of witchcraft. If
they found out what I was plotting, they would only see a
witch when they looked at me. They did not know God's
will, but that did not stop their speculating. Even Governor Bradford wanted Squanto alive to translate.

It would be a sign from God if I could catch Master
Hopkins alone whilst no one else would see us.

As I neared Hopkins' home, I saw Mistress Hopkins
in the garden, tending her herbs. Then, praise God, Master himself came out the front door. Without any time
to think, I blurted out, "Well met, Master. I need a brief
word with thee."

He looked surprised, to say the least, and glanced about, no doubt wanting to protect his own propriety as well as mine. "Very brief, then. What is it?"

Reaching into my basket, I exposed the jar. "This is a heathen poison—an expedient way to dispose of the danger Squanto poses to our treaty."

Stephen Hopkins' eyes widened. "Whatever are ye talking about?"

I burst into a rapid description of what Attitash proposed, ending with, "You can use this to poison Squanto's drink."

Master Hopkins took off his hat and rubbed his hair. "We call black cohosh snakeroot. But whatever you call it, you can't do this, Elisabeth."

"Pray tell why not?" I sensed that Stephen Hopkins was simply afraid a young woman could not carry out an execution. He was a soldier, hired by Myles Standish, used to killing. Hopkins and Standish still worshipped the King and had not renounced King James's rule.

"It puts thee in danger of great harm." Master Hopkins stepped closer to me. "*Mistress* Howland, have you already forgotten how close you came to being hanged or burned as a witch? I'm not a Puritan, but I know the fever burns in your Separatist people." Hopkins pointed to my left hand, still resting on the bottle of poison. "See how you've been marked, Mistress? They'll watch whatever you do."

I hastily withdrew my hand. How could I forget to use my right in such an important encounter? My eyes widened as I noticed Goodwife Billington and Widow Ford, coming from the goat pen carrying milk pans. Hopkins turned to see them too and waved me to go away.

My chest burned. This chance encounter had seemed an indication that God blessed Attitash's plan. I turned as Hopkins' loud whisper followed me. "John Howland must deliver it. Only your husband can decide if this is worth the risk to you." I drew a deep breath. Hopkins was giving us the chance if John was involved. Another hoarse whisper followed me. I strained to hear, "And give me the poison in a Christian jar, nothing from the heathen."

The women were almost in earshot. I turned back to him and spoke in a loud voice. "Thank you for asking after my husband, Master Hopkins. I miss him, however, rest assured he is always in concert with my own wishes."

Master Hopkins eyes flicked, indicating his understanding.

I greeted the women, taking one of the milk pails from Widow Ford. I have no idea what we chattered about.

Desire was deboning the fish Black Whale had brought. I put the jar of cohosh up on the shelf, behind other remedies, telling her only that Attitash had delivered some medicine for the Hopkins household. Desire expressed no curiosity, being too busy with the fish. We filleted enough for the Brewster table and Governor Bradford's.

A fierce rainstorm blew in as Desire and I came back from our fish supper with Brewsters. Little Humility had insisted on coming home with us so all three of us were squashed in our bed. Between thinking of Master Hopkins' words and images of our men caught out in a storm at sea, there was no sleep for me. Fear for my husband on the stormy sea suppressed my prayers for discernment about God's will for the poison. Just as I was finally growing drowsy, Humility wrapped her little arms about my neck and I had to shift in order to breathe.

Then I remembered Elder Brewster's comment at supper. I had made bold to ask if our governor, the Brewsters' foster son, would change his mind and behead Squanto.

"Do not fret thyself, Elisabeth," Elder Brewster had admonished me. "Captain Standish was talking with Bradford about Squanto just before the expedition left for the Massachuseuk."

I tried not to look too interested and Elder Brewster continued. "Standish was saying one of his men could accomplish the execution during the voyage home. That way we'd have traded for corn and furs before they killed him."

Evidently, my face showed my thoughts as Mistress Brewster scolded her husband for giving us foolish rumors which were unlikely to prove true.

As sleep continued to allude me, I wondered why my John had said nothing about this rumor to me. Did he not know?

My fearful thoughts were interrupted by Desire's coughing. She fumbled in the dark 'til she could ladle some water. After she came back to bed, we listened to the rain on the thatched roof and talked about the fancy house she'd lived in before her father died.

"Strong brick so ye'd never be wet and a huge fireplace." Desire's voice was so soft it was nearly lost in the noise of the storm. "Father taught me to read, ye know. Mother disputed this, saying maids who could read would not memorize their Bible verses. Mother said I'd not be able to bring a verse to mind when I needed it." Desire laughed wryly. "Of course I did remember the verse when Father died, but I don't know if she did." In the dark, I felt Desire's slight tremble. "There was NO verse I wanted to remember when Mother's new husband caught me alone and tried to..." Her voice was so low I could not hear. She'd told me the sordid tale before. Desire snuggled close to me. "Ye are so fortunate, Elisabeth, that thy mother and father died almost the same time." She must have felt my body clench, as she added. "Even though ye were only thirteen, ye never had to endure a stepfather."

"Yea, I did not. And thanks to John I did not have to be indentured." I could not imagine that being indentured to someone like Isaac Allerton would be much better than a nasty stepfather. I'd avoided that, but would his tentacles still destroy me if I passed on the cohosh? I was considering an action that would give Allerton an excuse to avenge my escape from his rule over me.

"Thy John shall return, dear friend. Ye shall have thy babe. None of that is meant for me." Desire pulled me close and I stroked her hair, just as I used to when my sister Rose and I slept together.

RAIN CONTINUED TO SLUICE DOWN the windows when Humility woke up. She was fussy, probably not having slept well either. When she asked for the third time, "Why Uncle John not come?" I hurried her back to Mistress Brewster's care.

Later that afternoon, I went to the shore, taking Humility with me and my gathering basket on my arm. We saw Attitash coming down her path and went to meet her there.

"Netop," we greeted each other. She leaned down to brush her hand on Humility's cheek and the child accepted it, then put her own little hand on Attitash's belly beneath her soft leather wraparound. I pulled at Humility's hand to stop, but Attitash laughed and pulled Humility closer. I silently said a prayer that this time her delivery would go well. She settled on a large rock and I sat next to her. For a few lovely moments we just held hands and laughed as Humility chased the shrieking gulls who dipped into the sea as the tide crept up the shore.

The heavy air was warming fast. Attitash let go of my hand and pulled her hair off her bare shoulder. "Hop-kins get cohosh?"

"Cohosh," I tried the word again, not yet being accustomed to it. "Yea. Ahhe"

Attitash put her hand protectively over her small bump. "Where is big cohosh?"

I assured her it was at home and would be taken to Hopkins soon. "I need to talk to John Howland."

Attitash gave me a look I could only interpret as she knew I was too young to think for myself. She asked, "Can Jon-owland?" she put a finger on her lips.

"Keep a secret?" I said.

She put her hand over her mouth. "Not tell others."

"Ahhe, yea," I assured her. Whether John would approve of the whole venture I could not say.

Near suppertime a shout came that the shallop was coming. I hesitated before I went to meet them. Should I tell John of my foolishness? I had already caused him so much trouble with my reckless behavior.

Most of our village came down to the shore. As the shallop drew near, the men all called out their "halloos" and Squanto held up a bag of corn, crowing as if he'd planted it. He was still alive.

18

Attitash

Cap-tan San-dish had not dumped Tisquantum into the Big Salt Water. The traitor sauntered up the shore, flaunting the Strangers' protection. Black Whale and my father stormed back to our wetu and our family talked late into the night.

"The Massachuseuk people have every right to be hostile to all Cloth-men," Papa said. He described the Strangers who lived in Massachuseuk territory as not only lazy, but without any honor. We'd stayed away from those Cloth-men, who our friends called, "Westons" when they came across the Big Salt Water to Plimot before the cold moons. They abused the hospitality of our own Strangers before they took their small wind canoe and went north to Massachuseuk territory. "They stole Massachuseuk women and keep them captive. They expect the People to do the work for them. These Strangers want all our beaver-brothers' pelts."

I asked if these Strangers brought women and children with them and was not surprised when the answer was no.

"And what does Tisquantum think of those Clothmen?" Mama asked.

"I believe he looks to how this could provide more power and goods for himself. The Massachuseuks found nothing but squalor and laziness in those 'Westons' Clothmen, so they let down their own guard. The Massachuseuk are ripe for spoil and all their furs with them." Papa paused to make certain we followed his thinking. "Tisquantum

could use Bad-ford's warriors for his own gain. If Tisquantum could convince Sachem Bad-ford to help his own kind,
lazy and evil as they are, then Tisquantum could join with
our friend Bad-Ford to take over Massachuseuk's beaver
pelt trade with other Cloth-men who come from across
the Big Salt Water each warm moon." Papa's lips pursed
as if he'd taken a taste of poison himself. "If Tisquantum
could do this, then Tisquantum, a mere servant to our
Massasowet, could push our sachem aside and be seen as
hero by all Wampanoag who fear the Strangers more than
they honor our Sachem." Papa spat into the fire. "With
such treachery threatening us, we must do something."

That night, questions kept all my sleep away. Did Hopkins understand what to do? I could never be sure Esapett understood me when we tried to talk. Sometimes her
eyes looked uncertain, but she would not ask me to use
her language instead. Other times I could not understand
her words and the words she evidently thought were mine
sounded like rocks scraping. Would Hop-kins now give
Tisquantum the big dose or would Win-sow and Papa
convince Bad-ford to kill Tisquantum? When I finally
slept, bad night spirits spoiled my dreams.

Elisabeth

"I thought ye might have thrown Squanto into the sea," I
said as John stripped off his sea-crusted clothes.

"Nay, though I wanted to. It's none of thy worry, Dear
Heart, but the Weston men who live amongst the Massachuseuk make our efforts almost impossible. They make
no friends, and are enemies with everyone." John shook
his clothes off by the fire and took up the clean shirt I'd
laid out. "And Squanto does not help. Instead, he insults
the Massachuseuk." John dipped into the water pail and
splashed his face. "Standish is even worse. Some men, even
heathen men, think muscles are the only method to win

over others. They either don't have brains and speech or don't know how to use them." John pulled the clean shirt down, covering the brief glimpse I'd had of his secrets at rest. "Edward Winslow says he will convince our governor to use his own knife to execute Squanto now that we have corn."

I added some of the new corn to the mussel porridge, then asked, "What chance is there Master Winslow can change our governor's mind?"

John grimaced. "'Tis a hard row we must hoe now, Love. Don't trouble thyself." He took the bowl of porridge and sniffed appreciatively. "Take a big bowl for thyself. Ye must eat lustily now." John wiped his mustache. "We must fatten thee up so my seed can become fruitful." He laughed as if conceiving was a great joke. "But we'll not plow that furrow 'til I've slept. I'm sore weary now and no man can do right by his wife in such a condition."

Truth be told, I was relieved that's all we would do. Sleeping in his arms was all I wanted. Weary myself, I was in no mood for any further attentions from my darling. But I did have an essential errand to run before dark and John needed to help me. I sat down on the bench next to his chair. "Before ye sleep, there's a plot afoot I must inform thee about."

"Something my dear wife is involved in? Let me guess, thy heathen friend, Attitash is also involved." This response was deserved, but certainly didn't make it easier for me.

"Yea, but wait, John. Do hear me out." Honesty produced speedily was my only chance.

"I'm sore tired. Are ye sure it can't wait."

"It cannot. Ye know how everyone says we must have the treaty to survive?" I did not even wait for an answer. "Attitash and her family brought me a concoction. They call it 'cohosh,' and she said her family wants us to give it to Hopkins to dose Squanto with and then Squanto will die, but there will be no blood and no one will know anything and so our governor will no longer have to lose face with their kings and so we will all…" I ran out of breath. I sounded like a small girl chattering away about goats in the pasture, not like a married women charged with saving our plantation and our Wampanoag friends.

John closed his eyes and sank back in his chair. "Dear God," he murmured. I thought he'd never open his eyes again. Mayhap his weariness had overtaken him and he was asleep.

"I must take the cohosh to Hopkins," I said.

John opened his eyes. "Tell me again, slowly."

Taking the jar of cohosh off its place on the shelf, I showed it to John. I began again, starting with Black Whale arriving with fish for us and the message to meet Attitash. John did not interrupt, and a few times he closed his eyes. It occurred to me that morning might have been a better time to divulge all this, but I could not imagine sleeping next to him with this between us.

John even smiled when I told him I used the word 'expedient' with Stephen Hopkins. When I finished, John sat quietly a moment, then rose from his chair.

"Ye think Hopkins should get this tonight, so this can happen before any further trouble with Squanto develops?"

"I do."

"Well, ye are not gallivanting about at night carrying poison by thyself. We must bring Hopkins here, so no one sees us carrying the potion to him."

"That's wise, John." My words did not reveal how my heart was lurching. Would both of us be brought to trial? Or burn in hell? Did God truly favor this?

It was still light out, the spring sun slow to go down over the hills. John went to the door and called out to William Latham who was chopping wood. When the boy was close, John sent him off to bring Master Hopkins with some excuse about needing to exchange information on what transpired while during the trading. I remembered Master Hopkins wanted a new container. As quick as the thought came to me, I recalled my father's beaker, still in the trunk where I'd placed their few belongings. Stephen Hopkins arrived just as I pulled Father's beaker from the trunk. I put it on the table, next to where I'd placed Attitash's jar.

Master Hopkins' eyes gleamed and he bobbed his head in excitement when I showed him the jar, using my right hand. "How did ye get so much?"

"From Hopamoch's family."

"Bloody good work!" Master Hopkins bit his lip. "Pardon, Mistress Puritan, if I've offended thee." He made a mock bow. "If we can cram enough down Squanto's snake-gut we've saved Bradford's face and Massasowet's too."

I showed him Father's beaker and he agreed it would work. He sniffed the jar, then poured some into the beaker. "I can fill the beaker with my aqua-vit and then plenty of snakeroot." He sniffed it and smiled. "Did ye smell it?" He held the jar out to us. I turned aside, having already taken a good sniff. John breathed deeply and coughed.

"Can you do this, Stephen?" John asked. "Will this mad scheme work?"

"Ye can trust me to get the job done."

"Tell no one else, Sir," I said, feeling a bit forward.

"Nay, only ye and Hopamoch's girl." Stephen Hopkins took a long sniff from the jar. "We call this snakeroot," he said to John. "The heathen call it 'black cohosh'. Once I've done in Squanto, I'll save a bit for my wife. She's troubled with female sweats sometimes and a bit of snakeroot helps." It embarrassed me that he spoke of Mistress Hopkins so plainly, but I said nothing. Mayhap women going through the change were what Attitash meant by women who don't bleed.

As soon as Master Hopkins left with the jar and my father's beaker tucked beneath his cloak, John sat down on the bed. "Help me with my laces, Wife. We must sleep now."

Mice gnawed at my back and lower tummy. The smell of bitter roots permeated my body. Something sticky between my legs and my fingers were red with blood.

"Elisabeth." John was patting my shoulder and I woke up, but the smell and the feeling were still there. "It smells like blood. Are thy courses flooding?" He got up and fumbled to light a candle from an ember in the fire. I knew what it would show before he brought the light to me. Deep red on my nightgown and sheets and rusty streaks on his shirt.

Attitash

I tried to shake my dream of Esapett crying blood tears as Black Whale untangled from my arms in the early light. Big Salt Water was red with Nippa'uus' early light. My husband had gone to our Massasowet with a message to send his translator. The message was that Toka-mahamon must help convince Sachem Bad-ford what a threat Tisquantum was to all of us. But if the black cohosh worked, we would need a translator to replace the snake.

My field work waited. The bean vines were climbing the weachimin stalks and the squash would soon cover the ground.

"We're chopping Tisquantum's head," White Flower said, working her hoe furiously.

Little Fish yelled, "Tisquantum, go," as he clapped his sticks to shoo the blackbirds away. The birds rose from every direction, forming a grand twirling cloud. Papa waved them away when he passed by on his way to Sachem Bad-ford.

As we chopped, I kept an eye out for Esapett to join the other Strangers working in their field. Her friends, Peh-silla and Con-sance were not working either, only the young men and boys and Spotted-face girl and her little sister. Had Esapett given the black cohosh to Tisquantum yet? Maybe my sad dream told a truth.

Nippa'uus was high overhead when my father returned. "Win-sow and Sachem Bad-ford told us that during their journey to the Massachuseuk, Tisquantum insisted that I, their trusted man, was the true betrayer and had told the lies."

"Matta! Did Win-sow believe him?" Mama demanded.

"Win-sow did not. He said this convinced them Tisquantum was indeed never to be trusted." Papa finished our water jug and grabbed Little Fish, who was still yelling at the crows. My brother played with Papa's topknot, which always made Papa smile. When he was calm, Mama and I asked Papa our questions. He told us that since they returned, Tisquantum could not be found. Win-sow had looked for him in the Commonhouse, but the men there said he'd not returned last night.

Before Papa could explain more, Suki barked and ran up the path to greet Black Whale and Toka-mahamon. They were both carrying big loads of beaver pelts. "Massasowet will give all these pelts to Sachem Bad-ford if he kills Tisquantum," Black Whale said.

"Do the Strangers demand payment?" I asked.

"They've not said so, but they always want more pelts to send across the Big Salt Water. We'll try anything to get Bad-ford to send Tisquantum to his grave." Black Whale stroked my belly lightly. "We must get rid of the betrayer and bring our sachems back to their treaty."

The men filled their tobacco pouches and went to see

Sachem Bad-ford. I wanted to follow them, but Mama knew what I planned by my eager face. "You stay here, Attitash, and keep your new-life safe! We'll find out when they return." She was right, as always.

Elisabeth

The sun was warm on our south window when I woke up. It took a moment for me to realize my bad dream was a sad reality. I remembered that John had been all sweet solicitation, helping me out of my soiled shift and bringing me a bowl of water. He'd asked nothing and I could not speak except to say over and over, "I'm sorry." John had no idea I was sorry for so much more than the mess.

Now, I found the stained bed-sheet and my shift soaking in a pan of water on the floor. The odor still proclaimed blood. I dumped the foul water and replaced it from the rain barrel. It was tepid from the sun and I washed myself thoroughly, then soaped the stains. My shift would never be clean again. I'd have burned it if I had an extra. My body ached and I wanted to go back to bed, but forced myself to sit down and eat some of the cold corn mush.

Priscilla arrived before I'd finished eating. "My John told me ye took sick."

Without a warning, sobs shook me. Priscilla held me close and I felt a faint ripple where her belly pushed against mine.

"Ye feel life, Priscilla?"

"Yea, can ye feel it too?"

My words rushed out. My hopes, my sniff of snake-root—saying only it was a heathen remedy—and now, my despair. I did not mention my fear that God took my bud of a babe for plotting poison. When I finished, Priscilla poured me a small cup of ale.

"Whether 'twas sniffing the heathen remedy or not, many of our first attempts go awry," she said. "Mistress

Brewster told me God takes the ones not fit to be born. When my courses were a month late, she said not to count on being with child until I was at least three months gone." Priscilla began scrubbing the stains. When I objected that I would do my own work, she ignored me. "Ye must rest, I'll help 'til thy husband can come."

I knew I must tell John what happened to me before rumors spread. "When will he be back? What are the men doing?"

"Do ye wish me to interrupt their talk with Hopamoch about Squanto?"

"Squanto?" The cramps in my belly intensified. "Is he with them?"

"Nay. But Hopamoch and Master Winslow are insisting that our governor kill Squanto. Hopamoch says King Massasowet is sending Toka here to explain his need to have Squanto executed." Priscilla poured more ale for me. "If ye want thy husband, I can tell John Howland thy illness is more than he might think."

"Nay!" I took another sip of ale. "I'm fine for now, thanks to thee, good friend."

Priscilla insisted I get back in bed and I dozed off again.

I woke to find the door open to let in a breeze against the hot summer sun. A swarm of flies buzzed over the covered ale bucket. Moving slowly, I went out into the garden. My shift and bedding draped on the fence were dry, so I gathered them up, then felt so weak I sat down on the stump. When John arrived sometime later, I was still sitting on the stump. Without asking, he took the clean washing out of my lap and put an arm around me to help me inside. John poured some tea for both of us, then finally asked what was ailing me. I started to say it was only my monthly courses, but he stopped me. "Ye must know something's amiss, Love. Ye've never been laid so low."

The truth I began with was that I was indeed three

weeks late and had hoped I was with child. His eyebrows lifted, but he did not interrupt. After an empty silence, I told him my fears. That smelling it and handling the jar of cohosh had washed away my pip of a babe.

John waited for me to wipe my tears. Taking a deep breath, I told him Attitash hinted that cohosh was not for women carrying a child. John's face followed my story, his eyes changing from dark to bright. He put his hand gently on my cheek as I gave way to more tears. Finally, I told him that Priscilla said 'twas common to lose a babe before it caught fast in the womb.

"John, I will be an honest wife to you. I had not told you this because I wanted to be sure." When I ran out of words and tears at last, he gathered me into his arms.

"Dear Heart, God would never take away the chance for an innocent babe to grow in exchange for an evil heathen's death. Ye must rest now." He carried me to our bed and adjusted the clean bed sheet over me. "We will have babes, so many I'll lose track."

I WAS UP AND AROUND in a few days, for the first time since my travails, and I went to the shore that evening. The summer sun hung low over the hills in the west. Attitash was already collecting clams and rewarded my return with her beautiful smile. I made an attempt to convey my loss to her and she seemed to understand.

As the sea sloshed toward our feet, Attitash took a cask from her belt and took a small drink. "Nipi. ni-pi." She poured a drop in my hand and I repeated, "nipi." Then I motioned drinking and said, "nipi—drink?" Attitash looked puzzled, then poured some of her cask water into the waves at our feet. "Nipi."

I dipped my hand into the waves and flicking the water playfully at her. "Water. Wa-ter."

She smiled and repeated "wa-ter—nipi. Hop-kins take

nipi?" She motioned drinking and I knew she was asking about Squanto. I lifted one shoulder, shrugging to indicate my ignorance. Not knowing troubled me, but Attitash's calm question made me feel less agitated. It seemed more like simple curiosity than the complicity of aiding and abetting a murder.

Attitash reached into the small leather bag on her belt and brought out a small blue berry. "Attitash."

That stopped me. I pointed to her, "Attitash."

She laughed again, "Ahhe, "and pointed to herself and repeated, "Attitash," then to the blue berry, "attitash," and popped it in her mouth.

We were both still smiling, when our husbands appeared. Attitash asked her husband something in Wampanoag that must have been my same question to John. "Has Squanto been found?"

Attitash
Black Whale put his hand on my new-life-bump. "Our child will be safe from Tisquantum's evil."

"Did they find him?"

"Not yet." He moved his hand as if he could feel our baby's movement. "But Sachem Bad-ford has called for Tisquantum to be brought in. It's just a matter of time.

"Did you think Esapett looked sick?" I asked.

He shrugged. "All the Strangers look sick."

We walked side by side up our path.

"I think she was trying to tell me she was carrying a New Life and lost it," I said.

"She couldn't have been very far along yet, but I never really look at her." Black Whale stopped and put his arm around my waist, settling on the swelling under my navel. "It must be easier to lose one so early."

I leaned against him. "She smelled some of the black cohosh. It's never easy if you think it's your fault."

"Was she trying to lose her New Life?" Black Whale asked as he tossed a stone onto the lapping water.

"Matta, she was not trying! She is sad," I said. "The cohosh must have been strange to Esapett. I tried to distract her a little by teaching her more of our words."

He looked up the hill to where they'd gone. "You just keep trying, don't you? She'll never really understand us."

19

July, 1622
Elisabeth

Mother sat in my new house, looking about as if she intended to help prepare breakfast. She reached to the shelf and found Father's bottle. Peering inside, she sniffed and made a face. "Have ye considered which kind of sinners test God's will by trying to take a life?" I knew she asked me the question, but she kept her back to me. "Even if an enemy needs killing, you should not take it upon thyself to kill. Our Lord, Jesus, sits at God's right hand and Satan rules thy left hand." Mother looked me full in the face. Her eyes flashed anger. The rod she'd used to chastise me was held firmly in her right hand. "The savage blood is on thy hands if it is not God's Plan."

The sun hit my eyes, and I forced them open, ending the dream. My entire body was rigid. My left hand burned as if Mother had once again taken the rod upon it to drive Satan out. Closing my eyes again, I forced the dream from my mind.

I went outside and bent to my work. John worried that I was not recovered enough to hoe. But I persuaded him I was indeed healthy again. Only a royal lady would malinger, willing to rest on others. If my work was needed, I would work.

It felt good to hoe alongside Constance Hopkins and Mary Chilton. I was the only married woman working in the field, everyone else had children to care for or, as with Priscilla, was close to childbed. As the sun beat down and my hoe worked to reveal the little corn plants hidden under the weeds, I actually hummed.

Remember Allerton and her little sister Mary came up the row towards us. This was the first season Mary, now six years old, worked in the field. She frequently stopped chopping weeds to watch seagulls weave and call above the field. Remember neglected to chastise her sister, but took her own break to lean on her hoe. Now, she asked Constance, "Did your father give some medicine to Squanto?"

Constance dropped her hoe. "Why do ye ask that, child?"

Remember drew herself up as if to become a woman. "Father mentioned that Squanto and Master Hopkins were having a drink with Father the night before Squanto disappeared."

So Hopkins *had* given Squanto the drink. I vowed to demand the full story from my John. Surely he'd talked to Master Hopkins by now.

Remember Allerton grinned. "I know your father would not give a heathen any remedy, but...." Her voice trailed off and she giggled as she prodded her sister Mary with her hoe. They started toward the next row, but Constance called after them.

"Oh la, Remember. Ye would have no idea what a remedy is," Constance taunted. "Thy father is as ignorant of our remedies from England as the least informed savage."

The glare Remember shot over her shoulder was one that could maim if not kill. I thought she might turn around and hit Constance with her hoe, and leaned over my work for a moment, composing my face. Was Remember Allerton implying more than a 'remedy'?

"Here come the Abominations," Mary Chilton hissed.

Mary was attached to Master Winslow's household and proud it contained no one that could be labeled an Abomination—our name for all the sluggards who took our food but loathed work. The Billington boys sauntered up with some of the new men. Of course John and Francis Billington were an abomination in ways more dreadful than their work—or lack of same. Although their mother cooked, they depended on the rest of us to put food on their family's table. They were a bad example that the new men easily followed.

"They're not only useless in the field, I doubt if any of them would be willing and able to take up arms if we or the Wampanoag were attacked by the Narragansett," I scoffed.

"Which ones are our friends?" Mary Chilton asked. "Wampa...or Narragan...?"

"Oh pay attention to thy master, Mary," Constance chided. "Surely he's spoken of Hopamoch and Massasowet as Wampanoag."

Mary flushed. As servant to Susanna White Winslow, she was busy chasing after little Peregrine and containing young Resolved's constant mischief. She heard little of the men's quiet discussions of the dangers to our settlement. Mary might not have realized that there was no assurance we would defend Massasowet or that he would defend us against the French.

As soon as John came in the door for supper, I dropped the ladle in the soup and faced him, hands on my hips, my voice coming out in a screech. "So what did Stephen Hopkins say about Squanto? Did he keep Father's bottle or give it to Squanto?"

"Why must ye know?" The crease between his brows revealed my husband was attempting to calm himself down. "Just forget it happened and don't stir up the fire."

"Tell me! It's been weeks and the bad dreams persist." My words spewed out vehemently. "I need to know!"

John sat down and tried to pull me on his lap. I resisted and sat on the bench facing him.

"Yea, he did give him the drink." John ran his hands through his disheveled hair, spilling wood chips and shavings.

I waited for more details. None came. John sat back as if he'd just told a long tale.

"Well?" I demanded. "Did he give him the whole dose? Did Squanto get sick? What about the bottle? Where did he go?"

"Something's burning." John said it calmly enough, but I jumped up and moved the crane so the soup was off the fire. After giving it a stir to free the liquid above the burned bottom of the pot, I returned to my seat and waited.

"Ye are a demanding wench, ye know."

"I am, and ye can be an infuriating man, so do tell me everything ye know."

"Well, I was not able to speak alone with Hopkins for a couple of days." He glanced at me quickly. "No one has seen Squanto. I finally caught Hopkins alone walking back from guard duty. He said Allerton showed up just after Squanto had arrived."

"Oh no!"

"Don't worry, Hopkins said he'd already prepared Squanto's cup—in the beaker ye gave him from thy father's trunk."

"Did Isaac Allerton recognize Father's beaker?"

"Allerton was focused on getting a drink himself. Of course, he'd brought his own beaker." John reached toward the cornbread I'd laid out. I gave him a look, but did not insist he wait for prayers or for the soup. "Squanto took a good long drink, but then made a bad face. Hopkins was hoping Allerton wouldn't notice, but Isaac asked Squanto what was wrong."

I couldn't help wringing my hands. John either told very short stories or very long. Resisting my urge to demand he get to the end, I took a piece of cornbread myself.

"So, Squanto said something like 'Hopkins gave me bad drink.'"

"And what did Allerton say?"

"He told Squanto he'd finish it for him, so's not to go to waste."

"God in heaven, what did Hopkins do?"

He told Allerton in very fine English, so proper he hoped Squanto would not understand, 'the savage's tongue was most affected by the disease which causes the bowels to shrivel and the blood to seethe so that one's very organs seize up and the soul doth depart. Anyone who durst touch the slightest portion of the same cup would be afflicted.'"

My cornbread was sticking in my throat from the image of Squanto attempting to translate this language. "And did this ruse succeed? What happened to the bottle?"

"Allerton finished his own and asked for more from Hopkins' big jar." John reached for our ale bucket and poured himself a large cupful. "Squanto took no more, but he seemed to get sleepy. Hopkins did not want him to pass out or expire on the premises, so he helped Squanto out the door and saw him stumbling toward the palisade gate.

August, 1622

AS MY BODY IMPROVED, so did my heart. John's assumption that God had destroyed our enemy calmed me. His outpouring of unconditional love when we woke in the dark of night brought light to my soul. I no longer attempted to remain composed. When his kisses covered my body and brought me to paroxysm of delight, I called out his beloved name with no restraint, then lay collapsed in his arms without a blush.

Our crops did not thrive, but not for lack of sunshine or rain. Not enough beans had been planted and an abundance of weeds grew faster than the corn in some parts of the field. Because we were still without the assurance of our treaty with King Massasowet, Captain Standish posted guards. But we needed the men who guarded to also work in our fields.

Many grown men who had come on the Fortune without wives and children even complained that they should not have to do extra work to feed the mouths of other men's families—and yet they ate our stews and cornbread as if God himself had given it to them with no woman's hand involved. Some men came to the fields late each morning but still left early. Many of these were the men who had come with Master Weston late in the past autumn. Thomas Weston, one of the London financiers, planned to establish his own colony and had requested our hospitality for his "settlers" until they could establish their own settlement north of Plimoth. His men had only been in our village a few hours when we all began to wonder how Weston ever expected that lot of scum to "settle." They profaned God and none of them were of the Lord's Church—only the King's church. They brought no women, no families. The motley parade of lazy, coarse oafs ate up our stores and many still lingered with us.

SUPPER HAD COOLED, been put back on the fire and cooled again when John finally came home. His face was animated, neither a smile nor frown told me whether it was relief or fear that made his eyes bright and his cheeks glow.

"Surgeon Fuller and Captain Standish determined cause of death."

"And?"

Now John finally smiled. "They declared a plague was

the cause of death. Elisabeth, God has shown his mighty hand."

"And the bottle?"

"We saw nothing."

I fell into his arms in relief. John's trust in the Lord was proven true again. "But will it bring peace?" I asked.

"In Good time. In God's time, His handiwork will be shown."

When I was with him, his words assured me. When I was alone, sometimes my dream with Mother's warning clenched my memory.

Attitash

Black Whale's smile told me there was good news even before his words.

"Where did they find him?"

"Our dogs—Mowi, Suki and the Strangers'—went sniffing around some bushes near the forest. They started to bark and we went to investigate. Tisquantum's body was stinking."

"Was Tisquantum killed by cohosh or their Sachem Bad-ford?" The question had been seared in my mind for too long.

Black Whale put a finger on my mouth. "Matta! We will not speak of medicines and raise suspicions. There was no sign of injury and no one will ever know."

"Does Esapett know?"

"I assume her people told her. Your father and I informed Sachem Bad-ford. San-dish. Their healer observed the body and declared Tisquantum died of the bad spirits they call 'plague.'"

"Where would the plague spirits come from? There was nothing but their firestick powder in those barrels."

Black Whale shrugged. "If we knew where those spirits are, neither we nor the Strangers would have died from it."

"What was done with his body?"

"The Strangers took Tisquantum's body. Sachem Bad-
ford says their god took Tisquantum's life as punishment.
If his soul goes anywhere, it would be to the Strangers'
Spirit Place."

Many questions spilled from my mind. I had never
known anyone denied a burial except when Tisquantum
tried to leave Yellow Hair's body on the ground for ani-
mals to destroy. I'd forced him to allow burial and now
Tisquantum himself might not have a proper grave.

Black Whale reached into his journey bag and pulled
out a brown bottle, a Stranger's bottle. "We found this,
but brought it back without showing it to the Strangers."
He handed me the bottle. Whether it was Hopkins or Esapett's, it would raise questions.

Black Whale stood watch while I carried the bottle bark
to the edge of the woods. I put the bottle between layers
of bark and then stomped on it until the bottle cried out
as it broke in many pieces. Taking my big quahog shell, I
then dug a hole to bury the broken pieces.

20

Elisabeth

The "Weston men" seemed to think everything belonged to them without as much as a 'by-your-leave.' Mistress Brewster and Goody Billington nursed the men who fell ill, without receiving a smidgeon of gratitude. They had now overstayed their welcome by months.

Before the corn was even ripe, the Weston Abominations began stealing it from the field to hoard for themselves. Worst, as far as I was concerned, they were rude to all of us women unless we had a husband nearby. One of these men, whose lank blond hair hung unrestrained, reminded me of the Cur on the Mayflower when he looked at us maids and women. His face was mottled as though he had survived the pox. I called him Pox Cur. He seemed younger than my assailant, though perhaps it was only that I was now a woman of sixteen instead of a maid of thirteen. I made certain that Humility and the other young girls were kept away from him, and told Attitash to guard her sister, White Flower.

All summer the foul men had deprived us of sufficient food. Now most of them had finally gone north when Weston sailed up the bay in pursuit of land for his colony. Those taken ill had been left behind and were still causing us trouble. Unfortunately, Pox Cur had stayed on, saying he continued to get fevers and needed to recover. I had my doubts that he had ever been sick. Malingerer was more like it.

As the meager crops grew into fullness, our governor

and King Massasowet still would not meet—or even com-
municate. All the trauma, the danger, the worry seemed
for naught. Had we not followed God's word? Or had
the time not come yet for God's will to be fulfilled? I
tried to take comfort in my husband's assurances that in
God's own time all would be fulfilled. But we lived in the
hope our governor and King Massasowet would renew
their trust.

Attitash

Our Plans did not bring the aquene, the peace, we sought.
It did help to have the rotten Tisquantum no longer plotting betrayals. But our grandmothers' council and Massasowet agreed that Sachem Bad-ford should show more
respect.

Despite our fears, or perhaps because of the protection Black Whale and Papa provided, there were no attacks
and we had a good harvest. However, the Strangers' fields
were not ready as early and the weachimin had small ears
and only one or two on each plant.

When we met by the sea at the end of our harvest, I
could easily understand Esapett's gestures and words that
described her concern about sufficient food. She put a
gentle hand on my swelling belly then rubbed her own
flat one.

"I want to be…" Esapett's face turned rosy. "Be…like
you." She sensed my own fears when I clasped my arms
over my belly. "Attitash, have good bebe."

I took her hand and joined it with mine so she felt the
sudden ripples caused by my little one's kicking. Esapett
giggled, then took my hand and put it on her belly. "I
too—good bebe."

Reaching into my bag, I pulled out the many colored
kernels and said, "weachimin," pouring them into her
hand.

She shook them lightly. "We-achoo-me?' I laughed too and we sat watching the small black whales chase each other in the Big Salt Water. But when the little girl, Humility, came to Esapett crying, I had difficulty understanding what Esapett was saying. "Sick—matchanni?" I asked.

"Ahhe." She pointed to the child's tummy, then to her little bottom. "No poop." She tried again, "Matta," patting the bottom and shaking her head. Now I understood, the child had a belly ache from not clearing her body of waste.

"We need to find strawberry," Esapett said pointing to the little child's red cheeks. "Not blueberry—Matta attitash—Red berry—straw-berry—where?" She raised her hands and her eyebrows questioned. I finally understood and led her near the spring where the wutamineash leaves grew. The red fruit was long gone now, but I dug up the root, knowing that seethed in hot water it would make a purging drink. Esapett beamed. "Like at home, like England." She pointed out over the Big Salt Water and I understood she meant the place they came from.

"THE STRANGERS HAD wutamineash back where they came from," I told Mama. She looked much more interested than I expected and questioned me closely to make certain they used it as we did. When I asked why she wanted to know, Mama answered briefly that the grandmothers were making a plan that required the Strangers use a remedy. "It's a plan you will learn later, Attitash, just put your mind on your New Life and don't worry about this."

Elisabeth

Mistress Brewster showed me how to boil the grated wild strawberry root and we gave a small cup to Humility. The child cleared within the day and her belly felt fine. Mistress was delighted to discover that the plant grew here in the new world too. "But don't let it be known that the Indian woman showed thee where to find it," she said.

"You needn't remind me, Mistress," I answered. "I made certain no one followed us, and I stayed well behind Attitash on the way there."

"Now we can treat those that need purging. When the berries come next spring we will make juice for fevers and the morbid throat." Mistress poured the remains of the remedy into a jar and tied a cloth over to seal it. "At least Weston's men won't steal this from us."

Next morning, while Mistress and I were tending to Humility's recovery from the dose of strawberry root, we heard shouting and when I looked out, John had joined a small group of the Billington boys and two of the Weston intruders. John seemed to calm them and I went back to the mess of a young girl's piss pot.

When John came home, he said the Weston men were demanding extra rations of fish and fowl. He had refused, telling them that he who would eat must hunt himself. Myles Standish had finally arrived to settle the argument, with quick results. "Captain Standish looked into their packs and found out they've stolen our corn and furs we'd gained in trade. Then Hopamoch came, telling us that they had been stealing from the Indians up and down Cape Cod."

"We're almost out of corn here," I said, and began pulling the feathers off the goose he'd shot that day. Without any warning, the room tilted. I sat on the bench and put my head between my knees. John picked me up and laid me down on our bed, concern wreathing his face.

"Take a deep breath. Again."

I did as he said and then took the cup of ale he handed me, telling him, "Mistress says 'tis common at this stage."

A warm smile cleared his face. "When a woman is six weeks gone, yea?"

"Yea, she says it happens when women who are with child get tired."

"Have ye fainted before?" The concern was back.

"Nay, not I. Priscilla fainted early on." I drank deeply but felt the room swim a little and lay back down. "But we have to cook the goose or it will surely go bad!"

"Sleep now. I'll get someone to help," he said and opened the door to let more breeze in. "Should I tell Priscilla or Mistress Brewster to cook it?"

I was too tired to answer and let sleep take me, knowing John would sort it out himself.

Attitash

It was almost time for us to go home to Poanoke for the winter. Wanting to be settled in before the snow started, we were busy grinding weachimin and drying squash.

When Seafoam and her husband arrived, she said they'd already finished their harvest at Nauset, and would travel back to Poanoke with us. We made our relatives welcome, but had not thought to see her husband again. Since Tisquantum died, Shimmering Fish, and others who had sided against Massasowet, were scarce as weachimin when the river ice melts.

Seafoam came with White Flower and me to the field to gather the last of the squash and bean vines. Mama and Grandmother worked behind us, chopping up the soil to sleep during the cold moons. Black Whale and Papa had gone hunting a few quail for supper. When we left our homesite, Shimmering Fish was sitting by himself, carving away at something.

Elisabeth

John was chopping up the corn stalks to rake into the soil and it was warm enough for me to enjoy being in the field. I did a bit to help, but he watched carefully to make certain I did not overdo. Several of the children were playing under the trees on the edge of our plots, watched by Remember Allerton and her sister. Mary, now almost eight years old was carrying the little Ford babe. Three months ago, Widow Ford had given birth to little John the day the Fortune arrived. He'd not gained much flesh and was small and a fussy babe. Humility played with the babe as if he were her poppet. Since they all lived at Brewsters, she was rather possessive of the babe and we laughed when she told Mary Allerton, "My babe." Now, Widow Ford was helping the Brewsters with their plot and had asked Mary to watch the babe. It gave me a start to see Humility, the child I sometimes thought of as 'my babe,' clinging to Mary Allerton's arm in order to share in the Ford infant's care.

Attitash and the women of her family were working in their field and I waved to them. Attitash's belly pushed out her poncho more every day, but she seemed to do as much work as her cousin, Seafoam, who was with them. I liked to see her looking so strong and fearless. Surely that would mean she would avoid any bad luck with her new one.

Another dispute with the Westons broke out on the far side of our fields. John went to help settle it and I took advantage of his absence to go see Attitash. We sat down to rest and Attitash let me feel her belly.

"It's kicking hard!" I told her, surprised at the strength of the bumps beneath my hand. When her little brother ran across to where the Allerton girls were playing a clapping game with the children, White Flower chased after him. Refusing to go back, Little Fish joined in tossing stones with the boys. White Flower relented and stayed to watch.

"Come, play with me," Humility tugged on White Flower and got her to clap with the little girls. They all laughed, even Remember.

Seafoam stood apart from Attitash and me, watching the little girls. I listened with my eyes averted as Attitash explained that Seafoam and her husband, Shimmering Fish, had recently come to visit. Evidently the Fish husband no longer aligned himself with the rebels and the couple had reunited.

Humility called to me, holding the water jug, shaking it to show we needed more. As I came to them, White Flower offered to go to the spring to get water. Humility, holding the Ford baby, danced alongside her, begging to go. White Flower took the baby up in his blanket, tied it around herself so he was on her back, and took Humility's hand.

Remember Allerton rudely tried to grab hold of Humility, her eyes turning hard with her fear of the heathen.

"They are safe with White Flower," I called out. "Let them go."

As they ran up the path, I reminded them to hurry, hoping White Flower understood me. Attitash called out too and seemed to repeat my warning in her words. They had just disappeared through the woods when I noticed the Pox Cur, slinking along toward the spring. Shimmering Fish came running past us. I noticed Seafoam following her husband with her eyes and assumed she knew the danger the Pox Cur might pose. But an unusual expression, a tightening of her eyes, made me suddenly anxious.

Attitash

I should have known. I should have watched Seafoam's eyes and seen the distrust when she looked at her husband. Should have listened to Black Whale when he told me he still did not trust my cousin's husband. Should have been suspicious when Shimmering Fish offered to accompany the girls to the spring.

The screams were so faint I thought it was the sea

gulls. Or the crows chasing a hawk up high 'til the hawk screamed her anger at the pests. Seafoam jumped up though, and ran toward the spring. I plainly heard her scream. Esapett and I both scrambled up. Remember Allerton tried to calm the other little children, who sensed the fear and were wailing.

Esapett called across the field to Jon-owland and the other Strangers to follow us. Mama came running with Jon-owland and the other men, full of questions. "Is someone hurt?" "Who is missing?" "Who was with them?"

Seafoam, hurrying back from the spring—her eyes wild—informed us, "No one is there. There are tracks in the mud going into the shallow water, but none coming out."

The men and Mama ran to the spring. Esapett and I followed. I reached the spring before Esapett and looked carefully at the tracks. It was as Seafoam said. Mama and the men were thrashing through the grasses on the opposite side. Then I heard a faint whimper from the bushes near me. Parting the reeds, I found the little baby. He was wrapped in his cloth. Calling out to Esapett, I picked up the infant and handed him to her.

"Little Moses," she said.

I did not understand her, but wrapped the cloth tighter around the limp bundle in her arms. Jon-owland reached us and took the child from her and we all hurried back to our houses. All except White Flower and Humility.

21

Elisabeth

It could not be true, but it was. Humility was gone, carried off. I closed my eyes in prayer. This could not be God's plan.

"Howland, we must gather our forces." Captain Standish stood before us, suited up in his armor, with sword, pistols and a musket. "We believe the girls were taken by Narragansett." Captain Standish wiped his hands on his pants, then picked up his gun. "Get your weapons, Howland, and meet us in the Commonhouse."

"Was it Weston's men who did it?" I asked John when Myles Standish was gone.

"We don't think so." He grimaced. "Hopamoch found the one you call, 'The pox cur,' lingering by the field. Hopamoch brought him to Captain, but he claims he saw nothing." John stood to go gather his weapons and glanced at the babe in my arms. "Better get him to his mother."

I went to Martha Ford, who snatched the babe from my arms so fast I feared he'd fall out of his blanket. "Who let those savages steal our children?"

I could not conceive of a coherent answer.

Attitash

I had just sat down by the fire outside, when Shimmering Fish appeared.

"Where were you, Seafoam?" he asked glibly before she or anyone else could question him.

Mama grabbed his arm. "Where is my daughter?"

His face slid into a mask of ignorance. "I thought she came back to you."

"Tell me where she is!"

Shimmering Fish did not answer, but wrenched his arm away and held out a hand to Seafoam. "Come with me, wife."

Seafoam shot a look full of despair at Shimmering Fish, then shrank within herself and turned away from him. "You are no longer my husband."

He whirled around and ran down the path toward the water. Black Whale appeared from the western path, just after Shimmering Fish disappeared. Upon hearing what happened, Black Whale grabbed his club and bounded down the trail in pursuit.

I wanted to take Seafoam and shake her until the truth came out. She must have known what Shimmering Fish would do when she brought him. Little Fish ran to Mama, his boyish bravery disappeared and clung to her leg until she picked him up.

The rain was starting to splash all over us when Black Whale returned, Papa by his side. They told us that Shimmering Fish took our only dugout canoe and was already out of sight, up one of the rivers that flow up with the tide this time of day.

"With the rain, we'll never catch him now," Black Whale said. "We will have to run upstream and see if we can find where he lands."

A clanking on the path alerted Papa to check outside. He held open the flap for Cap-tan San-dish, followed by several of his warriors, including Jon-owland. My shoulder burned in memory of the last time I met them fully armed as they were now. Cap-tan and Jon-owland crowded in with us while the others waited out in the rain. The smell of the Strangers and the black sand they use to make fire with their shiny rock sticks was overpowering.

Cap-tan spoke so fast I was not certain I understood, but I heard "Narragansett" and "fight." But Papa did not look confused.

"Before you fight them," he said, "we must find where they took the daughters. The rain is washing away all tracks. All you'll get by clanking into the woods now is to send them further into Narragansett territory." He tamped his pipe, making no move to find his bow and arrow.

Cap-tan's brow creased in anger and he huffed like a wolf before he spoke. "If you are afraid of the Narragansett, you can wait here. We are soldiers." I understood everything except the last word, but I knew he was insulting my father.

Papa did not take Cap-tan's bait. "We are not even certain if it is Narragansett or our own Wampanoag rebels that captured the girls. It is time to listen. Time to learn. When you've finished playing 'soldier' come back to us."

Cap-tan turned his back and clanked away. His other warriors followed, but Jon-owland stopped. "Did you see Shimmering Fish?"

Papa nodded. "Ahhe, you know much, Jon-owland. The rebel has taken our canoe and may be upstream. Black Whale and I will see if we can find where he comes to shore."

"Catabatash—thank you. I will not tell Captain Standish or he will try to find the rebel along the river. There's no way this many men trying to march along a muddy bank could catch him." Jon-owland glanced at me, then asked Black Whale if we would step outside. The rain had let up under the trees and we followed him. Though I was around him often when with Esapett, I had not spoken to Jon-owland since I was shot. Moving a little way up the path, out of sight of both Cap-tan and our longhouse, Jon-owland paused. He spoke slowly, in his words.

"Please for-give."

I did not know this word. "What is give-for?" I looked at Black Whale, but he shrugged his shoulders.

Jon-owland flushed. "Give me, um, mercy." Jon-owland could see we did not know 'mercy.' "Do not think me bad."

I understood their word, "bad." Bad meant like spoiled venison or fish left out too long. Bad can't be fixed. Black Whale took my arm and led me a few steps away. "What does he want? Should I send him away?"

"Not yet," I answered. "This word, 'bad,' is confusing. Our people are not bad."

"All Strangers are bad." Black Whale shifted his arms as if he would take up his knife from his belt.

"I thought so too, before Esapett." I knew Squanto became rotten when the Strangers kidnapped him. He was bad that could not be fixed, so Massasowet called for his head to be cut off. "I did not think Jon-owland was bad, but he did wrong, shooting women and children."

I stepped back to where Jon-owland waited. "Matta, not bad," I said to him. "Not good."

"Matta. Not good." His green eyes were dark, like the winter moss in icy spring-water and full of sadness. "I want good. I want Humility and White Flower safe. I want to help."

I could smile at him now with my heart, not just my mouth. But I could not speak. The lump of fear and sadness for my sister mixed with a swelling of relief that my dear friend's husband did feel compassion for my loss. Black Whale was not smiling, but he no longer had his hand on his knife.

"Go with Cap-tan now. You are his warrior," he said to Jon-owland in our words. "But tell him not to go far into the woods. The footprints and smells are washed away by the rain. Tell him we will learn from our spies where they are. We must use our minds." Black Whale pointed to his head.

Jon-owland seemed to understand. He hurried to catch up to his leader, his stride much longer than the strutting-turkey cap-tan's.

Black Whale and Papa gathered their clubs and stowed a quiver of arrows, then slung their bows over their shoulders.

Elisabeth

Humility and Attitash's sister could not escape. We had to find them. But how? As the sun rose, crossed the sky and sank toward the western hills I kept looking west to the vast dark forest where they'd evidently been taken. I was told this wilderness stretched so far it was as if the sea we crossed was covered with tall trees. Would even Hopamoch and Black Whale know how to find a village in the gloom? Trolls and fairies were said to lurk in the woods, not to mention all the vicious beasts. And the Narragansett.

While Priscilla and I were cleaning up the governor's supper, I listened carefully to him talk with my husband and Master Winslow. "There are those who would use this child's disappearance to attack our friends, or malign my ability to govern," our governor said. "We must be vigilant about ending these rumors as soon as they arise."

"Master Allerton will surely say this," I told my John when we were alone. "Praise God the Ford babe was left behind and we found him."

"Yea, that babe is too small to survive away from his mother. Thanks be to God for saving him," John said.

"But I was the one who let Humility and the babe go with Hopamoch's daughter, and argued with Remember Allerton when she objected." My words spewed out unbidden.

"Did ye not think before ye did that?" John was honing

his knife and did not look up to see the effect of his words.

"She *was* safe with White Flower!"

"But not with Shimmering Fish." Now he looked at me.

I gave him a wounded look. "Ye are using thy sharpened knife on me, John. I thought Shimmering Fish would save them from the young Cur!" As soon as I said it I realized my own fears had painted the young Weston cur with the wrong color and had ignored the danger of Shimmering Fish. My protests welled up into a near shriek. "How could I stop Shimmering Fish with his own wife sitting there, and Attitash not stopping him from going with her sister?"

John did not answer, and it was his silence that dissolved the fit of fury that fueled my defense. I put my hands over my eyes and fled to the garden, not able to face any more accusations.

Attitash

ALL DAY WE WATCHED. Not until Nippa'uus settled over the western hills did Black Whale and my father come down the path at last. We were relieved to have them home, but hopes that they would bring news of White Flower were dashed when we saw their grim faces. Papa had met with Pniese at nearby villages and the word was spread. It would take time.

22

March, 1623
Elisabeth

Three months passed and the only thing that kept me from succumbing to despair over Humility during the long confinement of cold and snow was the warmth deep in my womb. I knew that my tiny bud of a babe would not live to be born if I did not nourish it with hope. But until the snow was piled high around our house I struggled with letting go of my fear.

One night I woke from a dream of Attitash which showed her glowing with light from within. She looked calm, and touched my body gently, showing me with each touch that I also glowed from within. For the first time, I woke feeling my babe would be safe, wrapped in the light of my love. I lifted the heavy wool rug that covered the window to keep out the fierce gales. The moon was a crescent, the stars gleaming with light and wild swoops of colored lights bouncing around the heavens.

"What is that?" I shook John awake.

He mumbled, then sat up and looked out. "Northern Lights."

"Is it a sign? Do you think Humility and White Flower can see them?"

"Surely they can." John pulled the covers over our shoulders and we leaned our heads together to witness the glory in the sky. John's face was faintly visible as the brilliant lights cascaded across our little home, enough to see the smile on his face.

The lights were fading. John did not comment on Atti-tash. He did not have dreams that carried any message—or if he did, he did not confide them to me. I closed my eyes, picturing Humility sleeping with White Flower in a snug home like Attitash's. I prayed that the Narragansett mothers were good to their children. Even captives.

Attitash
We'd been at our winter home for three moons now and there was no word about White Flower. Finally, Sea-foam's brother came with rumors that the Narragansett wanted to ransom the girls back to us or the Strangers. He had done his vision quest during the last cold moons and this was the first time he had come to us without his father or Clan Uncle. "They want our wampum for the girls, which they would trade for beaver with the northern Abenaki. There also were rumors they would only trade my sister and the little girl for firesticks." He had grown tall and I realized he was just a little older than White Flower.

"Whose rumors are these?" Papa asked.

"Toka-mahamon said only that our spies had informed Massasowet."

"If only Massasowet trusted their treaty again, we could plan what to do together."

We all knew that since Sachem Bad-ford refused to kill Tisquantum and send his head, Massasowet would not speak with Bad-ford. We'd hoped finding Tisquantum's body would change that, but fierce pride in both Sachem Bad-ford and our Massasowet kept them apart.

"Even if our leaders speak with each other, what the Narragansett want and what can be offered will not be the same," Grandmother said. "We want our daughter back, but not with an exchange that brings the firestick-death to all our people."

Without a settlement for White Flower and the girls, the Narragansett grew bolder. And without the Strangers' agreement on our treaty to bring their Sachem's men and firesticks to our defense, not only the Narragansett, but the Massachuseuk or other nations could overwhelm us. They would take our land, and steal more of us women. If other big-wind canoes brought new Strangers with their firesticks, we would be slaughtered. Or we might be overtaken by all the new men that had crowded into Esapett's village during the last warm moons. Many of these men left when the cold moons came, but they were not far away.

I reminded myself that Mama and Grandmother had a plan to bring our Massasowet and Sachem Bad-ford back together. But it seemed as likely to fail as to succeed.

It was not yet light when I woke to hear a young boy's voice calling through the flap of Grandmother's neesh'wetu, "Massasowet matchanni," he said. Hearing that Massasowet was very sick did not frighten me. The Grandmothers' Council understood that pretending our beloved Massasowet was dying could bring the Strangers' Sachem to his side. Grandmother had not told me of the plan until the brooks were full and my time was near to give light to my New Life.

"It's the only way we can get those bear-headed Clothmen to give up their false faces and come to Massasowet," Grandmother had explained. Esapett's men were afraid to show trust to my people. Papa had sent word that Sachem Bad-ford and his people would wait for Massasowet to send for them. Our Massasowet could not go to them with aquene—with peace—because they would turn away. "Only if he becomes sick, and they come to visit and decide to heal him, will both sides be able to speak as friends again," Grandmother told the council.

"How will Our Massasowet get sick?" I said.

Grandmother laughed. "He will eat nothing but bear

grease and beaver fat," she said, "and no one will give him any remedy. He'll bind up fast."

Elisabeth

A few days later. Hopamoch and Master Winslow came to see Governor Bradford. The men sat smoking in the sunset. I was outside with them, scrubbing the pots with sand. Hopamoch was very agitated, explaining with gestures as well as words that King Massasoit was very sick.

"Hopamoch wants to know if we could bring a remedy to cure their king," Master Winslow said. "They have used all their heathen methods but he is worse."

I looked at Hopamoch and White Cloud,who had come with her husband but sat near where I worked. She returned my gaze and making a tiny circle with her thumb and finger said, "Wutamineash."

"I don't know what that means," Master Winslow said. "Perhaps it's their word for gout, belly ache, or morbid throat."

Wu-ta-min-eash, strawberry, I thought. When Humility was with us it was a simple cure. I spoke up.

"She suggests a remedy, I believe," I told him. "You could take a tincture of strawberry root for roiling belly, and a confection of the fruit for his throat. I'll ask Mistress Brewster what to send for gout."

Governor Bradford looked slightly startled. "Would you ask the other mistresses if they have remedies on hand, Elisabeth?"

Mistress Brewster said that Massasowet's healers should look near a spring for watercress or sassafras to ease gout, if that was his trouble. "Gout doesn't usually kill us, but the heathen die from many things which God preserves us from," she told me.

The springs have watercress in March, but it is not a good season for finding strawberries. Mistress had little left of the root tincture and only Goodwife Billington had a jar of the berries boiled to make a paste. She refused to give it to me.

"Why should I give the savages what I made for my family?" she said. "After the way they kidnapped my boy John I'd give them nothin'!"

I tried to explain to Goody Billington that it was the Narragansetts who had kidnapped her son, almost two years ago and that it was King Massasowet's people, the Wampanoag, who rescued him. And that we now wanted to return the favor.

"Ye can say what ye want, 'twas our soldiers and Standish what brought my boy back."

It was useless to convince the woman by reminding her that our work last summer provided food for her that her own husband and sons had done little to help grow. She had a cone of salt set out and began furiously grating.

It was on me to find the strawberry. Constance Hopkins went with me, with her brother Giles as guard. At first we could find nothing but a few early tiny blue flowers. Combing aside leaves near the spring, I finally found the green leaves and dug out a few plants to get the root. I dug more close to the water and at last found a few tiny berries. Mistress Brewster helped me grate and brew the tincture. We used a bit of that to seethe the few little berries into a paste. I wrapped the little bottle of tincture and the concoction of berries in a cup in a cloth so they would not break during the journey.

White Cloud, Attitash's mother, beamed when we brought them to Master Winslow. She motioned rocking a babe to me and I understood enough of her words to know she was accompanying her husband to be with Attitash at her childbed. Surely Attitash and her family had expected we'd have White Flower home before the babe came. Not to be. They would depart by sunrise next morning to climb over the hills and then walk two days.

Attitash
When my family arrived, the women around the fire with me parted to let them through. Papa was in the lead, with Win-snow and Jon-owland behind him. My mother and siblings followed and I hurried to embrace them. My father gave me a quick greeting, then went into Massasowet's home, leaving the cloth-men by the opening.

"Attitash!" Mama stroked my belly. "I'm in time." We both wept as Little Fish begged to be picked up.

"Is there any word of White Flower," I asked.

"Not yet. When Massasowet recovers and works with Sachem Bad-ford, then they will be able to bring her home." Mama would not let me see any crack in her belief that White Flower would come back to us. "You must put all your heart to your child now. Bring it to the light."

Black Whale came from inside Massasowet's neesh'wetu and waited with Win-snow and Jon-owland, gesturing and speaking slowly with them. Jon-owland smiled at me and I wondered if he knew the ruse. Papa came to the opening flap and gestured to Win-snow to come in.

The women tending the fire told us that Massasowet's wives were rubbing his legs. "It makes an impression that we are attempting everything we can think of to heal him," she whispered to me. Mama and Grandmother came out of the neesh'wetu and welcomed Mama. "It's working well," she whispered to Mama and me. "Our Massasowet acts as though he can't see, so the cloth-men are convinced he's about to die." She smiled wryly. "Win-snow asked Massasowet's first wife what she'd already used. She told him only willow-bark tea." She laughed. "He probably thinks Strangers are the only ones who know how to heal." Grandmother took Mama through the crowd to join our beloved leader.

Black Whale waited by the flap, listening and reporting

to me. "Win-snow's taking Massasowet's hand." I kept my face calm, as did Black Whale. We were not sure who knew of the deceit we were practicing upon the Cloth-Men, and upon Massasowet's betrayers.

"Now Win-snow is looking inside Massasowet's mouth. He's scraping his tongue with his knife and now pasting the wutamineash on his tongue and throat. He's mixing the tincture with seethed water and Massasowet is drinking it." My husband put his arm around me, "The medicine will work, my wife. The Strangers feel welcomed here. Our peoples will soon join hands against the Narragansett."

As if in response, my back was wreathed in pain that moved around to the front. My contorted face and hands on my belly told him what was happening. With Black Whale's arm around me, I moved slowly toward the edge of the crowd, no longer able to think of anything but my New Life.

By the time I reached the Moon Lodge, Grandmother had everything prepared and helped me settle into the nest of furs lined with rushes. But sleep would not come.

"Are you hurting?" she asked.

"It comes and leaves again."

All was momentarily quiet with my body when the pains came quickly and made me cry out.

"Breathe fast, pant," Mama said.

Grandmother, Mama and Aunt Blue Sky held my legs, letting my feet push against their hands. "Almost ready. I see some hair. Now! Push!" They held my hands and I pulled against them. A great pain surged, then sudden relief. "The head's out! Now push, push, push."

I was strong. Strong for my baby. Strong for my husband. Strong for my people. With another pain that swallowed the whole moon lodge, I pushed my baby into the light. Tears flooded my face. Grandmother laid the wet bundle on my belly. I felt the hair, the shoulders and little belly. I felt the tiny bundle of manhood and knew this was a son. Grandmother snuggled him up to me and tweaked my nipple. She pinched his mouth open and he sucked. As he sucked, he opened his eyes. He knew me and I knew him.

23

Elisabeth

I opened my eyes just as my beloved's hand reached down to mine. Neither of us spoke, though our hearts were saying plenty as he pulled me into his embrace. Finally, he sat back, the candlelight showing the joy in his face.

"We have peace, my darling. We are now in a position to negotiate together for the release of the girls."

A smile from deep inside filled my face. "So King Massasowet is healed? The strawberry concoction worked?"

He pulled me back to him, chuckling. "Well, the rift is healed. Winslow is convinced it was all a show so Massasowet could prove to his nation that we are indeed their friends." He kissed me slowly then stroked my cheek.

The bubble of relief and delight filled me so that I could hardly speak, but I had one more question. "And Attitash? Any news of her?"

"Yea, good news. She delivered whilst we were in their village. Her father says 'tis a lusty boy and that she's up and about already." He turned his back on me, presenting the point laces holding up his breeches. "If ye can help me undo the points and get these off, I plan to lie down and not get up until sunrise—or maybe even longer."

He brought the candle closer so I could see. As I worked, John explained that their delay was due to Massasowet's request that they take the dose of strawberry paint to cure others. "None of them seemed sick. Winslow wondered if this was Massasowet's ruse to demonstrate our renewed friendship to all his people who had doubted it."

I tugged the last lace out of the waistband so his breeches could be pulled off. "Can we finally put Squanto's death behind us?"

"Yea, we can." John stood and shed his breeches as a knock on the door came, accompanied by Love Brewster's voice announcing that he'd brought firewood and asking if Master Howland was safe home. John sent him off with thanks, took his breeches to the door to shake out, then came back to bed. He blew out the candle and lay down next to me. "Do not tell anyone—not Mistress Brewster, not Desire, not Priscilla, not anyone—that King Massasowet was perhaps staging his illness and recovery." Before I could ask why, he added, "We have regained their trust, and any such speculation could put us back where we were before. There is still some blood to be shed, but I need sleep now," he mumbled, pulling up the covers.

"Just one more thing," I said. "I think I felt the babe move today." But his heavy breathing and lack of response told me this too would have to wait. And to wonder what blood must be shed.

WHEN I WOKE ALONE IN BED, sunlight on my face, it took me a moment to move from dream to reality and remember John was indeed home.

Just then he came in with fresh firewood, dressed only in his shirt. "Stay there until the fire warms up."

I was happy to do so, especially when he joined me. It was immediately obvious he was recovered from his adventures. When we finally were spent and lay snuggled beneath the covers, I put his hand on my belly. "Ye can't feel it yet, but I'm sure I feel the little butterfly moving."

"Butterfly? You mean OURS?"

I laughed in assent. "Priscilla says in a month its kick will be so strong that even its father will feel it."

John's smile lit the entire little house. "He will be a lusty boy."

"Or a strong little girl. Ye know butterflies are strong even though they look fragile."

"Yea, I've watched them fly against the wind."

I let his image move in my mind, but the lingering warmth was chilled by a sudden reminder of his words before we slept. "What did you mean, 'blood must be shed.'?"

"Not yet, do not worry."

"I must know if ye are part of the shedding." Now the chill became lodged in my throat. "'Are ye speaking of how to rescue Humility and White Flower? Tell me."

John ran his fingers through his thick, black hair where it collected on his crown. "Hopamoch informed Edward Winslow of something Massasowet told him."

"What?"

"Massasowet had kept it from Governor Bradford, but after we healed him, he wanted us to know. Remember the trouble with Weston's men and the Massachuseuks?"

"Yea. Were they involved in the kidnapping after all?" I was surprised when John smiled.

"Not Englishmen." His smile disappeared. "Massasowet says that one of the Massachuseuk warriors, Witawumat, leads a plot against us. He planned an overthrow of Massasowet, but with Squanto dead, the Massachuseuks have taken over the plot against us. Standish will take a couple of men and go up there to strike first."

"This has nothing to do with the kidnapping?" I did not understand the necessity to get involved in anything that did not restore Humility and White Flower.

"Not directly, but it's all connected. If the Massachuseuk attack us, how do we survive? Or at least not waste ammunition and men on repelling them?" My world was too filled with complicated troubles. "But you just came home!"

"Don't worry, I'm not going." He traced my belly. "Is there anything to eat? I'm starved."

As I cooked up corn mush, he reminded me that last year we'd not had a good harvest due to lazy people. He reached into his coat pocket and pulled out a wrinkled, folded paper. "Winslow has written down what he considers the problems with some of our people and I'm copying it out so he can send his copy to our financiers and we'll have one here." He then read.

1. The vain expectation of present profit, which too commonly taketh a principal seat in the heart and affection, though God's glory is preferred before it.

2. Ambition in their governors and commanders, seeking only to make themselves great, and slaves of all that are under them to maintain a transitory base honor in themselves, which God oft punisheth with contempt.

3. The Carelessness of those that send over supplies of men unto them, not caring how they be qualified; so that ofttimes they are rather the image of men endued with bestial, yea, diabolical affections, than the image of God, endued with reason, understanding and holiness.

I plunked the trenchers filled with mush on the table. "I have no idea what any of that means. Does Master Winslow want to impress someone or make it plain?"

John grinned as if my ignorance were a joke. "He does indeed write in the manner of the books he reads. But he told me more about what he means." He took a big mouthful of mush and gave a satisfied sigh. "Real food again, though it will be nice when the fish run and the fowl come back." He took another bite. "The point is, our financiers in England have no understanding of how difficult and complicated it is to secure trading rights, nor any patience for us to bring them profits. And I suspect some here also seek profits for themselves."

"So, 'vain expectation of present profit taking over the heart and affection', is greed. That I surely understand. Women bear the burden to satisfy men's greed. Most men would take advantage of our submission for their own gain." Too late I realized from his tight mouth John assumed that he was taking my comments as directed at him. I put my hands on his shoulders. "Don't think I am speaking of thee. Think instead of how Master Allerton, Goodman Billington, and many who are not as cruel, but still consider all the women here as their slaves, washing their clothes and cooking for them." My husband relaxed, a small smile indicated he considered himself above that lot. I went back to my work and continued. "The part about their governors' ambition and base honor? Winslow's not speaking of Bradford, is he?"

"Nay." John looked at the door, making sure we would not be heard. "I'm not certain if he refers to our deputy governor, Allerton, who is also the financier of our plantation, or of someone between us and King James—someone in England working for himself. Of course, he speaks of the dunderheads Weston brought over too." He put the paper in front of me. "Try to read it."

I looked at the writing, rather smudged and not easy to decipher. "Bestial men were sent to us? That seems a coarse way to describe them."

John smiled, "Yea, 'tis. But Winslow wants to make his point."

"What does this have to do with how we plant? Will we plant with squash and beans surrounding our corn, like the Wampanoag?"

"Nay, we may have a mutual aid treaty and the Wampanoag are our friends, but we won't be planting their way, which is against the Bible's instructions—each crop to its own field." He cleared away the mush bowl and took the cup of tea I offered him. "It means that these 'bestial men' do not have the milk of human kindness in them, the God-given need to work for the common good." He savored the hot tea and took another long drink. "Bradford, Carver and Winslow were convinced by reading Plato that we could live together communally, so we tried to have all work the fields and all share the harvest. However, mayhap men were different in ancient Greece. Here, too many care only for themselves and did little or no work."

"And how will ye make them work?"

"Each will work for their own good. Each of us, every man and woman in each household, will be given a plot. We will draw lots so that no one is favored with fair or poor land except by chance."

"I will have my own land?" The thought was so strange I had to run it back and forth in my mind. "Does that mean I have to work my own plot?"

"Well, I am thy husband, of course, I'll do most of the work. Ye will do what ye can, without endangering the babe or thyself. Ye both require food—so ye should have a plot. All the boys and men without family here will be assigned to a household, and each household will work their plots together. We'll have some assigned to our household."

I let it settle in my mind while I finished my mush and cleared the trenchers. "But I thought in the New World we would no longer have gentry owning the land—that all of us together would work and share alike." "We don't want to go back to the English ways of landed gentry. We want all to have an equal share. Lots will be drawn and only for this season. No owning of the land. Every year we'll draw lots again to see which land we farm." John stood up from the table. "I think most of us will agree. Only those who lived off the work the rest of us did will object." He pulled on his cloak and hat. "Surely, ye don't want to go back to feeding others with the sweat of our own bodies, do ye? And those that did not work do not have a majority."

He left me to clean up and ponder the new world. Each of us with our own plot. I wondered if Hopamoch and his family kept their own harvest or shared it with all. Attitash would be coming in the spring, bringing her new babe. Would her sister, White Flower, be back to meet the new babe? To work in the field? Would she and Humility be released when the negotiations succeeded? All my thoughts were underscored by the suppressed worry about Humility and questions about their release.

24

Attitash

Papa teased Mosk's cheek with a finger, gaining a chortle from the baby.

"I never did like the chief warrior, Cap-tan San-dish. But he killed a much bigger man with his own knife."

Papa had gone back to Plimoth with Win-snow and Jon-owland, but he returned by the time the river ice was melted. He was greeted with great warmth by everyone as word had already come to us that my father had helped Sachem Bad-ford and our friends to put down the Massachuseuks.

"One of the Strangers that preys upon the Massachuseuk?" I asked.

"Matta." He shook his head. "His name is Witawumat, he's a Massachuseuk."

"Who is he? And why was he killed? Did San-dish shoot his firestick?" My old wound burned, though I usually did not feel it anymore. Whoever Witawumat was, I pitied him such a shameful, violent death.

Papa handed my son back and lit his pipe with a burning stick from our fire. "Witawumat was fool enough to think that because the Cloth-men who came to his land were lazy and evil that he could also mock our friends. I could not believe that the short, little Turkey-Cap-tan was strong enough to grab Witawumat's knife which hung from his neck. It was a Cloth-man's knife Witawumat got when he killed one of them. Cap-tan San-dish called it "Fench". Like that yellow-haired one you tried to save."

I nuzzled my son's hair, hoping Mosk would never have to meet someone like the yellow-haired Stranger who died while I tried to save him. And I hoped Mosk would never have to see someone like Yellow-Hair be torn from their grave, robbed of a chance to journey to the Spirit World. I pushed aside those old memories, but I could not push away my hope that Mosk would get to meet my sister before the summer ended. Tears welled behind my eyes. I kept them focused on my son, so my father would not see.

Papa continued his story. "Cap-tan San-dish killed Witawumat with his own knife. And other Massachuseuks with him. A lot of blood was spilled. Cap-tan also told the evil, lazy "Weston" Cloth-men to get out. He gave them corn and they sailed up north in their wind-canoe." Now my father seemed to notice my face. "He did save their women, but the other Massachuseuk were either killed or ran off. Even sachems who were our friends are afraid of us now, because our protectors killed without needing to."

I wondered if the Massachuseuk's grandmothers' council was able to meet. And if they would now consider us were their enemies. My father must have read my cloudy thoughts in my face.

"What I had to do is not easy to explain, Attitash. I had to stand there watching the turkey-strutting Cap-tan San-dish kill Witawumat. It did pain me, knowing how badly the Weston cloth-men had treated Witawumat's people. But we are the only People who have the Cloth-men's protection and we will need this reputation to deal with the Narragansett. That is how we'll free White Flower."

I wondered who might get killed trying to rescue my sister. My old wound from the Strangers' rescue attempt burned. I had ignored what my father was saying, but now heard him talking about getting many, many beaver pelts from other nations. Our Massasowet is now a great leader, with other sachems now paying homage to us.

I did not remind my father that what he'd witnessed was what he'd predicted Tisquantum would do. I knew my father was caught between the friends among Esapett's people—like Win-snow and Jon-owland—and the ones looking out only for themselves. Esapett herself suffered from some of these Strangers. Papa had ended up in the wrong place. White Flower and Humility had been in the wrong place many moons now and who knew what they suffered. Maybe there was no right place in such a time. Never a right place for us since my grandmother's grandmother saw the first Cloth-men coming across the Big Salt Water.

Grandmother had been listening silently. She'd heard the story already when my father and Massasowet had told it to the Grandmothers' Council. After Papa left, she put her arm around me. "Witawumat may have been filled with the Cloth-man's greed too," she said. "But your father did tell us that the Weston strangers who lived with the Massachuseuks did much harm. They took their women, stole their food, pulled up their crops before they bore fruit and ate the green stalk before the weachimin had formed." She patted my head, as though I were as small as Mosk. "Our people's way is to take care of all—every child, woman and man. When such evil comes among us, perhaps only evil will work against them. But I will never trust this turkey, the one they call 'Cap-tan'."

"I hate him already," I answered. "He is insulting to all our women. And he even insults my friend, Esapett." I pushed away the memory of how Cap-tan had stared at my cousin and me during the harvest feast. I kissed my baby's warm cheek. "I do trust some of the Strangers, but your wisdom is always true. I will not trust this Cap-tan, but we need him to help bring White Flower home."

Elisabeth

My fervent expectation that the girls would be returned to us come spring became my bitter disappointment. Now, even the Ford babe was gone, having succumbed to the morbid throat. The boy had been weakly ever since his birth but had managed to survive even being left in the reeds by the Narragansett. He was buried in the softening spring ground.

The remaining snow had melted, leaving mud everywhere. We were confined to the house, but I slogged to Brewsters and found young Martha Ford singing and clapping. Widow Ford and Mistress Brewster were in no mood to endure a small girl's shrill chatter, however. They were attempting to make use of the sun to scour the house clean and air it out.

"Shall we take Martha for a walk to the shore?" I asked Desire. "I need a mud-break," We wrapped up in shawls. The widow did not seem to notice we were leaving with her daughter. Young Martha carried her rag poppet, which she had not let go since her baby brother died.

We settled where the beach was sheltered from the westerly wind. The tide was low and the girl ran about mimicking the screaming birds overhead. When she settled down with her poppet, I paid no attention until I noticed Young Martha had her poppet covered in sand, so only the yarn hair showed. "Don't bury your poppet." I told her. "It's getting filthy."

Young Martha gave me a look through hooded eyes. "My baby brother had to be buried. He got sick from the heathens when they stole him and gave him back."

The girl's words seemed to stick between my shoulder-blades. I rubbed the crick in my neck. "That's not why babes die." I did not disguise the scolding tone from my voice. "Do ye not listen to Elder Brewster? God giveth and God taketh away. Thy brother died because God took him, not because some strange Indians had him for a short time."

Martha's mouth turned into a pout. She pulled her poppet out of sand and shook it. I asked for the poppet so I could clean it and told her to look for shells.

Desire laid a hand on my arm. "Gentle with the child, Elisabeth. Are you so certain you are right? She just quotes her mother and you quote yours."

"I know, but it's as if they don't trust me to take care of my own babe someday."

"You are not on trial or locked in the stocks, so save thy breath." Desire kept her voice low and continued, "I'll bring the child's words to Elder Brewster. Without the widow knowing her daughter passed along this accusation, Elder can find a way to assure Widow Ford 'tis our Lord's decision to take the child, not the enemy who held the babe." She made a wry face. "And the lack of sufficient food that made Baby John so weak might also be the Lord's hand."

I busied myself with cleaning the sand off the poppets. Young Martha found a few shells, and seemed to recover her disposition by cavorting in the rising tide, her dress splashing. When I called her in, she came stepping knee high through the water, then retrieved her poppet. Proclaiming, "My baby's hungry," young Martha pulled up the shawl and put the poppet to her skinny chest.

25

Attitash

Grandmother tucked sphagnum moss around the baby before we added the furs and laced up the cradleboard. We both giggled at the sight of Mosk's little nose and eyes peeking out. His calling name was a good one. He did look like a little bear cub.

Black Whale wrapped his arrows in the quiver, discussing our journey with his Turtle Clan uncle, Seekonk. Mama had already gone to Patuxet to get the soil ready for planting. Seekonk promised to bring Grandmother and come visit all of us at Patuxet when their own planting was done.

We left early morning and walked fast. Mosk slept well in his cradleboard and I felt strong. But after stopping to eat at high-Nippa'uus, my shoulders felt tired and I lingered while suckling Mosk. He drank so fast he dribbled milk, and then slowed to a suck, sleep, and suck rhythm. I'd drifted off myself when Black Whale woke me. "I hear Sky-Fire spirits out on the Big Salt Water. We want to get over the top of the hills before they come after us."

I could hear them too, but they seemed far away. I could only hear the low, faint rumble and saw no streaks of fire in the sky. Nippa'uus was hidden, the clouds blue-black. We walked fast. Black Whale did not have to wait for me. When we reached the top and could see out over the Big Salt Water, I caught my breath. The rumbling turned to crashing and above the northeast coast, angry streaks of fire crossed each other in the sky. The rain would reach us soon. We ran lightly, our packs bouncing. The baby wailed in his cradleboard. I swung it front so he faced me. It was harder to run, but he quieted down.

We reached the tall trees just as the rain hit and took shelter, Black Whale bent branches beneath trees that were upwind of the tallest trees. They would catch the Sky-Fire but fall away from us. We pulled the skins from our packs and threw them over the branches, securing them with lashings and rocks, then crawled under. Mosk was screaming by the time I got my breast exposed for him. He stopped mid-scream to grab the nipple. The Sky-Fire spirits had never frightened me, but now I had a baby to protect. I hoped my fear would not spoil my milk. In spite of the noise and my fear, by the time Mosk slept, the Sky-Fire Spirits left us, traveling above the water down the coast. We wrung out the skins and continued walking until the first stars came out, then made our fire and shelter, ate journey cake and slept.

During the night, Black Whale cried out in his sleep. The baby woke up and by the time I got Mosk back to sleep Black Whale was breathing the deep sleep breath again. I silently wished him good dreams but it seemed a long time before I could sleep myself.

As soon as Nippa'uus showed his first rays, we quietly broke camp and got on our way. It was late afternoon when we finally saw our Patuxet homesite. We heard the calls of delight from Mama and Papa and they came up the trail to meet us. Mama took the cradleboard from my back.

"I was so worried about you, little grandson!" She nuzzled him, and then opened her arms to me. "And about you, Daughter."

"We are fine, Mama. We can take care of ourselves."

"No one can defy the Sky-Fire Spirits, you can only try to avoid them." She looked at Black Whale as he set down the packs. "I am glad to see you all well, Daughter's husband." Mama's eyes searched his face. "But you are still worried. While the Sky-Fires were battling, I envisioned you weeping, Black Whale. I feared it meant something happened to Attitash."

"Matta, nothing happened to her." Black Whale did not sound persuaded and I looked closely at him. His mouth was a tight line, the mouth of a worried man. Black Whale closed his eyes for a long moment, and then looked at Mama and us. "I too had a vision. The Sky-Fire spirits took their battle along the coast to Nauset. My vision was of Aunt Blue Sky, Seekonk's wife, screaming. I worry Fire Spirits ran in her body and burned out her blood."

NONE OF US slept well that night, though we'd tried to convince Black Whale that his vision was not true. We woke up early and prayed as Nippa'uus rose from the Big Salt Water. Mama had the soil well prepared to receive the weachimin seeds. Papa and Black Whale went to the brook and brought back a few fish that were caught in the weir. We were chopping them to put in the hole with the seed when I heard a call. I looked to see Esapett coming to our field, her smile big and her obvious belly pushing out her skirts. We both laughed as I brought Mosk's cradleboard out from its shady place.

Esapett rubbed his hair, clearly taken with its abundance. She held out her arms, and I put the baby in them. She propped my baby on her own bump and kissed his fat little cheek. Turning to me, Esapett patted her chest with both hands over where her heart beat. "White Flower, Humility." We both knew there was nothing more to say. Until we could rescue them, they were in our hearts. I put my hand on her belly and felt her New Life and we both understood our hearts were strongest to keep our babies safe. Jon-owland came, carrying his hard-stone digger. He smiled at my son, then asked after Our Massasowet.

"Catabatash." I replied. Jon-owland knew I referred to their medicine of wutamineash, but I detected a teasing in his smile. He might understand our little deception, I thought, but he would also understand why it was done.

Papa pointed to where they were planting near our field. He and Jon-owland talked and Papa explained to us that each of the Strangers' family now had its own land to plant. "Their sachem says we have our own too." Mama and I exchanged looks. Why was Bad-ford explaining what we'd had ever since our creator, Kiehtan, sent crow with the weachimin seed for us? But we only nodded to Esapett and her husband as they went back to their field.

We'd almost finished for the day, when a runner came into view from the hills. He went straight to Mama.

Elisabeth

We heard loud wailing from Hopamoch's field and I looked to see Attitash and her mother clinging to each other. My first thought was that they'd heard bad news about White Flower and my stomach dropped. If it was bad news about White Flower, it would be bad news about Humility. Black Whale and Hopamoch came running, strings of fish in their hands. When they got close they dropped their fish and wailed themselves. I could see Attitash's baby swinging in its pack from a tree, so I assumed at least the disturbance had naught to do with the child. John had paused in his work to watch. "Can you find out what's going on?" I asked him. "Do you think they heard something from the Narragansett? Something about the girls?"

"Nay, they would seek our counsel if it were." He turned away from the spectacle of wailing. "I can't ask them now," John said. "I don't have enough words to understand people who display their feelings so openly. I could easily say the wrong thing."

The group quieted a bit, then collected their tools and left. White Cloud helped Attitash take the baby and follow the others.

I seethed with frustration, wanting to know what happened, but no way to find out. "Sometimes I feel like there's always a wall between Attitash and me," I told John as we walked home.

"That's because there is," he replied. "Several walls."

We were joined by others tending to their own lots as we all trooped back to the gate and to our houses. I had become somewhat accustomed to the hideous sight at the main gate. The northern Indian whom Standish killed with his own knife was still with us. His impaled head, often filled with pecking birds, mocked us from the tip of a pale. The boys threw rocks at it and made up disgustingly cruel rhymes. I wondered if Attitash had seen this and it was keeping her away.

There was much speculation as word spread that "the heathen are setting up a terrible noise." John and I caught up with Edward Winslow and his brothers. John talked quietly with Master Winslow a moment. When we arrived home, he put his arms around me. "Quiet thyself, Eliza. It's naught to do with Humility or Hopamoch's daughter. Whatever it is we'll find out soon enough. And in due time ye'll have the chance to sit with Attitash and discover her situation"

Life was certainly not simple. I shook off my thoughts as I fried up the fish John had caught early morning. John gave a brief prayer and we ate in silence. The late April sun went down slowly and we were sitting on the bench by our door when young Resolved White came with a message from his stepfather, Master Winslow. "Father says to tell you that Hopamoch came to let him know he was going to Nauset for a few days. His wife's brother was killed by lightning and he goes to bury him."

Truth be told, my first reaction was relief. I had not met this relative of Attitash and the death of an uncle was not the worst that could happen. The relief was erased by the horror of death by lightning. Of course it was common. Death itself was common. The storm had frightened me, but I felt safe once John and I reached our home that afternoon. The thunder shook our little home and crashed about like the sound of kegs full of ale rolling about the sky. To realize that the storm had struck Attitash's uncle made me quiver.

As Resolved ran off, John put his arm around me and held me close. I took his free hand and pressed it on my belly. "Do you feel that?"

John's eyes tightened then opened wide. "I do! I feel it!" He laughed out loud and leaned over to kiss my apron-covered belly.

Attitash
When we first heard what happened, Black Whale stood rooted, waiting for the realization to sink in. Not only was Seekonk his clan uncle, but since Black Whale's father had died, Seekonk had acted as both father and clan uncle. We all let our voices carry our shock and sorrow to the sky. The Sky-Fire Spirits would hear us, but it would not change their ways. They burned up trees and killed people and other creatures without regret.

"We must prepare for the journey," Mama finally said. She wiped her tears and took a deep breath. "Attitash," she touched my shoulder, "Your baby calls you."

I had not even heard Mosk's cries. I released Black Whale from my embrace and took my child's cradleboard from the tree, kissing his baby face and opening my poncho to comfort him with a teat. My sorrow did not touch him.

We all moved slowly, shock hindering every muscle. It

was decided with little discussion that I could manage the rest of the planting while Mama and Black Whale went to Nauset to bury Seekonk and bring Aunt Blue Sky, her daughter, and Grandmother back to live with us in Patuxet. That night, as soon as the baby slept, Black Whale and I melted into each other. Grief and love blended our bodies. After we were spent, Black Whale wept silently in my arms. The sighs and quiet sobs from my parents, told me they were comforting each other in the same way.

The next day, I worked furiously planting weachimin. When it got warm in the afternoon I took Mosk from his cradleboard and carried him to where Esapett and her husband worked. Her eyes shone with both joy and sad memories when she held my baby. I knew she felt a shadow of my feelings, both welcoming little Mosk and mourning my first New Life. We rested in the shadows with fresh spring water in the big jar. We both drank deeply. Esapett opened her mouth, closed it, then spoke carefully in her own words, "Who died?"

I understood, but did not answer—wondering how to say, "My mother's sister's husband," or "Black Whale's Clan Uncle," in her tongue. "Black Whale's Noe'sho," I tried, using our word for "father", thinking she might understand that word. She took my hand and pressed it to her heart. Sorrow and sympathy are easy to show.

Putting our joined hands onto Esapett's belly, I said in my words, "When will baby come?"

"Pa'poose?" she asked, using the name for baby used by people of the north who live by the big fresh waters.

"Ahhe, pa'poose Towwankeeswuch—summer?" I answered, remembering her word for the warm-moon season to hill the corn.

"Yea, July."

I did not know this word, but it was enough talk. Mosk had fallen asleep and we both had work to do.

THE WEACHIMIM WAS ALL PLANTED when my family returned. We all crowded into our little wetu the first night.
Next day we worked to strip and bend branches in arches
to form our new two-fire wetu. The mats from our one-
fire wetu were placed on the new frame along with the
ones Aunt Blue Sky and Grandmother brought from Nauset. Grandmother was settled at the end with Aunt Blue
Sky, little Ice Feathers on one side and Little Fish on the
other. Mama and Papa were by the entrance on Aunt's
side and Black Whale and I on the other. We stowed all
our belongings in bags by the fires in the middle, then
went to the outside fire to rest and tell stories.

As Nippa'uus sank below the western hills, Aunt Blue Sky
began. She told us how Uncle Seekonk had been collecting fish from the weir in the brook. "The Sky Fire spirits fought each other and then attacked the water where
he stood. Fire burned out his life-blood." She'd told the
story many times and was just able to finish the whole tale
before weeping took away her words.

Grandmother held her until she was quiet. Then we all
told our stories of how brave and good Seekonk was, how
he lost his first wife and children in Patuxet when the
Strangers' bad spirits took them. "And now I survive here
in Patuxet," Aunt Blue Sky said. "Four Otter Clan women
now live here." Grandmother, Mama, Aunt Blue Sky and I
were all women now. Maybe White Flower would be now
too. It would be too cruel if she became a woman with
only Narragansett women to welcome her. She'd been
gone so long, so much had happened. White Flower did
not know Uncle Seekonk had died. She had not held my
baby. Maybe she had forgotten us.

26

Elisabeth

"Hopamoch has two wives, living there," Governor Bradford announced to the table as I served supper. I almost dropped the pan, but caught it in time. Nausea flooded my throat at the thought.

Master Eaton laughed. "Old Testament style. That's one way to make sure the bed is always warm."

He had lost two wives of his own and slept in a cold bed now, but it hardly seemed a laughing matter that White Cloud must now share her husband with another woman. I banged the pan down hard and gave the entire table of men an evil eye. That only produced more laughter and my own husband joined in. When John and I were back in our own little house he continued to think it was a small matter. "The heathens have such different ways," he said. I kept quiet, but found myself not wanting to see Hopamoch or even Attitash.

When the fields showed a faint green haze a week later, our hopes for a good crop were high. Only those households which had been too lazy to finish their planting complained about having to be responsible for their own plot, citing all manner of excuses why they needed help. Their pleas were ignored, like the seeds they spilled at the end of the row.

John and William finished quickly, but not before the women at Hopamoch's homesite had planted their entire field. Attitash, and the new wife dug, added the fish chunks, planted the corn and tamped it down in no time.

William Latham made a crude comment about the advantage of two wives at planting time. I cuffed his ear and told him to keep his thoughts to himself. Even joking about this hideous practice made me gag. But we were still sowing the corn and theirs had grown two hands tall. They were already planting the beans and squash to climb the cornstalk.

Attitash's little son was on her lap, her dress pulled down shamelessly to suckle him. Deep inside my womb, my babe had settled down. I reminded myself that all the godly men in the Old Testament had at least two wives. If the rumors were true, Attitash's family was simply following ancient tradition and hadn't caught up to God's ways. My anxiety about the two wives eased away. Leaning my head against the tree, I closed my eyes.

Attitash

At first I was so burdened by grief that I did not notice Esapett's distance. Our beans did start up the weachimin stalks and the squash grew around. But Kiehtan did not send more rain and the three sister-plants were not blossoming. Esapett's field was much worse since they still planted the weachimin by itself and there were no beans and squash to cover the ground and keep it moist.

Aunt Blue Sky was wary of all the Strangers, of course. Win-snow did come to speak with Papa, giving his sympathy. "I told him I am fortunate to have three women cooking for me," Papa said. "He seemed a bit surprised, probably because they have so few women."

Esapett still did not approach me. Her New Life was getting so big it looked difficult for her to hoe. She had nothing to hoe anyway and she stopped coming to the field. I prayed to Kiehtan and to the rain gods to save the crops. I fed Mosk and listened to Mama and Aunt Blue Sky settling my little brother, Little Fish, and Aunt's little daughter, Ice Feathers. The babies were our distraction, but nothing could keep away the heavy emptiness of our home.

The squash ripe moon waned and came again to shine over the hills in a sliver, but still no rain. We spent an entire morning praying. We burned sweet grass to bring all the spirits and burned sage to drive away any bad spirits. We sang our prayers, clapped our sticks, and waited.

Elisabeth

No rain and no word of our dear little girl or White Flower. The Weston men were as oblivious of our heartache as they were ignorant of civil manners. I was hanging our washing on the fence in front of our house one morning when two of them came sauntering by. I tried to be civil myself with a curt nod and mumbled, "g'morning," They responded to my decency with indecent leers at my burgeoning stomach.

"Looks like you've had a busy winter," followed by guffaws and more rude comments about the heat of the summer showing a hot bed last winter. I spied my old four footed friend, Rogue, sniffing about my muck heap and called on the dog to defend me. She nipped at one man's ankle and barked twice. That drove them out of my path, but comments came back, "both bitches are foul this morning."

The only work that calmed me down was tending my vegetables and herbs in my garden boxes. I watered them and the chives, rue, and dill were thriving.

At last we were rid of the remaining Weston lot in mid-June. With little fanfare and relief on our part, they left in a shallop to settle on land Weston had arranged for north of the Cape.

But still no word of the girls and no rain. Few weeds grew, but neither did the corn. As the dry spell continued, the young plants barely stood upright. When I stole a gaze at Attitash's field, their corn was taller and stood straight, with tiny beans inching up the short stalks. Squash covered the ground, but all the plants were shorter than they should have been by late June. A godly punishment kept rain and the girls from us. It seemed we would not save our girls without saving our fields.

Mistress privately told us women that she worried God was angry because we no longer worked the fields as one community, but in separate households. Her husband, Elder Brewster, argued forcefully in his sermon that it was because greed had led too many of our men to spend all their time trying to arrange trade for more and more beaver. "We are neglecting our duty to pray, to beg God's forgiveness, and to be fruitful and multiply. In the fields and in our homes."

I smiled, glad I could take that personally. Priscilla and I were indeed blessed with husbands attentive to their duty to be fruitful. And Susanna Winslow already had a new son by Master Winslow, adding to the two boys by her late husband, Master White.

We needed an all-day prayer service to bring God's mercy for the stolen girls and to our fields. Sitting all morning in service made my back and nearly everything else ache. I tried to ignore it and pray. God would not return our girls or provide rain until we showed our repentance sufficiently. I had to stop the morose thoughts and concentrate on God's mercy.

At least my babe stayed strong, judging by its kicks. John kept glancing at me from the men's section, so I tried to put on a pleasant face. Mistress was keeping a close eye on me too. When we rose to sing another hymn she leaned over to whisper, "I'll go with thee for a little walk, Elisabeth. Ye must drink and relieve thyself."

"But I must keep praying," I insisted

Mistress took me firmly by the arm and led me out. "Do ye think our Father must listen to a woman close to childbed with all these men to pray? Ye must take care of thyself to take care of thy child."

I could not argue with that and gratefully lay down to rest after Mistress made certain I'd drunk the tea she made for me, followed by some ale. Concluding that I looked close to labor, she bustled about my little house making sure I had sufficient clean rags and dry rushes to put on the bed.

Attitash

At last the time had come. Before the grind-the-corn moon, Towwankeeswuch, we would be prepared to rescue my sister and Humility. Hoping the scum enemy had not already taken White Flower as a wife, our Papa had gone to the grandmothers to seek their council. Tokamahamon was here, talking with the Strangers about what could be offered to the Narragansett. Sachem Bad-ford said they had to pray before they could decide.

The Strangers sang a slow mournful tune. They were not in their field but in their large house, were praying to their spirit. Would our Sky Spirits clash with theirs? They say they only have one spirit, although they gave it three names. One of the names must be for the mother of earth.

After an entire day of praying, we went to the shore to see if Kiehtan and the Sky spirits would at least bring us rain. Thankfully, there were many more spirits in the trees, the woods, the water, the stars and the moon. They could help us find White Flower and Humility.

Elisabeth

When my husband returned from services I felt rested enough to fix a little supper. John insisted he need only a biscuit, but took a bowl of the leftover corn mush I'd saved. We carried our food out to the garden to escape the oppressive heat inside. The little breeze barely cooled my face. I suggested we find more relief from the heat on the shore.

"And walking helps my back."

John was reluctant, but I persuaded him when we saw several others going, including Priscilla, her John and their babe. Once we got down to the shore, I settled on my favorite flat rock with Priscilla. The men took their pipes down by the water. It was indeed much cooler there and there were clouds in the northwest.

"Esapett."

I looked up to see Attitash, her mother and the other woman coming past the A shaped rocks that formed the natural barrier between their part of the shore and ours. Often when we were alone, I would go to their area, but it was rare to see Attitash on our part. She saw me struggling to get up and motioned me to remain sitting. Priscilla put a protective arm about me, but Attitash greeted her as well.

Attitash

It seemed our prayers were heard as the Sky Spirits had begun assembling in great roiling clouds. Mama walked toward the Strangers' shore and called to me, saying that Esapett was sitting there looking as though her time was close to bring her child to the light. I did not ask my mother how she knew, but as we drew near, I could see from the look on Esapett's face and the way her belly stuck out that Mama was right. Aunt Blue Sky hesitated to come with us, but Mama told her it was time she met our neighbors.

Esapett glanced very quickly at Aunt Blue Sky and then away, as if she were afraid of her. I introduced her as my mother's sister. I could not tell if Esapett understood.

We all sat down on the sand and began the awkward

attempt to talk with few words. We patted our hearts and they did the same, saying "Humility. White Flower." We understood that they also prayed for rain, easy enough with big clouds and smiles to show our encouragement. I had Mosk in his cradleboard and I unlaced it and pulled him off. Priscilla's baby was a bit bigger, dressed in their cloth and looking much too warm. Priscilla called her baby "Esapett," smiling when I pointed to Esapett and then the baby, saying their name the only way I could.

When Esapett suddenly bit her lip and uttered a low moan, clutching her belly, Mama instinctively reached out her hand near the trembling of her belly. Esapett understood the gesture and let Mama put her hand gently down to stroke the quivering mound.

"White Cloud, be careful," Aunt Blue Sky said quietly, but Mama ignored her and continued to rest her hand against the movements of the New Life.

"Her child is very big for such a small mother," my mother murmured. "I hope they have a moon-lodge woman who knows what to do."

Elisabeth

"What is she doing?" Priscilla demanded. "We should go, Elisabeth."

I knew she was right, but it felt so calming to have White Cloud massage my belly. Our only midwife on the Mayflower was Mary Chilton's mother. Since her death the first winter, we depended on the Grace of God and the experience of Mary Brewster and Susanna Winslow. Both mistresses had been delivered of babes themselves, but I doubted they knew as much as White Cloud did. The pain in my back had diminished and I took several deep breaths. "Catabatash," I said to White Cloud and Attitash. Priscilla and Attitash gathered up their babies. I held out my hands to be pulled up and White Cloud did so slowly with her strong hands. It was then I realized we had a crowd of people watching me. Remember Allerton's hands were clapped over her mouth. I turned my back on them all as John arrived to take my arm. Priscilla urged us to "hurry but not so fast that ye fall," and I had no chance to bid farewell to my heathen friends.

I was quite distracted at the time, but did still notice that White Cloud seemed very comfortable with the new woman. If I understood Attitash, this was her aunt. Mayhap it was like Leah and Rachel and all the other sister-wives in the Bible.

By the time we arrived home, Mistress had already come and put the clean rushes under a worn sheet on our bed. Priscilla and Susanna Winslow were the only guests at my childbed. Constance, Mary Chilton and Desire were all older than I, but were unwed and could not attend until they'd given birth themselves. Mary made a groaning cake for her mistress to bring. John came by with sufficient ale for my friends to wash down the cake, handing it through the door and blowing a quick kiss to me before Mistress Brewster sent him away. Humility was in the back of my mind, but I had to concentrate on my delivery. When my pains intensified, I paid no mind to what my friends were doing, but as the pains lessened I was glad to be with them.

Dozing off between pains, I was awakened by the crash of thunder. Susanna Winslow opened the door and the smell of fresh rain filled the house. Everyone was laughing and praising God. Somewhere inside I was praising God for the rain too, but my body overwhelmed my mind. I had no voice for my thanks. Mistress sat by the bed, reminding me to hold my breath when the pain was strongest and to release it and take a deep breath when it lessened. The sound of rain on our roof assured me that God did indeed bless me and my husband. Our first babe would come into a land of plenty.

The pains started coming so fast there was no pause between. My awareness of rain, cake, ale and friends was lost in pain and exhaustion. Mistress Brewster kept telling me to breathe, breathe, breathe, but I could not get more than a tiny breath. I forced myself to pull in air and it came right back out in a great groan that challenged the thunder.

"She's not big enough for her babe. Its head shows, then it goes back again. She can't deliver!" I opened my eyes to see Mistress Brewster wringing her hands. "Her John said he'd bring the Indian woman if we need her."

I opened my eyes and forced my words out. "Get her. Now!"

Pain took over. *I was in Mother's bed back in Bedfordshire. There were sheep bleating in the shed. I could curl up and stay with Mother. John was calling me from somewhere, but I was too tired to answer him. Father came in the door and smiled at me. Mother told me I was no older than she'd been when she birthed her firstborn.*

"I help." White Cloud's voice. Mistress was moving aside and White Cloud's hands were massaging me. Her hands were slippery. One was on my belly, pushing down and the other hand where my babe needed to get out. I saw her motion to Attitash and Mistress to each take one of my feet and give me leverage. Pain was my friend and pain was my enemy. Pain kept my babe safe. Pain tried to push it out.

"She's got hold of the head! The crown is showing!" Priscilla called. She gripped my hands.

White Cloud grunted hard and I understood I needed to push. But my strength was gone. There was only jelly where my muscles used to be.

"Esapett! Come!" White Cloud's voice broke through the fog of my mind.

"Netop. Give light." It was Attitash, using her word for

friend. My mother seemed to be holding me, telling me without words that I was as strong as she was "Push, push, push," all the women in the room cried out. Drawing a deep breath, I pulled on Priscilla and Susanna Winslow's hands and pushed against Mistress Brewster and Attitash with my feet. I felt as though my belly was turning inside out.

"It's head is out," Mistress proclaimed. "One more push, come on!" I gathered my strength again and groaned with a great push. Unbelievable relief and the sound of a little squeak. Every bone in my body ached and my muscles all collapsed.

"It's a girl." Priscilla announced as the squeak became a little wail.

Someone put her on my belly and I stroked the little wet body, murmuring to my squealing babe, "Hush, hush. Ye are with me now, hush." There was some business about pushing out the bloody mass, then all was quiet. I could see a faint light through the door as someone opened it. The rain was now slow and gentle on the roof.

I thought I heard my John's voice outside.

"Elisabeth is fine, John, and ye have a beautiful daughter," I heard Priscilla say. "Take the heathens home quickly, before someone sees them."

Attitash touched my face in farewell and left with her mother.

Mistress tweaked my nipple and it stiffened on command. My babe rooted around and found it. She sucked as though she'd been taught. The sucking pulled on my belly. I was now a mother.

27

Elisabeth

My babe was sucking noisily when John reached my side, his face alight. We both laughed at her determination though there was surely little to drink. Then she popped off, her face quiet in the sleep of an innocent babe.

I wrapped her up and handed the little bundle to him. He held our babe very gently and nuzzled her cheek. "Did ye think of a name?"

He was not surprised when I told him 'Desire,' though I think he'd only considered what we would name a boy. "Ye will get a son next time," I assured him.

John breathed deep of wee Desire's scent. He raised his eyes to mine. "As long as ye deliver safely, we'll not worry. God will give us daughters and sons if He chooses."

"Was it you who brought White Cloud and Attitash here?"

"Yea. Hopamoch came and told me his wife would help if we needed her. I brought them to wait at Winslow's house."

I stroked his strong finger that our daughter clenched with her tiny one. "Thank God ye brought her. I did need her."

"Yea, White Cloud knew that. She insisted on coming out in the rain when Susanna Winslow came to fetch her." John kissed the babe's little cheek. "She has a big head." He looked outside. "Ye heard we have a good rain. Our crops are saved." When I nodded, he continued. "Let's hope this miracle detracts from anyone finding out about

White Cloud. Someone is bound to conclude that there were heathens practicing witchcraft at thy childbed." Seeing the flurry of fear come into my face, John leaned over to kiss my brow. "Nay, Love. Do not worry. With this rain there is naught to complain. And if they do, we'll show them this little miracle."

The door opened and Desire Mintor came in. "May I hold her?" Tears filled her eyes and her thick dark hair swung beneath her coif. "That I lived to see this day, as ye promised me!" Desire kissed my daughter's cheek.

William Latham burst in. "There's a ship coming in, and it's ours. It's English. "

Priscilla couldn't wait. She took her babe and ran out to see.

I closed my eyes and dozed off again, waking later to find I was no longer alone. Desire was back and offered me a long drink of fresh spring water. "The Lord is merciful indeed," she said. "The crops are standing tall." She held my little Desire's face in her hands. "Surely God will bring Humility back." Flies buzzed lazily on our table and Desire waved them out the open door. "And the Ship Anne has come. It brings ninety people, many of them women and children." She started to rattle off those I would have heard of, the Brewsters' daughters, Fear and Patience, wives of several of the men who'd come alone, like Samuel Fuller's wife, Bridget. And two widows destined to become wives of William Bradford and Myles Standish.

"And who for Isaac Allerton?"

Desire laughed. "Mistress Brewster says her daughter Fear is already pledged to him."

Attitash
"Wait." Mama said when I started down the path again. Nippa'uus was fully up now, shining on the water. Something caught the light and flashed at us. It was very small

and bouncing on the water. I could not tell if it was the cloth of the Strangers' Big Wind Canoe. Mama and I looked at each other a long time moment. "More Strangers."

Dread spread in my heart, covering my delight in Esapett's new daughter. We could not keep the Big Wind Canoes from bringing more Strangers. In the circles of seasons since Esapett and her people brought women and children for the first time, we had learned a bitter truth. More and more and more would come. Even now, many among our friends were too eager to fil their own bags with the gifts Kiehtan brings to us. They take too many beaver pelts and cut down ancient trees. They do not take only what is needed to build a village for the ones here in our land, they also send much back across the Big Salt Water.

My throat clenched as I gazed out on the Big Salt Water. Our forests would disappear, the beaver dams gone, streams running too fast, carrying Mother Earth with them. Even the soft path we traveled would turn to hard rock.

Mama took my hand. We had no words of comfort. We walked home in silence.

Aunt Blue Sky took Mosk from her breast as we entered. "My own little Ice Feathers doesn't take much anymore and there's little milk for yours. He just wanted to suck. He was almost pulling my nipple off," she laughed.

My baby reached for me and latched on, milk dribbling down his chin and onto my breast, relieving the pressure. Grandmother stirred the fire and began cooking. Mama and I were so tired we could hardly speak. Black Whale pulled me against him, allowing me to rest as I fed our son.

WE STAYED AWAY from their village, but could not avoid the swarm of new Strangers when we went to our field. Many new men and a few new women now chopped out the plants that threatened to grow above their weachimin. If they'd only plant the beans to grow up the weachimin stalk and the squash to cover the ground beneath, they would not need to be chopping so much. The Strangers' weachimin was growing, though each plant had only two ears instead of three or four like ours.

Little Fish and even Ice Feathers helped chase crows away by clapping sticks. Was White Flower hoeing Narragansett crops now? I wondered if she was with Narragansett women who treated her well. Grandmother told stories of women becoming attached to the enemy after being stolen. But I knew White Flower longed to come home to us.

Little Fish called out that some of our people were coming down the hill. We dropped our work to run see. It was Uncle Red Hawk, Aunt First Star and Seafoam. I was glad to see her with her parents, which meant she'd given up looking for her rotten husband and was living at her mother's fire again.

When they reached the path coming to our homesite, we rushed to them. Papa and Black Whale had met them near the spring and we all gathered with questions. "How are you feeling? How are your crops?" And then the hard one, "Have you heard anything about White Flower and the Strangers' child?"

"That is why we came." Aunt First Star glanced at her daughter. Seafoam looked as though she was about to rebuff an attacker herself.

Uncle Red Hawk took the jug of water I offered and drank deep, then told us his news. "A messenger from the Narragansett Sachem, Canonicus', came to Massasowet. He brought an offer from Sachem Canonicus to release your daughter and the little Cloth-men's girl."

I caught my hands from flying to my mouth. Would it be an offer we could fulfill?

Uncle Red Hawk continued, telling us that Sachem Canonicus had used Shimmering Fish to kidnap our girls. "He said Shimmering Fish was eager to leave his own people and align with the Narragansett." Uncle Red Hawk glanced at his daughter and Seafoam shrugged as if warding off a blow.

"But why did they take White Flower?" Mama asked.

"The messenger, Grey Owl, took your daughter to replace Sachem Canonicus's daughter, killed by the Clothmen's bad spirits soon after she became a woman."

If only I could see this Grey Owl and pull his tongue out. Canonicus took White Flower to replace his own daughter. We would never see her again. Nothing we could offer for her—no tools, no wampum, not even firesticks—could replace her.

"Why did Shimmering Fish want the Strangers' little girl?" Grandmother asked.

"Grey Owl said the Cloth-men's girl was needed to trade for the Cloth-men's bounty. The Narragansett want a firestick in ransom for their captives. They will continue to demand this, but we will not let the Narragansett get what would be used to kill us. Not until Clothmen give us enough firesticks to keep away our enemies."

We were all full of questions, yet Uncle continued. "This Narragansett told us his people have not yet avenged Tall Elk's life, but Shimmering Fish could replace Tall Elk."

I still could not draw a deep breath. What would Sachem Canonicus take for White Flower? And who was Tall Elk? Why had this Grey Owl come to our Massasowet if his Sachem wanted to keep both girls?

Uncle Red Hawk looked at Papa and then Black Whale. "Remember the man you killed to rescue Attitash and White Flower," he said.

My stomach lurched. I had never heard the name, Tall Elk, but I could see Papa and Black Whale, pounding our kidnapper on the head, his body twitching, while White Flower and I watched in terror. That had been three years ago, when White Flower was a mere girl—a nun'squa.

"We remember the man." Papa's arm muscles tensed, as if reliving his club smashing this Tall Elk's head. "So, the Narragansett accept Shimmering Fish alive instead of avenging with another death?" Papa asked.

"So Grey Owl said." Uncle Red Hawk took another long drink then glanced at my cousin. Seafoam kept her eyes down and I could not tell what she was thinking. "They are using the Fish my daughter married for their own needs—to kidnap the girls, and now to attract another woman in exchange for the two he stole."

Mama's face was impassive, but the look in her eyes when she caught mine revealed the horror this possibility raised. What new woman? Another Wampanoag? Me? Another one of the Strangers? But Seafoam was the only woman Shimmering Fish could attract.

"Another woman?" Grandmother spoke for all of us. "Get White Flower back, and lose another?"

"Sister," Uncle Red Hawk said to Mama. "We have prayed, danced, sung, and taken the terrible loss of White Flower to our Grandmothers."

Mama and Grandmother nodded their heads. Grandmother spoke. "My son, even if the Cloth-men would be willing to give a firestick to our enemy—and we could not believe they would—and if the Narragansett had weapons, it would be the death of our people, not just our dear White Flower."

"Of course, Mother," Uncle said to Grandmother. "We can't give our enemy a firestick, but the Narragansett will instead take wampum, Cloth-men's tools, and another woman in exchange."

"Who would go?"

Seafoam opened a journey bag and spilled onto her

lap a pile of beautifully polished wampum. The purple shone against the gleaming white in the shells. This display had taken many hours of gathering, washing, cutting and polishing. Seafoam's face was still, but there was both pride and pain in her eyes. She glanced at me, and then looked down at the bounty as she spoke. "I will go."

No one responded to her. The low cooking fire crackled, as my son gurgled in his cradleboard. Ice Feathers crawled onto Aunt Blue Star's lap, watching us all.

"Why would you do this?" Mama asked. "We would gain our daughter only to give you to the enemy."

Seafoam wiped her eyes, the first sign of what this decision cost her. "I have put my husband out from my fire. He caused your daughter to suffer—and the Cloth-man's child."

We waited again. It seemed like I was in a very strange dream. The three-note bird sang and my dog, Suki, turned around three times then settled in a cool spot under a tree. But despite this, nothing felt normal. Nothing was familiar. A heavy, dank, dread hung about all of us.

Mama finally spoke. "Do you offer this because you think you should pay back the harm caused to White Flower? Shimmering Fish harmed my daughter. Not you."

Seafoam let a faint smile into her eyes, though her mouth stayed grim. "Catabatash, thank you. But that is not why I go." Seafoam flicked her eyes at me, then lowered them again. "But I do not do this as payment. My heart still turns to him. Maybe Shimmering Fish is right." She heard me gasp and turned to me. "Attitash, we know our people are weak. The Wampanoag can't keep the Clothmen away. They have killed too many of us with their bad spirits and their firesticks. The ones who live north of here do not even work. They make our people feed them and worse. They rape our women."

The truth she spoke made a bitter taste on my tongue. But these Weston men were not like Esapett and Jon-owland. Seafoam knew this, but she continued boldly. "The Narragansett are still strong. If we join forces, we can send the Cloth-men back where they came from and we will have enough beaver, enough land, we will have aquene."

Mama stood up. Her eyes shot fire at everyone. "Do not bring this defiance to our fire!"

If only I could take Seafoam by her pretty hair and drag her away. How could she speak of our entire clan as rebels? After all Shimmering Fish had done, she still listened to his dangerous words.

"Sit, Daughter. We must keep our heads clear." Grandmother's voice carried the wisdom and weariness of many years. "You know Seafoam still speaks for that rotten Fish." She took out her pipe and filled it, and then reached a stick into the fire to light it. "The Narragansett have always been our enemy." Grandmother said. "Shimmering Fish stays with the Narragansett because he wants their abundance. We all hope the rot in Shimmering Fish will be burned out." After taking a long puff on her pipe, she passed it to Seafoam. "Don't let his endless hunger for more become your own hunger."

Seafoam accepted the pipe, but held it in her hand. "Grandmother," her voice was only slightly less strident. "You tell stories yourself about when your grandmother was in the cradleboard—before the Cloth-men began to come looking for our beaver and demanding everything we have. You tell us that before they came, our enemies and the Wampanoag had only small battles, one or two kills in exchange for a wrong done. But since the Cloth-men came with their bad spirits, we have lost so many people, so many deer and beaver, that we now fight each other for land and for our very life."

I wanted to put my hands over my ears. There was truth

in what she said, but only part truth. If Seafoam went to
the Narragansett, it would be easier for us to keep our
treaty with the Strangers. She caused nothing but trouble.

Grandmother was silent for a moment. "What you say
is true, my son's daughter." She spoke firmly now, not
with anger, but with strength. "But the Narragansett is
still our enemy. We would no longer be the Wampanoag if
we joined the Narragansett. We must survive on our own.
The Narragansett would make you a wife and would keep
you even if the rotten Shimmering Fish leaves."

Seafoam passed the pipe to her mother and Aunt First
Star took a puff. Seafoam ran her fingers through the wampum. "Who would be my husband if I stay here? I am one
of the rebels now." She passed her hands over her eyes.
"I could not sleep until Grey Owl told our Massasowet
what Shimmering Fish asked me to do. I have decided to
offer myself to the Narragansett. Working on this bounty
is the only way I could make my heart beat calmly again.
I must go." Seafoam turned to me. "You will accompany
me, Attitash and Black Whale. You will bring home the
girls." She held out her hand to take the pipe back from
her mother. She inhaled.

I wondered if Seafoam would ever sleep again. Was
there a hunger for more than she needed? Or only a hunger for enough food? My own hunger was for my sister
and my heart quickened with the understanding that perhaps my sister and little Humility would be returned.

"Do what you must, Cousin," I said as I accepted the
pipe from her. Taking a puff, I looked at Black Whale. His
shoulders were flexing as though he was already holding
his bow and arrow. Black Whale and I might be in danger
if we went with Seafoam. She must have seen the thought
in my face.

"You will not take Seafoam there without the Cloth-
man who is husband to your friend," Papa said. "We can

trust him and he will bring his firestick to keep you safe."

"Should not Win-snow go?" Mama asked. "He speaks more of our tongue."

"Matta. It would draw too much attention from the other Strangers and our own people if Win-snow went. He is known to speak for Sachem Bad-ford and some of the other Strangers would insist on coming," Papa said. "We would have many firesticks in Strangers' hands instead of one. This Jon-owland can be trusted, but would not be assumed to be doing anything for Sachem Bad-ford.

"Ahhe," Mama agreed. "And Jon-owland will bring their little girl home."

"Grey Owl will make certain this Cloth-man understands what his people must continue to provide to the Narragansett so that another of their girls is not taken." Uncle Red Hawk added.

"And what will that be?" Black Whale stood up, his hands clenched in a fist.

"Only a few shiny-stone traps and other tools. No more than what they now give us," Uncle Red Hawk assured him. "No firesticks."

My baby wailed softly, I took him from his cradleboard and set him to my breast. I hoped my roiling belly would not curdle my milk.

Seafoam turned to her parents. "Your Otter Clan niece, White Flower, will come home to her mother," she said to her father." I will find a way to visit you," she told her mother, though Aunt First Star could not make her face accept this deceit from her daughter.

Seafoam rose. "I am tired from our journey and I need to sleep. Let me know when you are ready to leave," she said and left.

Mama and Aunt Blue Sky wept as they said goodbye to their brother and his wife. Uncle Red Hawk and Aunt First Star left with their heads down, ready to go home to their son and their crops. They would mourn Seafoam as if she had died.

Elisabeth

Telling us only that Seafoam and her family were here and we had an important decision to make, Governor Bradford asked us to assemble in his house. He did not want to use the Commonhouse, "Because some I choose not to involve would attend."

John and I found Edward Winslow and Elder Brewster with Governor Bradford. We hoped, of course, that that a plan was being hatched which should release Humility and White Flower. When Attitash, Black Whale, and Hopamoch arrived, it became evident that was indeed the case. Perhaps our prayers were finally being heard.

We all crowded into the house with the men taking all the chairs. Attitash and I sat on the bench, my little babe on my lap and Attitash's on hers. She'd not seen my Desire since she was born. Attitash's eyes took the babe in warmly, but this was not the time to play with infants.

Hopamoch and Seafoam's father took turns speaking. The lump of ice that had been in my throat since the abduction diminished greatly when I understood that the kidnappers would consider a ransom. Hopamoch pointed to the muskets standing in the corner when he told us this was one of the Narragansett demands. Before any of us could protest, Hopamoch made it clear that tools and wampum might be part of the requirement. I took a deep breath. That could be arranged. Attitash was holding herself very tightly, her arms around her son were rigid with tension.

When her father told us the Narragansett demanded a maid in exchange, her back stiffened and she shot a quick glance at me. Did they want an English maid—or girl? Attitash whispered, "Seafoam" to me. I confess my first reaction was relief. I had little affection for Seafoam, though she and Attitash were obviously close. She was very shy of me and had seemed to be present for all or most of the troubles Attitash had suffered.

When Winslow had finished questioning Hopamoch on the details of the trade, he then repeated it, with translation as needed, for us. "The Narragansett took our little Humility to force us to trade more. They won't give her back unless we promise more beaver traps, more knives, more axes." Master Winslow noted that Governor Bradford and Elder Brewster nodded in agreement. I noted that my John did too. "A relative of Hopamoch's wife has offered to go. She was married to that rebel who came to us bloodied and filled with a lie, the same rebel who stole our girls and sold them to the Narragansett. This niece of White Cloud is willing to be the ransom for our Humility and for Hopamoch's daughter." Winslow looked at Hopamoch to make sure he'd gotten the translation right.

It was decided that they would leave in two days, during the festivities to celebrate our governor's marriage. In the midst of the feasting, no one would question my John's absence. It was obvious to all of us that only Mistress Brewster need know where he'd gone until the rescuers were back home safely.

28

Attitash

I collected several wampum shells and polished them, then made a wristlet for Sachem Bad-ford's new wife. I also made a small one for Esapett's new daughter. I'd only had a chance to glance at her babe when we met at Sachem Bad-ford's house. Today I could give the gift. We would go to the feast so none of the Strangers would ask why we were not there. Only Seafoam and Grandmother remained at home, packing all the food and wampum to leave that afternoon.

I carried the wristlets in my bag and tucked Mosk into his cradleboard. There was plenty of sphagnum moss to catch all his pee. Aunt Blue Sky noticed we made certain that our one-shoulder dress covered our breasts. Mama explained that we used to think the women Strangers had no breasts or legs as they never showed them. "We saw their legs when they searched for mussels in the Big Salt Water," Mama said. "And now we see Pahsilla and Esapett's breasts when they feed their babies."

"So why do they cover up now, when it's so warm?"

"They cover up a lot, their hair, arms, legs, breasts," I told her. "But we can't figure out why." I smoothed my own dress, checked all the strings wound around my legs and tied my hair back. It was almost as long as before I'd become a woman and it was cut to my ears. At the time, I wondered how long I'd have to wait to for it to grow to my shoulders so Black Whale and I could marry. It had been snowy, the first cold moon, Pepe'warr, when

Mama cut it and we were married when the river ice had all melted.

Mama, Aunt Blue Sky and I followed Papa and Black Whale along the path to Pli-mot village. We could look at the Big Salt Water, where the new wind canoe sat. We walked up the hill to the wall the Strangers had made from tree branches. The gruesome head of Wituwaumat, the Massachuseuks man, was still stuck on one of the poles. I kept my eyes down and was glad Mosk, happily riding on my back in his cradleboard, was too little to know this was the dreadful remains of the man Cap-tan San-dish killed.

We went in the gate and I was pleased to find Esapett and Jon-owland outside the longhouse. Esapett greeted me with a smile.

I could not follow all her words, but she held up her little daughter and I took her. The baby opened her eyes and I gazed into them. They were not like her mother's, quiet water in the woods, reflecting the colors around it. They were dark blue, like deep water of the lake.

"What do you call her?"

"Desire."

"Desiah? Like your netop—your fa-rend?"

"Yea—ahhe."

I put the little wristlet on baby Desiah's arm. It was much too big, but Esapett took it in her hand, obviously delighted.

"Catabatash," she said, touching each little wampum shell with her finger.

"She can speak some of our words," Aunt Blue Sky whispered in surprise.

The door to their big longhouse opened and Mis-tess Bews-teh came out, with the friend Desiah. Mis-tess greet-ed Mama and me, and nodded at Aunt Blue Sky. I told Mis-tess my Aunt's name and she nodded again, but her face was not warm as it was when she greeted the rest of us. Pahsilla looked down too, probably out of respect for someone older than she. By this time many people were coming out the door and Papa and Black Whale had found Win-snow and were talking to him.

The feast for Sachem Bad-Ford's wedding was even bigger than the feasts we'd attended for their harvest celebration. There were many more tables set up as many more people now lived there. Two new women did not hide their surprise at seeing Mama, Aunt, and me. Esapett introduced us, telling us Mis-tess was their mother. I used Esapett's words to welcome them and was proud to see their surprise.

The Pniese who came with our Massasowet had hunted when they came through the forest. Mama and I sang our prayers of gratitude to our brother deer before we butchered them. Esapett and Pahsilla waited quietly 'til we'd finished. They stood back while we sliced the deer through the belly and let the guts and blood run out. Both knew how to slice the skin and pull it off and cut out the tastiest parts. We were all tired by the time we'd finished butchering and the meat was simmering in several big pots on the fires inside Mis-tess's house and two outside. I sat down to rest and feed my baby, keeping my eye out for Jon-owland. We'd agreed that he would find Black Whale as soon as the feast began and arrange where to meet on the path to our rendezvous. Until then, I would have to act calm. I'd learned from my mother and grandmother how to keep my face calm, if not my heart.

Elisabeth

There was much preparation for Governor Bradford's wedding to Alice Southworth, the widow who'd come on the *Ship Anne*.

All the light-hearted chatter was carried on with the thin layer of civility which covered my heavy heart. John and I had said our farewells before we went to the wedding ceremony. Everything after that was pretense.

When Attitash and her family arrived, I took them with me to Brewsters' garden. The two Brewster daughters, Fear and Patience, stared at my Indian friends. I'd not had an opportunity to be with the Brewster daughters since they arrived on the *Ship Anne*. Their mother was distracted, so I informed them that these Indians were special friends. Attitash nodded her head politely and said, "Well met," which made their eyes open wide as a giggle escaped Patience.

"Sachem Bad-ford and Cap-tan San-dish new women?" Attitash asked, which made the daughters laugh out loud.

I tried explaining to White Cloud and Attitash in their own tongue that the ceremony had taken place and the brides and their husbands were having a glass of aqua vit together. There was no way to say most of that in their words, of course. I don't know what they understood. Attitash made a circle with each hand, then put them together to make a whole. I remembered Master Winslow telling us their wedding vows included joining both sides of a hoop together and nodded to affirm that the marriages were sealed.

"Tell the heathen friend we all pray for little Humility and for her sister," Fear Brewster said kindly.

I mumbled something in Wampanoag about "nun'squas,' which I thought was their word for young girls. Attitash had understood most of what Fear had said, but kept her face clear of both her anxiety and new hope for the girls.

Attitash had to be at least as worried as I was. I looked at her resting from the considerable effort to butcher the deer. She would leave her baby behind to go into dangerous territory to rescue the girls. But at least she would be in motion, not stuck here wondering.

It tore at my nerves that I would have to sit back waiting and not even able to express my fears except with Mistress Brewster and Desire. We'd agreed I would stay at their home until John returned with Humility. I looked forward to being alone with them at the end of the day. Pretending that I had neither hope nor terror was exhausting.

When Attitash and Black Whale slipped away, I knew John was gone. The gossips around me chattered. I listened half-heartedly.

"The ship's captain told us he always carries as many beaver pelts as he can get for the return voyage." Fear Brewster was eager to tell all she'd learned. She certainly did not seem a bit frail. Mistress had told me once that they'd left their daughters in Holland, believing young maids were too frail for a long voyage. If that were true, then Priscilla, Constance, Mary Chilton and I would not be here.

"My father told me that we used to have beaver in England, but that they were completely destroyed— trapped out—way back in the time between King Henry the Ist and Henry II, by Anno Domini 1200." Fear Brewster paused to see if we were surprised. I certainly was. I'd seen a few beaver hats, but had no idea what the animal looked like. John had told me they built houses of mud and sticks that made dams. And that they were thick as flies up in Maine.

Fear Brewster continued, "I heard Father tell Master Allerton that this killing off could happen here in the Promised Land if the Natives get enough iron traps instead of snares." Fear scraped more salt off the big cone and dumped it in a bowl. She glanced at her mother, who had not stopped smiling since her daughters arrived. "But Isaac Allerton says there are far too many beaver for that to happen here."

At mention of her father's name, Remember Allerton's ears perked up. For the first time, Remember was old enough to help with the feast. Her sister, Mary, now eight years old, was in charge of my babe and Priscilla's Elizabeth. They were laid out like poppets on bedding in the shade of the garden.

The older boys were out setting up planks and sawhorses to make tables in the common square. Resolved White was helping, but his young brother Peregrine was underfoot. Their mother, Mistress Susanna Winslow, was giving a final kneading to the bread dough. She set it in two pans, all she could make from the last of the rye. These rare loaves were for the bridal couples. As she set the pan packed in warm ashes above the lowest fire, Susanna gave us her views on why Master Winslow would be returning to England with the *Ship Anne*.

"Something is rotten. My husband says the goods recorded by the financiers are not nearly equal to what was sent back with the Fortune and with Weston's ship." She put one small log on the fire and blew softly. "None of us can trust Weston, but since he is one of the financiers, the others would believe him. My husband must go himself to bear witness to the truth. If our debt with the financiers is not reconciled, we will lose all supplies and any additional settlers." Susanna Winslow looked at our faces. "They could take the land away from us. We would be back in Holland or England, persecuted by King James again." She yanked Peregrine away from the dough bowl. "We'd all be in the same kettle as the poor little girls."

Did she know about the rescue attempt? I understood now why she submitted to being left alone here without a husband. Only Edward Winslow, whose word was true and his charm in negotiating recognized, could save our plantation from ruin by the financiers. Enemies on all sides, I thought. Narragansett, French, and our English financiers.

Mistress Hopkins and Goodwife Billington arrived, bearing more bowls and we began setting everything up as the boys finished the tables. Our gossip stopped as no one wanted to say too much around Goody Billington, whose wagging tongue was her only defense against her own husband's continual failings. I took advantage of my new babe to excuse myself and spent the remainder of the feast sitting where I need not participate in the talk.

WHEN WE WERE FINALLY settled in Brewsters' house that night, I was ready for sleep but not ready to succumb to night terrors. Desire and I settled in the garden, watching the sun in the west light up the waves in the eastern sea. It would be dark soon and wherever my John and the Indians were they would be bedding down in the forest.

Desire held the baby, cooing in her face. "When Humility comes home she'll be wanting to hold this one."

I was glad Desire could speak in the positive. I felt more like *if* Humility comes home, but would not express my anxiety.

"Elisabeth, have ye looked at the letters that came with the *Ship Anne?*"

The letters had completely slipped from my mind. I told her there had been a brief letter from my brother. "I do wish my sister Rose could see my babe!" I swallowed the lump of homesickness that had returned in small measure since all the troubles with the kidnapping and then intensified when my Desire was born. "That would make it a little easier to bear that Mother did not live to see her." I felt selfish mourning my own family when so many had lost theirs. I forced my mind to return to her question. "Did ye get any letters?"

"Yea, from my friend in England. She would have me come there and live with her." Desire started to cough and paused to compose herself. "Since Master Winslow is going, he can be my chaperone, I'm going back to England."

I sat rooted, unaware of anything but the friend in front of me. Tears obscured my vision as my eyes went to the *Ship Anne*, anchored out in deep water. Desire had been my friend since the voyage over on the Mayflower. After my family died, Desire and I lived together with our guardians. She was a sister to me. Now I would lose her, just as I'd lost my sisters, Rose and Joan. She would not see my daughter grow up.

"Come home with me, Elisabeth!" Desire put her arm around me. "Surely your John could travel with Master Winslow and then remain in England. All of our settlement might all have to go home soon, if what Susanna Winslow says could happen is true."

"John would never go. He always talks about the opportunity here, the promise of land, the promise of trading. And John believes all will be settled with the financiers. He'd never go back to the poor circumstances of England."

My words were strong, but Desire saw the confusion of my emotions and pressed on with her temptation. "Thy husband has some means of his own since he inherited our late governor John Carver's worldly goods. Ye know, Elisabeth, this place will only make thy husband greedier. The more they get, the more they want."

"But, Constance Hopkins says her parents tell her the bounty of this land is God's blessing on us!"

"Oh, fie!" Her vehemence made Desire cough again. "Do not forget that Stephen Hopkins is not of the Lord's church! He was hired by Myles Standish. He calls us 'Puritans', making fun of our desire to rid the church of the King's rule and the Papist dominance and return the church to our Lord."

I said nothing. Desire swept her thick dark hair clinging

to her neck back under her coif "We do not believe that God 'blesses us," it's more like He uses Satan to tempt us to exhibit worldly goods. All the rush to get more beaver and wampum, that's what's behind kidnapping Humility and the Indian girl. We are as bad as the heathen, thinking we can earn God's salvation. God knows before we are born whether we will dwell with him forever. Nothing that happens to us is a reward. Those who accumulate wealth should not flaunt it. They should share with the poor." She drew a deep breath, then coughed. "Have ye listened to nothing Mistress and Elder Brewster say?"

"But England is full of greed too!"

"Yea, but only the gentry and the monarchs. Think of how ye grew up. Were ye not in a small village where everyone made their living by hard work of their hands? Only the lord of the manor owning the land was greedy."

I wondered how much Desire knew about our hard work back in Bedfordshire making cloth. Dye, water, scrubbing, wringing had all roughened my hands before I left when I was thirteen. On the Mayflower, I had noticed that Desire, like her friend Catherine Carver, had lovely, smooth hands. Desire's hands were more like mine now, but her cough prevented her from doing the hardest work.

I did want to see my sister Rose. And I did not want to lose Desire. My John might be willing to travel later, when our babe was old enough to endure the voyage. And I had to admit that, God forbid, if my John did not return from the rescue, I would be on that ship home before its sails were raised.

29

Attitash

The climb up the hill took all my strength with my pack full of the Strangers' ransom bounty. Seafoam walked quickly, her wilting spirits of the past few weeks gone. She was obviously exhilarated with finally being again with her husband, the rotten Fish. I paused for breath, observing my husband's muscled thighs and legs. Would I still desire him if he'd betrayed everyone? But Black Whale would never betray, so it was useless to imagine how my cousin could still want her husband.

We were soon out of sight of the Big Salt Water. This was the first time I'd been on this trail since White Flower and I were captured by the Narragansett. I was still a young girl then, and White Flower a child. We'd walked tied to each other and to the Narragansett called Tall Elk. There was little I remembered about the trail until we reached two boulders where the path split on the way up. We were now in Narragansett territory. My muscles felt rigid, as if I were still tied to a rope as I'd been when we were captives and I could not take a breath. My chest felt like it was full of porcupine quills. To release my fear, I pictured my Spirit Grandmother and gave my fear to her in a lump. She laughed and threw the lump of fear up and it broke into shining little pieces, as it had when I gave her my anger the first time. My Spirit Grandmother's hair streamed out as she shook with laughter and I joined her softly. I opened my eyes to see Seafoam looking at me strangely, but I could breathe again.

We stopped for the night by the small creek and fire pit where we'd stayed when Papa and Black Whale rescued us. I kept my own grandmother in my mind and the fear stayed in the dark woods around us, but not in my heart.

Before Nippa'uus sank behind the hills, we sang our night-prayers. Jon-owland raised his eyes and spoke words. We all prayed for the safe return of White Flower and Humility. Which god heard us? Or did they all?

Seafoam and I wrapped ourselves in deerskins and lay down while Black Whale and Jon-owland kept watch by the low fire. The murmur of their voices—halting as they each searched for words—mixed with the shriek of night hawks hunting insects under the stars. I dozed off, then woke to hear them talking about beaver. Jon-owland waved his hands in the firelight and smacked them, describing how he'd seen one swimming, "with a round head above the water, then SMACK, it slapped its tail in the water." Black Whale chuckled, it was the first time I heard him do so with a Stranger.

"How many traps did you bring for Canonicus," Black Whale asked.

Jon-owland held up four fingers.

"Don't let Grey Owl know how many you have or he'll take them all." I knew Black Whale was right, and I was glad Jon-owland had plenty.

"How you catch beaver with no traps?" Jon-owland asked in our words.

I raised my head to watch Black Whale's demonstration, knowing how his hands moved so eloquently. He did not disappoint me.

"First you need lots of porcupine quills." There was some gesturing to make clear our word for the quill-throwers. Then he continued, "You take a hollow log just big enough for the beaver to squeeze in, put the bait well inside, then place the quills facing into the trap. The hungry beaver does not feel the quills going in, but when he tries to back out—he's caught. We just have to wait until he gives up, then grab him by his smacker-tail and pull him out." Black Whale paused and I knew Jon-owl-and was laughing quietly. "You need a partner to whack the beaver on the head as soon as he's out—they have very sharp teeth and will bite your hand off."

Jon-owland creased his brows in concentration, trying to understand. "So Abenaki want our traps?"

"Your traps are easier to set and they keep the bea-ver there until you get back to check the trap line." Black Whale shifted to get the smoke out of his eyes. "But the quill trap is much more entertaining." Seeing Jon-owl-and's look of confusion, my husband added in their words, "So merry."

"Ahhe," Elisabeth's husband agreed. "Merry. How you get plenty beaver before traders brought traps?"

"We had enough for ourselves. For sleeping robes, win-ter robes. We had plenty beaver 'til your people wanted more and more." Black Whale looked at Jon-owland, who wore a cloth robe over his cloth shirt. "What do your peo-ple do with them all?"

Jon-owland tipped his hat. It was shaped with a close-fitting cover over his head set on a broad brim. "Fur keep out rain and snow."

Black Whale stood and stretched, then threw another small log on the fire. "You sleep now?"

"Nay—matta. I watch, you sleep now." Jon-owland waved Black Whale off and propped himself against a rock.

When my husband joined me, I snuggled into his arms and whispered, "Do you think the Narragansett will try to ambush the rescue?"

"If I thought so I would stay up myself. Go to sleep now, I'll take Jon-owland's place before light."

After a quick, deep sleep, I awoke from a dream that my

baby was walking already and coming up the trail. It took
me a moment of listening to the quiet night sounds to realize where I was. Mosk was back home with my mother,
grandmother and Aunt Blue Sky. Little Ice Feather still
demanded the breast so Aunt had enough milk to satisfy
my son's demand. I had not slept without him near since
his birth. I moved closer to Black Whale, his familiar scent
soothing. He was breathing deeply, but I could not hear
Seafoam. I reached my hand to her and found her quivering like the birch tree in the wind. Moving closer to her, I
stroked her arm. "Are you dreaming?"

"I had a dream."

I put my face near her ear so we would not wake the
men. "Tell me."

For a moment her quivering grew even fiercer. "It was
about my husband."

"Was it a happy dream?"

"Matta. It was not happy." Seafoam leaned her forehead against mine and her trembling slowed. "He was all
pale, almost like Jon-owland."

The rest of the night there was no sleep. Black Whale
got up long before Nippa'uus rose. When we got up
to pray, we could not see the Big Salt Water. I realized
the Narragansett never saw the Big Salt Water because
Nippa'uus came to them over a hill instead of out of the
water.

We were near the top of the hill and were to meet Grey
Owl and the girls by a spring on the western slope. It was
an easy walk down the hill before Nippa'uus was in the top
of the sky, our rendezvous time.

There was no sign of anyone when we reached the
spring. Black Whale searched the surrounding woods and
trails for signs that anyone was hiding. Jon-owland questioned whether it was the right spring, but there was only
one spring on this side of the hill.

I hated waiting, but there was nothing else to do. Nippa'uus began descending. The wind picked up and clouds were moving in from the west when Black Whale pointed out movement on the trail below. Jon-owland poured the black sand into his firestick. The grey and white owl feathers in a man's topknot became visible. Then I could see another humped figure. The hump moved, so white it had to be little Humility. All the birds seemed to start singing, though they usually were quiet during the heat of the day. And I sang, quietly but sweet. Seafoam did not.

"I thought Shimmering Fish would be with them," she whispered.

They disappeared as the trail wound back in a loop and the trees sheltered them. Then all at once they were with us. White Flower was carrying Humility on her back. My sister was smiling so bright she made the water in the spring look dull. With the child still on her back, White Flower lunged to me. The rope connecting her to Grey Owl stopped her. He told her to wait until he had seen the bounty we brought. Humility began whining. White Flower turned to comfort the child and Grey Owl loosened the rope around her waist a little.

Seafoam and I began unpacking all the bounty. With a rigid set to her mouth, Seafoam laid out the wampum she'd worked so hard to make beautiful. I took out the Strangers' knives, an axe, two shiny rock traps and one kettle.

Grey Owl stroked the wampum. He said nothing, but his face flicked a glimpse of his approval. I did not understand his dialect easily, but he and Black Whale talked about the Strangers' offerings and Jon-owland was brought into the discussion. Grey Owl at last agreed this bounty was sufficient and turned his attention to Seafoam. He nodded to Black Whale, looking at my cousin with the same leer in his eyes as in Cap-tan's.

Jon-owland raised up his firestick. He had not lit it yet and pointed it toward the sky. "Give us our daughters."

Grey Owl smirked as if making us wait was funny, but he loosened the rope and White Flower picked up Humility and ran to me. I smelled her dear familiar scent, like the flowers she was named for. Then we hugged and hugged and wept and laughed. Jon-owland came and picked up Humility. He too was laughing with delight, but the little girl began asking for Esapett, then crying and pounding him on the chest with her little fists.

"Where is Shimmering Fish?" Seafoam demanded.

Grey Owl told her she would find her husband when they reached Canonicus's village. She looked slightly eased, but I felt White Flower stiffen. She was in my arms but now stood away, avoiding my eyes. I leaned to her ear and whispered, "What's happened to the Fish?" White Flower whispered so low I could hardly understand her— something like "Can't say yet."

Grey Owl's fingers seemed to seek Jon-owland's firestick. My husband reminded Grey Owl that our men were all skilled hunters with a bow and arrow and had no need of a firestick. The Narragansett understood he would not get one until we had our own.

As we readied to leave, Grey Owl put a rope around Seafoam's waist. She struggled to get it off and I yelled at him to let her go.

He ignored us both and pulled it tighter. "She might run away." Keeping her close to him, he started down the path.

White Flower and Humility kept quiet. Did they know what would happen now to Seafoam?

"Remember us," I called to her as they started down the trail. "Catabatash."

She did not reply.

WE STARTED DOWN the eastern slope. White Flower carried Humility, who would not let Jon-owland or me touch her. When we stopped by a stream to drink, White Flower finally spoke.

"Seafoam will not find Shimmering Fish."

"Where is he?

"Dead."

My throat clenched with an ache for my cousin. "How?"

"They killed him with a club, they said it was the same way Tall Elk was killed. She will be another wife for Canonicus or Grey Owl."

White Flower kept her head down and I asked no questions. Seafoam's evil husband would no longer influence her, but she was now in the hands—and arms—of our enemy. The ache in my throat intensified as fear came in a dizzying wave.

When we reached the top of the hill and could make out the gleam of Big Salt Water in the far distance, White Flower put Humility down. "See the Big Salt Water?" she asked in our words.

Humility nodded, still no smile on her face. "Nipi," she said. Our word for water. Jon-owland glanced at her.

"She won't be able to use these words when she gets home." His face was gentle, but I understood why his words were firm.

"Humility will miss me," White Flower said quietly to me.

"Ahhe, she will. But she has Mis-tess, and Desiah, and Esapett to remind her." Esapett had tried to explain Humility's mother to me and I thought she had died. Probably one of those many who died their first winter here. She now had family among her own people. And there would be rejoicing when we returned her. But my family would find a new reason to mourn—White Flower would come home, but Seafoam would not.

Jon-owland left us with our family and took Humility to hers. Or tried to. She screamed when Jon-owland took her from White Flower. He hurried away, the little girl's cries echoing back to us.

30

Elisabeth

The warm day made my babe fussy. I rocked her and sang, standing where the breeze from the sea came in the back door. I'd just put her down finally and lay beside her when I thought I heard excited voices. Not willing to be disappointed by checking every time I heard something, I did not rise to see who or what. When I heard a small child crying, I thought it might be Humility, but knew she would not be crying but happy, and decided it was Martha Ford's little one.

Knowing I should not look for my husband until near dark, I dozed off myself. I thought the kiss on my cheek was a dream, but turning over cried out in delight to find my John leaning over me. The stubble on his chin below his mustache was fierce, but I relished everything about him. When John released me from his embrace, we checked our babe and found her still sound asleep.

"Everyone home?" I asked.

"Yea, we are all home. The girls, Attitash and Black Whale."

"And ye."

He answered with a kiss that quickly turned to kisses. We had not made love since our babe was born. Before I could concern myself with whether I would once again welcome him, John had lifted my skirts, moved his hands slowly up my thigh and found me ready to be his wife again.

Attitash

WHITE FLOWER CRIED in our mother's arms, then our grandmother's. Black Whale gave our son a quick kiss on the head, then went with Papa to report to Sachem Bad-ford.

White Flower hugged Little Fish until he ran away laughing. I already had Mosk at my breast, but when he finally released, she took him too and hugged him tight.

"We had babies too, but no one like Mosk." She handed my son back to me.

"Who did you stay with?" I asked.

"My family."

"We are your family." I tried to quell the small knot in my throat. Of course it would take time for White Flower to adjust. "Did you stay with the Sachem Canonicus?"

"I stayed with his first wife's brother's family. They had lost a daughter too. They kept both of us."

"Will you miss them?"

"Matta, well maybe a little." White Flower took my hand. "I missed you all, but they were good to me. And they had a son, White Owl." She stopped and looked up in the trees. "Grey Owl's son."

"There will be other young men," Grandmother said. She was busy unpacking our journey bags, but she listened to everything.

When Black Whale arrived back from Plimot, he picked Mosk up, swinging him in the air 'til he laughed.

"Sachem Bad-ford declares a ceremony tomorrow to welcome home the girls."

WE WERE ALL so happy to be together again that we sat up late talking. I slept well, with my husband and my baby both in bed with me. The only time I woke was when White Flower cried out in a dream. I heard Mama go to her, so I went back to sleep.

WHITE FLOWER WAS usually quiet while I did her hair, but next morning she fidgeted so much I finally stopped combing. "Can't you sit still? We have so much to do before we go to the governor's wedding feast. Massasowet has already arrived."

She sat still for one short moment, and then shifted again. "My belly hurts. Maybe it's from all the climbing we did to get here."

"Did Grey Owl give you something bad to eat?"

"All I ate was journey cake and it was good." She pressed her hand against her lower stomach, just below her navel, but said nothing more.

We collected mussels for stew, cut up the fish our men brought and brought it all to the feast. Just before we got to their palisade, White Flower stopped.

"I have to make water. Right now." She put her pack down and stepped into the woods. Wondering if this was related to her bellyache, I followed her. I was not surprised to find her standing over her puddle, pointing to the strands of blood.

"Has your life-flow come while you were gone?" I asked, hoping she had not celebrated this occasion already with the Narragansett.

"Matta." She looked at me with shining eyes. "I am a woman now!"

We called to Mama and Aunt Blue Sky. They came quickly, embraced White Flower and Mama pulled some sphagnum moss from her journey belt to catch the flow.

"You need to be at the feast," Aunt Blue Sky said to Mama. "I will take her to the moon lodge and begin the cleansing."

"But don't cut her hair until we get home," Mama said.

Aunt Blue Sky and White Flower both smiled. "Ahhe, we will keep all the important ceremony until you and Attitash come home," Aunt assured her.

Mama took White Flower's hands briefly, both pride and a glint of regret in her eyes. I remembered wondering at that same look when I became a woman. Now I understood. Mama was saying goodbye to her little girl.

As my mother and I walked across to Mis-tess's home, I asked, "When White Flower's hair grows to her shoulders, she can marry. But does she have any interest in a young man?"

"Ahhe, she can marry. But she does not have to marry yet." Mama paused as we arrived at Mis-tess's home. We could hear the Strangers' sharp stone chattering from the women behind her house. "We are so alone here," Mama said. "I don't see her with other young people. We may have to wait until we are all together in Poanoke this winter."

"Well, her hair won't grow out until at least the coldest moon, so plenty of time."

Elisabeth

Attitash understood when I asked why her little sister and the other woman were not with them. She did not seem worried as she answered with gestures that would have been rude in mixed company, swooshing her hand from her secret place between her legs. It did occur to me that White Flower might have started her courses. There would always be mysteries between us, like what would they use since they had no cloth with which to sew clouts to catch the blood. Did they have stories about the first woman—the heathen version of Eve—sinning and thus being cursed?

Attitash

She had most of our food ready when Humility came running to tell Esapett her baby woke up. Esapett sat down and exposed her breast, cupping the baby's head. Humility leaned against Esapett, smiling at the baby and stroking her cheek. Two other Cloth-women came and helped with the food, shooing Esapett to the bench in the cool shade. Esapett was obviously happy to stop working and rest.

Some of the new women looked boldly at me when I sat near Esapett and Pah-silla. Ignoring them, I fed Mosk. We enjoyed the fresh breeze off the Big Salt Water, watched the birds wheel back and forth from the fields to the water. Now and then a small dark whale surfaced far out among the waves. Two women, dressed in cloth that covered their arms and looked far too warm for the day, arrived together. Esapett told me they were Sachem Bad-ford's and Cap-tan Sam-dish's new women. Neither looked very young. I thought they had probably lost a husband, as I knew their new husbands had lost wives when the Strangers first arrived here.

Mis-tess motioned to everyone to gather out by the tables. Her husband raised his hands to the sky, the way we greet Nippa'uus in the morning. He did not sing his prayer, just talked. Our Massasowet and the Pniese he brought with him raised their hands, so I did too. Sachem Bad-ford helped his new wife sit on a bench with arms and Cap-tan did the same. I remembered Cap-tan insulting Seafoam and me at the first feast we attended. Now his eyes were only on his new wife.

My own husband still had eyes for me but I wondered if Black Whale would want another wife if he became a Pniese. Papa told me the Strangers do not take another wife even if they become sachem. I felt a flick of envy. I looked to where Black Whale stood, talking with another Pniese. He glanced at me with love in his sparkling eyes. He was more handsome now than when I first kissed him.

Our little son reached out his arms. Mosk had his fa-ther's high forehead and eyes like the night sky with no moon. I bounced Mosk on my knees and sang him a song.

Esapett and Pah-silla laughed with us, then sang a little song which brought Humility running. She saw me and asked for White Flower. I told her in our words she would come later. Humility's mouth turned down and she would not sing with Esapett. I was anxious to get to the moon lodge and my sister's woman ceremony. There was no way to explain that to Esapett, so I simply gathered Mosk and said a goodbye.

Elisabeth
After Attitash and the other guests left the wedding feast, we cleaned up and finally took our ease. Humility was playing with young Martha Ford, whose mother had gone home to tend to her own house. No longer Widow Ford, Goodwife Martha Browne, now lived with her husband, Peter Browne. Martha Ford Browne arrived back with her husband's dog, my old friend, Rogue. The dog's teats were heavy with milk for her new pups, who trailed behind. I suspected Black Whale's dog had sired the pups. They had the same wolfish yellow eyes, instead of Rogue's dark brown. Goodwife Martha picked up one of the puppies and addressed me. "Mistress Howland, my husband says you have always been fond of his dog."

"Yea, I have. Since Rogue came with us on the Mayflower," I replied.

"He sent this pup for you, if you would like to have her, Mistress."

The pup wriggled and squealed. Holding my babe in one hand, I rubbed the pup behind her ears, then looked at Martha. Was the widow—rather, Goodwife Browne—trying to get on my good side after a year of snapping at my heels? Or did her new husband want a favor from my John? "You can still call me 'Elisabeth.' You need not call me, 'Mistress,'" I said. "I thank you and your husband for the pup, Martha." I moved little Desire up on my shoulder. "Could you keep the pup until my babe's a little older? Another week or two?"

Martha Browne agreed, only a slight sulk on her mouth. She took her leave with her daughter, followed by the dogs. Humility wanted to come with me to my house.

"Nay, nay, Humility," Mistress Brewster grabbed her hand. "Come with me now."

Humility wailed and looked back at me, pleading with her eyes. I turned my back. I loved the child, but needed peace and quiet to rest. Mistress had warned me not to get too tired or I'd lose my milk.

Attitash

Little Fish begged to come into the Moon Lodge with us, which made us all laugh. Black Whale took him off to the creek to toss rocks and we women settled into the ceremony to welcome White Flower. Her face was soft, filled with her joy at becoming a woman. Grandmother had prepared well. The sweetgrass smoke welcomed all spirits and the burning sage drove out the bad ones. Water was poured, prayers were sung. Then our mother took the sharp quahog shell and holding one strand of hair at a time, she cut White Flower's hair up to her ears. Gratitude thrummed in my heart for White Flower's return from captivity. I knew Mama felt it too. Watching her face as she performed the ceremony, I stroked my own hair, now covering my breasts. It was three circles of the seasons since Mama had cut mine.

Mosk woke demanding food and I left White Flower in her elders' hands.

31

Elisabeth

Back in our own quiet house, I fed the babe and slept with her until John returned. He brought home venison pottage and I ate another full plate. I was always hungry now, even when I'd had a decent meal earlier. Priscilla had reminded me that since we were making milk for our babes, we needed to eat for two.

John took an envelope out of his pocket and put it on the table. "Governor Bradford gave me this letter addressed to, 'Survivors of Edward Tilley and Agnes Cooper Tilley.' John broke the wax seal and opened the letter. 'On behalf of the Widow Joan Cooper.'"

"Widow Cooper? Humility's mother! She's still alive?" I'd forgotten the woman existed.

John smoothed the page and began reading silently.

"Tell me what it says," I urged John.

He looked up. "Widow Joan Cooper is married."

"Married? That's a blessing." Or was it? "What does she want?"

"*To Whom it May Concern. Joan Cooper, widow of Robert Cooper has received Word that her late husband's sister, Agnes Cooper Tilley, and her husband, Edward Tilley, have died. Lord have mercy on their Souls.*" John looked up, eyebrows raised.

"Keep reading," I said.

Widow Cooper is grateful for the care given her daughter, Humility, by Edward's niece, Elisabeth, and others who made the Pilgrimage to the New World.

However, since learning of the deaths of so many in the new colony, she fears that her daughter too will perish. With her approaching marriage, Joan Cooper's ability to care for her daughter has greatly improved. Her mother requires that Humility Cooper be returned to England. Send the child on the next ship which carries a guardian for the girl.

"Nay! It can't be!"

John paused, his face creased with concern. "Let me finish the letter, Love."

I nodded and he continued, "*Joan Cooper is most eager to be with her child again, if she still lives. With God's Grace, they shall be reunited.*"

"There is a mark, which must be Joan Cooper's." John showed me the rough mark. I took my eyes from the page. The truth was written there in cold black ink. I would lose Humility again.

"How can she want her sent back across the sea?" The letters swam on the page, but John had already told me what it said. "This woman can't decide now to drag Humility away from everyone the child loves. Not just torn from me, but from Desire, Mistress Brewster and even White Flower and Attitash." I could no longer control my tears as they rose from deep within me and spilled. "We just got Humility back from the savages!"

"Stop." John's voice was soft, but insistent. "Humility is safe again. Save thy tears."

I staunched my tears, but could not prevent my words from spewing out. "Does her mother expect Humility to remember her? Humility was a babe when the woman gave her away. Now she's four." I took a deep breath. "Desire will not want to risk taking her across. Humility might not even survive another voyage." Desperately searching for any way to keep Humility with us I continued, "We can write and say Humility was kidnapped. That would be the truth."

John's look stopped my chattering. He waited for me to calm down, then asked, "How is Humility related to you? She was with your family's household, so I thought she was your Uncle Edward's daughter."

"Nay. Uncle and Aunt lost their only child before we came." It was complicated to explain. I rubbed my forehead to stop the ache, then pushed back the curls which escaped my coif and clung to my face. "Humility's my family by marriage. She's not my blood family."

"Agnes's brother was the child's father and he died? So Humility's not thy cousin—not family?" John sounded as though he were filling out one of the governor's reports.

"She's family in my heart. We all lived together in one household on the Mayflower—ye remember." I stopped, willing my eyes to hold the tears. "Then they all died. All except Humility and me."

John put down the letter and reached for me. "'Twas a terrible time, that first winter. I was ashore building houses when ye still lived on the ship and lost them all. Ye almost died too."

"So they tell me."

"Do ye remember when I carried thee from the ship to shore?" The warmth of John's arms released tight muscles in my neck and I sank into his shoulders.

"Rather like a dream. I could scarce remember what was dream and what was not. Did ye carry Humility too?"

"I carried both of you. She clung to thee so tight it was useless to try to separate her."

I touched his strong arm and his muscle flexed automatically. "Have I ever thanked thee?"

John laughed softly. "We all thank God every day for life. And I thank Him for thee." He held me until I finally got up and began tidying up the dishes.

"We don't have to settle this right now," John said.

I had time to prepare my arguments for keeping Humility.

Attitash

"You stayed late with the Stranger Sachem and our Massasowet," Grandmother said, when Papa arrived home. Papa nodded. "Sachem Bad-Ford is a happy man to finally have a wife again. He spent little time with us, but Win-snow talked with Massasowet and me. Win-snow is going back in the big wind-canoe that brought all the new Strangers."

"Win-snow is going across the Big Salt Water? Why?" I asked. The traders went back every year, but none of our Strangers had gone back.

"He must visit his Cloth-men beyond the Big Salt Water. The big wind canoes carry our beaver and fox skins over and trade for more firesticks, hard stone pots, and tools." Papa looked out to where the Strangers' big canoe rose and sank with the waves. Its white cloth wings were tied down and the big canoe looked like the bones of a Salt Water creature "Win-snow braves the Big Salt Water journey to find out what happened to all the furs. The Cloth-men in the east claim they got fewer than were promised and refuse to trade more tools or firesticks."

After taking a long drink from the water jug, Papa wiped his mouth and added, "Win-snow said he will leave before the weachimin harvest. He will take a woman and a little girl with him."

"Which woman? What little girl?"

My father shrugged. My mind hummed with questions. There were only a few little girls in their village. I did not think Allerton's daughters would go without their father. Would it be our little Humility? She was so dear to White Flower now. The child seemed to be Esapett's clan. Could Esapett be the woman going back?

Elisabeth

Desire read the letter quickly, then again slowly. She put it down without comment. Desire did not look upset, in fact she looked rather pleased. "God works in mysterious ways."

"Desire! What do ye mean? God can't want this."

"Do ye think ye know what God wants, Elisabeth?" Desire asked me in a gentle voice, but I felt stung.

"We should not send Humility back," I protested. My voice shook with anger that Desire could not see the truth. "Humility loves us. Her mother gave her to my uncle and aunt—to us. She doesn't know her mother."

"I knew Joan Cooper in Holland."

That stopped me. "Ye knew Humility's mother? Ye've never mentioned her. Was she one of those heartless mothers who don't love their children?"

"I didn't know her well." Desire's eyes moved to the east, looking through her open door to the tall ship anchored in our bay, "I was young—and troubled by my own family. But I remember when Joan Cooper's husband died, soon after my own father died. And she had the new babe—Humility—along with other children. After she lost her milk, for lack of sufficient food, Widow Cooper was desperate. Agnes and Edward Tilley gladly took Agnes' little niece. There was enough goat milk on the Mayflower to Humility, but none at her mother's home."

"What gives that woman the right to ask for Humility back now?"

"Joan Cooper gave birth to Humility."

My bubbling wrath ebbed. That was the truth. I knew now what giving birth meant. Carrying your babe for nine months, the miracle of her birth, giving suck, your new daughter's smell, stroking her warm skin, the taste of her check, watching her grow.

Desire folded the letter and gave it back to me. "Joan Cooper has moved back to England. I can take Humility home with me."

"And God only knows if either of you will survive the

voyage." I held the letter in my hand. "I'm losing both of you."

"Elisabeth, pray on this." Desire took both my hands. "God gave thee a good husband and a little daughter—thy own Desire." She let go of my hands to wipe a tear, then smoothed her cheeks and composed her face.

I tried to compose mine too, but my heart was aching and the pain filled my eyes. "I will always remember thee, Desire. I will always love thee."

"Yea, and I thee." Desire took my hands again and drew me close. "We will miss each other, do tell thy husband to write me, and include everything."

We'd both lost so many to death. This was different, this is a choice. "I know ye need this friend back home, Desire, but I need thee too."

"Nay, Elisabeth. Ye don't need me. Ye like me, even love me, but God knows ye don't need me and ye don't need Humility." Desire looked me in the eyes, biting her lip. "But her mother needs her. What if you had hoped for four years to get your daughter back and then your circumstances made it possible?" And what if I'd not had enough to eat and lost my milk? What if my own little darling cried from hunger and I could not feed her?

Voices outside Brewsters' door alerted us to Mistress Brewster and Humility's return. Desire and I embraced quickly and I carried my sleeping babe home. When I unwrapped her, little Desire opened her eyes and looked into mine. Her dark lashes swept her cheek as she closed them again. What would my Desire look like when she was four years old? God must want Joan Cooper to see Humility's face again, to hold her child.

I was sixteen now, an upgrown. A mother with a husband and babe. I was old enough to say farewell with dignity to Desire and Humility. Tears should be saved for behind the bed curtains.

As I took Aunt Agnes's green shawl out of the trunk, I remembered when I'd given it to Attitash. We had been told we could never again meet together. I gave her the shawl to wrap her babe in when she delivered. When she lost her babe, Attitash returned the shawl to me.

Holding it to my face now, I detected both Aunt Agnes's lavender scent and a hint of the herbs Attitash used to cleanse me. I would send Humility a reminder of Aunt Agnes, and Attitash, and myself.

32

Elisabeth

The day before the *Ship Anne* was to sail, another rain soaked our fields. I took my little Desire, now six weeks old, to the open door and let her listen to the sound of soft rain. My daughter gazed deep into my eyes and seemed on the verge of smiling.

Just outside the door, our new pup, Rounder, chewed on a stick she'd dragged to the garden. John had just brought her from Goodman Peter Browne. He said a mongrel dog might be useful—she would know how to chase the rabbits and deer, yet would fetch the fowl and not spook at the sound of the musket like the Indian dogs did. Rounder did not seem to mind the rain, shaking it off with a wriggle from head down to her tail.

Back indoors, John was taking advantage of the wet weather to finish the letters he'd postponed while busy in the fields. After reading aloud the letter to my family he wrote on my behalf, I made my mark, "EH". He wrote *Elisabeth Tilley Howland*, beneath.

When the rain stopped after supper, John sat down to finish the letter to his brothers and I took my babe to see Desire and Humility. Desire was packing her belongings in a trunk. Humility begged me to take her to the shore. Mistress Brewster urged me to do so. "'Twill get the child out from under our feet while my daughters and I help Desire," Mistress said. She was about to hand Desire the shawl I'd brought over, but now put it on Humility's shoulder. "Keep the sea wind off her."

I stopped back at my house for a little wool rug to protect my babe from the sea winds. John had finished his letters and came with us, carrying our bundled up daughter. As we picked our way, the setting sun broke through the clouds over the western hills. I was watching the path when Humility called out, "Look! A sky bwidge." She clapped her hands. "Does it go to heaven?" Not waiting for an answer, she danced up and down. "Tell Auntie Desiah there's a bwidge to heaven for me. Is my mama there?"

Rather than answer all her questions, we gathered in the beauty of the rainbow forming over the eastern horizon. I explained to Humility it was called 'rainbow', and did not go to heaven or England.

"Wain-bow", Humility said.

"Nay," I laughed. "Ra-ra-ra-rain. It comes after the rain and makes a big bow over the sea. Rain-bow."

She said it correctly then and I told her the story of Noah and the promise from God. "God will go with you on the ship, all the way across the sea to thy mother," I told Humility. "There will be rainbows in England too. Think of us when ye see a rainbow."

By this time, we'd arrived on the shore and the rainbow was fading. We could see storm clouds pushing each other across the northeastern sky. Humility clung to my skirt, begging to hold my babe.

"I take my baby to Mama," Humility said. She pulled off the green shawl. "Put her in here. I'll keep her by me."

John and I laughed, but there was an ache in my heart. Humility did not know what she was in for, I was sure that she would forget all of us. We would be a short story that she might think was a dream.

Black Whale and Attitash called from down the shore. Hopamoch was with them. He and Black Whale came to talk with John while Attitash and her little son settled on a rock by me. We no longer worried about crossing the leaning rocks which divided their part of the beach from ours. Even Isaac Allerton did not trouble me. He was distracted with courting Fear Brewster, who to my dismay seemed to enjoy his attention.

Attitash adjusted her poncho to cover one shoulder. Her hair, pulled back and bound, was slick, as if she'd been rained on. She looked sad. John had told me the sorry ending to Seafoam's hope to rejoin her husband. I wondered if this was what troubled Attitash.

"Esapett, netop."

"Ahhe, Attitash, my friend, netop."

Humility looked up from my babe and smiled at Attitash. "Netop. White Flower?" The child looked around as if to discover her friend.

Attitash pointed back. Her sister was coming along the shore. Humility ran to White Flower, who picked up the child. Humility grabbed at White Flower's head. As they came closer, I could see White Flower's hair was chopped off to her ears. I didn't know if I should avert my eyes. Had the Narragansett assaulted White Flower? Or had she been punished? I looked to Attitash, but she was smiling calmly at her sister as if nothing was amiss.

Attitash caught my look and put a hand on her own hair, divided into two long tails. "White Flower woman now."

I understood that much, she had the breasts and hips of a young maid. But the hair?

Attitash smiled broadly. "When White Flower's hair to here," she pointed to her own shoulders, "she can marry."

Thinking back, I realized that Attitash's hair had been shorter than her mother's and sister's when we first met. And though it was longer now, was shorter than her mother's.

White Flower sat down near us, with Humility still clinging to her. She handed Humility a little deerskin bag and helped her open it. Humility laughed in delight to find some quahog shells, polished into wampum pieces.

"Be careful," I warned her. "Don't lose it." I wondered what Humility's mother would think of these beautiful savage pieces.

White Flower and Attitash sat quietly, watching Humility. Attitash shifted her gaze when the birds shrieked. We both watched them rise and fluttered, as they always did, as though they were connected to a huge banner flying in the sky.

Our attention turned to the arrival of men carrying huge packs of beaver pelts to the longboat, then setting out to load the ship. Attitash pointed out to the Ship Anne, riding the gentle waves up and down, then pointed to me. "You go?"

She thought I was going back to England! I shook my head, but questions filled her face, making her brown eyes look almost black.

"Esapett matta." She waited, so did I. She'd said, 'Elisabeth not,' but I was not sure what she meant.

"Matta—do not go with Win-snow." Attitash said. "Esapett, stay." Attitash put her hand firmly on my arm. "We need you, Netop. You need us."

"I stay," I tried to reassure her with my face. If we were alone, I could use more intimate gestures, even embrace her. I felt someone's eyes on me and looked to see Remember Allerton tossing stones in the water between glances at me. Well, let Remember look. She must have learned to trust Attitash a little.

"Who goes?" Attitash asked. Her hand gripped my arm.

"My friend Desire goes. Humility goes. Winslow goes. Winslow will come back." I put my hand on top of Attitash's and spoke slowly, the emotion in my voice surely conveyed what I meant even if my English words failed.

"You will miss your friend, Desire."

The knot in my heart tightened. "I will. But I am home here. With my husband, my babe, my other friends, with you."

Attitash smiled and turned to her sister. "Esapett stays."

Remember Allerton was looking at us again, so I beckoned to her. "Would ye like to join our conversation?" The girl took a step toward us, then recalled where we were. Glancing about the shore, Remember turned and ran so fast I thought her freckles would fly off her face.

Attitash and I giggled. She gathered her son and gestured to her sister they would leave. White Flower had to extricate herself from Humility, who still clung to her. The child put up such a fuss, I should have slapped her on the wrist or threatened a stick to stop her insistent screams. Truth be told, Desire would have her hands full on the voyage with this willful child. I did not want to imagine what methods Humility's mother and new stepfather might employ to drive the demons out.

NEXT MORNING Desire led humility, wrapped in the green shawl, to the shore. I gave them both kisses and embraced them.

"Thy friend will be so glad to have thee back," I said to Desire, pushing down the knot in my heart.

Her eyes were lit from within. "Yea, I keep Mary's letter close. God-willing we will be in each other's arms before snow flies."

"Will ye find someone to write me?" I got the words out before a sob could escape. Desire couldn't write. I couldn't write. This was our last true conversation.

Desire looked down at Humility, wriggling in her hands. "Mary can write a bit. She will send thee any news." She looked up at me. "Ye know I will miss thee!"

I nodded, "But ye will have Mary."

"I will. As ye have John. Do make him write with every ship that comes. Tell me all the news—how many more babes ye have, how many Priscilla has, how many thy Indian friend has."

I could not bear to watch their departure. Burying my face in my own little Desire's cheek, I walked back up to our settlement and sat down on a rock near the gate. When Edward Winslow returned, he would give us news of Desire and Humility and their new life.

Mine is a good life, I thought. When my parents brought me three years ago, I'd been eager, thinking it would be a great adventure. Now my childish ideas were gone. It was a great adventure, achieved only with peril and heartache. I looked to the woods looming dark and deep to the west. There was another wide sea far, far to the west, Stephen Hopkins had told us. It took a tall ship years to sail around all the land between. It occurred to me for the first time to wonder who lived in all that great forest. Before we came here, I'd only thought of the people living here as wild creatures, savages, like the bears, wolves and lions.

My reverie broke when Attitash appeared, carrying her babe's cradleboard. Little Mosk was asleep and Attitash hung the board on a tree, before sitting down next to me.

"Ship's sailing," John arrived, pointing out to sea, where the white sails were filling with wind.

My babe stirred and began to whimper, rooting for my nipple. Little Mosk awakened too and squirmed to get unlaced and fed. Attitash hummed a little song to him. She had taught me the song with motions and a few of our words. Now, I tried singing with her in English.

Rockabye baby, in the treetop.
When the wind blows, the Cradle will rock.
When the bough bends, the Cradle will fall.
And down will come baby, Cradle and all.

Attitash
We finished the song and smiled. Both our babes were safe. My friend and I sat together suckling our babes and watching the ship take the waves. Mosk only nursed a little bit before he wanted to sit up and watch the birds screaming overhead. When Esapett's babe finally had her fill, she let go with a pop. She was satisfied, for now.

Notes and Acknowledgements:

History is not just facts and events. History is also a pain in the heart and we repeat history until we are able to make another's pain in the heart our own.
— Julius Lester

HISTORICAL FICTION: The characters in the book are fictional, but I used the names of historical people for all Pilgrim characters and for some of the Wampanoag. I attempted to write what is plausible in addition to known historical events.

SOURCES: Primary sources I used written by Mayflower passengers are: William Bradford's *Of Plymouth Plantation*, and Edward Winslow's *Good Newes from New England* and *Mourt's Relation*. *Good Wives* by Laurel Thatcher Ulrich and *Founding Mothers and Fathers*, by Mary Beth Norton were most helpful describing female life in Plimoth. The living history museum in Plymouth, Mass gave me the full view of life at Plimoth Plantation with Pilgrim Village and Hobbamock's Homesite. The role-players in Pilgrim Village portray the Pilgrims in 1627. The Wampanoag people remain their contemporary selves while demonstrating Wampanoag life at the time Europeans first brought families to live in Wampanoag territory. Kate Waters' and Russ Kendall's book *Tapenum's Day*, about a Wampanoag family and their books on Pilgrim children's "day" are accurate depictions of family life at that time. *Facing East from Indian Country*, by Daniel Richtor is an in-depth book on events of North America seen through

253

indigenous people's point of view. Reader's interests about Wampanoag should be directed to Wampanoag people. There are many Wampanoag websites, including *www.pli-moth.org/what-see-do/wampanoaghomesite*.

RECORDS REVEAL: The English settled on a site in Cape Cod which the Wampanoag called Patuxet. It had been settled many years earlier by Wampanoag who cleared fields, grew corn, and built homes. A few years before the Mayflower arrived, all the inhabitants of Patuxet had been captured or killed by Europeans, or died of diseases. The new arrivals on the Mayflower did not seem troubled by the absence of any living inhabitants. They praised God for clearing and preparing this land for them.

Little was written by about the women beyond their birth, marriage and death. The record does show the historical Elizabeth Tilley was baptized in England on August, 1607 and came on the Mayflower in 1620 with her parents. The historical John Howland was born in England in 1592. He was Governor John Carver's servant—probably his clerk.

Following the signing of the treaty of mutual protection, the Wampanoag nation's leader, Massasoit, asked one of his warriors, Hobbamock, to live near the new settlement to ensure the English followed the treaty's terms. The record describes Hobbamock as bringing a large family with him. In their matrilineal society Massasoit and Hobbamock would have followed the instructions of the Wampanoag grandmothers' council. This aspect of governance was lost on the Pilgrim men. They referred to Massasoit as "king."

Edward Winslow vented his frustration with later arrivals when he wrote in 1624 that "three things are the overthrow and bane, as I may term it, of plantations" (see chapter 23, page 221 in the story). Winslow's description of those driven by personal gain and greed motivated me to tell the story of opposing views within the Pilgrims through the lives of the Elisabeth and Attitash in this sequel to *Strangers in Our Midst.*

The rescue attempt described in the book's opening scene is described by Edward Winslow. "Notwithstanding, some of them pressed out a private door and escaped, but with some wounds…though they procured it in not staying in the house at our command; yet if they would return home with us, our surgeon would heal them." I chose to portray Attitash in this story as the one wounded in Winslow's narration.

FICTION BASED ON RESEARCH: The character Attitash is pure fiction, as are her mother, siblings, aunts, uncles and Black Whale. The cross-cultural experience between Elisabeth and Attitash is also fiction. Although the English records do mention interaction between the Pilgrim and Wampanoag men, nothing is mentioned of women. Based on close cross cultural friendships of my own, I am convinced such interaction between two young women is plausible. Deepest gratitude to my late friend, Ethele (Tudy) Martin, whose children are now my adult godchildren. Tudy transformed from a young African American mother who would not look me in the eye, to an intimate friend who trusted me with her Tamera and Shay-Glorious.

However, it was clear to me that as a non-native person, I would have difficulty understanding Wampanoag ceremonies and rituals. My Native friends here in mid-continent—Dakotah, Lakotah, Ojibwe, and Lanape—advised me. Special thanks to Elona Street Stewart, Lavon Lee, John Pourpot and Prof. Anton Treuer for their combination of scrutiny and encouragement in my understanding indigenous people. On all my visits to Hobbamock's Homesite in Massachusetts, the Wampanoag staff answered many questions. Bob Charlesbois, director of indigenous programs at Hobbomock's Homesite was most helpful and encouraging. My apologies for all mistakes, they are mine, not theirs. When a ceremony is private to their culture, I imagined details, hoping they would be consistent with Wampanoag beliefs. One way the Wampanoag referred to Europeans is translated into English as "cloth-men." I invented Attitash's use of "Strangers' because it is consistent with how most people view outsiders.

English spelling was not consistent at that time; I have tried to keep my selected spelling Elisabeth consistent. To distinguish my imagined character from the historical person, Elizabeth Tilley, I used the spelling Elisabeth. The spelling of the Wampanoag leader is *Massasowet* in Edward Winslow's writing and *Massasoit* in Bradford's. This word is a title meaning "honored—revered", so I often use, "our Massasowet" when Attitash and other Wampanoag people speak, just as the Pilgrims describe Bradford as "our governor." The Pilgrims' view of the Native Americans is recorded using many historically negative terms, including "savages."

THANKS: The historical aspect of the novel, came alive with help from many people. Thanks to teachers at the Loft Literary Center, particularly Mary Gardner. Three writers from my early Loft class, Rosemary Jensen, Barbara Schue, and Peter Arnstein read every word weekly and have given me priceless advice and encouragement. My lasting gratitude to them. Laurel Yourke of University of Wisconsin at Madison brought order out of chaos. Readers from book clubs provided invaluable insight on the first book that was useful in this story.

I am so grateful that my husband, Jim, finished reading the draft manuscript a few weeks before his death in August, 2015. His instant feedback of dozing off or being moved to tears told me immediately if a scene was working. If not for the support that surrounded me following his death, I could never have brought the completed book to my amazing managing editor, Nick Dimassis and the terrific Forty Press trio of Nick, Joe Riley and Kelly Keady. Nick traveled from Wisconsin for Jim's memorial which gave me motivation later to get back to Elisabeth and Attitash. Deepest thanks for carrying me through this past year to my children, Tom, Charlotte and Carolyn, and their dear spouses, Julie, Carlos and Greg. My sisters Anita Cummings, Julie Christensen, Joan McDermott and Rita Vellenga provided unconditional support. My good friends Ruthena Fink, Terrie Brandt, Anne Brandt Anderson, Lynn Nelson, Theresa Rahn, David Stewart, and many others gave me sympathy when I needed it and strength to work on the book.

Thanks to the Mayflower Society for providing a venue to meet other descendants and hear their stories. Elizabeth and John Howland have a multitude of descendants today, including my awesome grandchildren: Stefan and Ian Landreau, Aidan and Brendan Vellenga, Hannah and Milly Berman—all unique twelve generations later and quite capable of telling their own stories.